Uroboros Saga

BOOK FIVE

By Arthur Walker

For Kitty

Get updates on my books by following me on Twitter.

@arthurhwalker

Over all things that are agreeable to his nature and genius, the man has the highest right. Everywhere he may take what belongs to his spiritual estate, nor can all the force of men hinder him from taking so much. It is a vain attempt to keep a secret from one who has a right to know it. It will tell itself.

~Emerson

CHAPTER 1

FINANCIAL DISTRICT, COMMERCE DOME, LUNAR COLONY

4:28 AM UTC/GMT April 16th, 2200

Ezra's War Journal, Part 10

The Lunar Colony has been in upheaval for weeks. It had been a complicated affair to get the criminal syndicate to work with the new interim government. It took Silverstein weeks to lay the groundwork for the first meeting. This had been further complicated by Ervin Carol's unwillingness to leave the Lunar AI's side. I had no idea that terrestrial intelligent agents could be so irrational. Taylor, the only other person suitable to the task, finally convinced him to venture out for the morning, and attend the sit down.

"Has Henry Scarsdale sent over notice that the meet is secure?" Silverstein asked, fumbling with his tie in front of the hotel room mirror.

"Yeah, notification popped up on the private network mobile he gave me," I said, glancing at the message one more time.

I was deemed a security risk by the organizers of the meet, being a Type One Drone. The best Silverstein could do was sign me in as his security detail. I could be on the premises, with a handgun, and only in designated areas. I didn't like it. We'd already had bombings, shoot-outs, and gangland assassinations just to get to this far. Syndicate goons tried to kill

Silverstein twice in the last thirty days, and even conducted recon on the facility that houses the Lunar AI.

I was pretty tired of it all by then. I knew trying to wipe them out wasn't an option, even with a whole team of Type One Drones. Still, after all I'd seen in the last couple weeks, I was angry enough to try.

"It'll be alright, Ezra," Silverstein said, putting on his suit coat. "Everyone has plenty of incentive to make this work. Henry's found all the funds I sequestered. All the payoffs should have cleared accounts by the time everyone sits down." Silverstein had carefully hidden resources throughout the colony before losing his memory.

"And if that isn't enough to sway everyone?" I asked.

"We do things your way," he replied, somewhat downcast.

"After what happened in the Port of Paris last month, I'm ready for that regardless of the outcome. Too many civilians have been caught in the crossfire. I don't like that the people responsible might get comfortable government jobs in the new lunar authority," I said, sitting down at the small breakfast table by the patio door.

Silverstein nodded, my words mostly echoing his own from the last few weeks. It wasn't a month ago we were stepping over bloody and wounded civilians in the Port of Paris, after an improvised device was used to force open a syndicate currency warehouse. Room service arrived, pulling me away from that memory, but the cold and empty feeling would persist the rest of the day. I hated the Syndicate.

I stared at the food we'd been brought, surprised at what Kale had been able to arrange since he had taken control of food distribution from Earth. I hadn't had a fried egg or a piece of bacon in months, and there it was, right in front of me. It was delicious. I felt terrible eating it, knowing many people were not so fortunate.

"I got a shareholder's notice that Kale took control of Uroboros Financial," Silverstein said, between bites.

"What? What's he doing?" I asked, a little annoyed.

"A damn good job," Silverstein said, holding up a piece of bacon, appreciatively.

"You don't care that he's basically stolen your company?" I asked.

"Not really. In the final analysis that isn't what he's done. He's basically me, remember?" Silverstein said, accompanied by his easy smile.

"Kale is nothing like you. He's cold, and unstable," I said, shaking my head worriedly.

"Not since taking Brook under his wing. She's changed him. He's actually kind of great now. He's even managed to track down Perfidy and enlist his aid. He's protecting the Earth, with very little help or appreciation given," Silverstein said.

"The cyborg from Madmar's warehouse in Midtown? He's alive? You've been keeping tabs the whole time?"

"Ha, yep, of course. We haven't been able to communicate directly, but I've been able to use my shareholder connection to track some of what Kale has been up to."

"How is Brook?"

"Kale has made her a VP of records and logistics, or something like that. Her special training makes her very detail oriented, ideal for tracking anomalous entries into the Uroboros Financial systems."

"I can't imagine her wielding spreadsheets and memos instead of a soup ladle," I replied, somewhat surprised.

We assumed getting the lunar colony stable would be a springboard for change and renewal across the globe below. Silverstein was taking it all pretty hard, something Brook had been concerned about. I think the only thing that kept him going recently was the prospect of a new lunar authority and reconciliation of repossessed property and assets as a consequence. If successful, it would unlock the portion of the global economy that relied on trade and tourism with the moon.

The prospect would be a small comfort compared to all the stress we'd be facing throughout the day. I had been feeling better lately, but I still carried a pair of peanut bars with me wherever I went. Nothing seemed to make Silverstein feel better, except those rare moments he and Taylor could find the time to be alone and do whatever it is they do. Their relationship had been close lately, even if still platonic on the surface.

"Is that handgun going to work for you? I know you prefer rifles, but it is all they would let my security detail carry," Silverstein said, sitting down across from me.

"It's .40 caliber, and the ammunition is custom, low recoil. It's pretty nice. You get it from Henry?" I asked.

"No, Ervin Carol got it from the security office at the Lunar AI facility. I figured there would be less liability that way, what with trackers and such."

"Good call."

We finished breakfast, both of us probably a little lonely for Taylor. She was always good at keeping a meal lively. We'd come to rely on her quite a bit in the last couple of weeks; she was seen to be inviolable by the populace, an instant celebrity. Silverstein worried it would change her, but all she had done was bring back fashion shows, museum viewings, and theater to the Lunar Colony. These were things I had only a glimmer of appreciation for, but that the regular work-a-day people really needed.

I think Silverstein needed it as well. Arranging the logistics and the venues had been a necessary distraction for them both. The human interest in such things wasn't unknown to me, and I never voiced any objection. All the same, lurking in the dark corners of those events made me long for the cold winter forests of Finland, where there were no people, or the tunnels where mine tend to dwell.

The hotel was quiet that early in the morning, the continental breakfast for the folks in economy rooms not even out in the foyer yet. The desk attendant smiled and waved at us as we went through the doors, a decidedly different reaction than the first time she'd seen me. Taylor's exposure had been good for Drones and Metasapients because she was often seen on video interacting with us like anyone else. There were those that felt she was a menace, or merely a machine or possession like a pen or a mobile, but those folks were in the minority.

For me, if I was going to be stuck somewhere that wasn't Port Montaigne, the moon was fine. At least it wasn't Mars. Stupid, stupid, Mars, and everything that had to do with that foul place.

"He is your security?" The driver asked, opening the limousine door for Silverstein.

"Yes."

The driver nodded, motioning for me to join him up front. I rounded the hovering vehicle and opened the passenger door. Once everyone was back inside, we began moving while Henry Scarsdale and a few other dignitaries chatted quietly behind me. The driver made a U-turn, heading back toward the prearranged route we'd discussed a week ago with Henry.

"Smallest security guy I've ever seen," the driver remarked, keeping his gaze on the road.

"Who was the biggest?" I asked, trying not to sound too annoyed.

"I'm kidding, Ezra. I know who you are. I drove back when Henry took you guys down to deal with Maurice Madmar. Followed the medical examiner back after recovery. You did the moon a favor," he said, batting me playfully with the back of his hand.

"What's your name?" I asked, looking over my shoulder through the glass at Silverstein as he talked with the other dignitaries.

"I'm Foster Lecce, been driving for Mr. Scarsdale for about seven years," he said, taking the corner, and keeping the route.

"Sorry, that day was a blur," I said, turning my attention to Foster.

He seemed to be genuine, but I couldn't understand why he wanted to make small talk, let alone about that day. Dr. Madmar's last stand. The deaths of the telemechanics he had kidnapped still haunted my dreams, the sound of them gasping for breath still visited me in the dark. Dwelling on it always led to recall the event in detail, and consider every move I made. I did my best not to think about it.

"I didn't mean to bring up a bad memory," Foster said, probably in response to my pained expression.

"Let's just do the job, get everyone there, back home, and with a minimum of talking," I said, resting my hand on the pistol in my inside pocket.

"Yeah, okay," he responded, taking the turn that took us toward the tunnel, situated between bio-domes.

The rest of the drive was blessedly quiet. The Lunar Colony was a different place than when we had arrived. Now, the lights were on, local colors on display, and people were walking the streets and taking public transportation to work. The slender buildings that occupied space with the supports holding up the biological enclosures overhead were bustling with activity. There were places Taylor hadn't been able to force open, and a handful of dark places that wouldn't come back to life with Silverstein's financial wizardry, but they were thankfully rare.

We arrived at the meeting place, a casino in the upscale entertainment dome, affectionately referred to as "Little Vegas." For someone with enhanced senses, it was the worst meeting place ever, the whole venue a contrast of darkness, bright lights, and holographic advertisements. It all ran together, dancing in the streets outside parlors, bars, and gambling establishments. Apparently, it was the only place the Syndicate considered to be holy ground, off-limits for violence. Degenerate jerks that they were, I wondered if that informal rule would be enough to keep the meet peaceful.

We pulled in beneath a huge well-lit canopy outside one of the largest hotels, taking our place in a line of other luxury vehicles and limousines. Silverstein, along with the rest of the VIPs, got out on the sidewalk, and after exchanging handshakes with a few people waiting outside, proceeded toward the entrance. The security detail formed a loose ring around them, hands inside their jackets. I preferred to keep my distance, walking where I could see the group and the environment. I kept my hands at my sides and my hand off my earbud receiver as I walked calmly with the flow of the rest of the crowd.

"I'll stay at this door. If there is trouble, don't call or waste any time, just come to me and we'll leave," I said, closing the distance with Silverstein as security checked him in at the entrance.

"Okay, I will. What about Ervin?" Silverstein asked.

"The process could survive without him, he has a successor. You do not," I said, trying to be as rational about it all.

"Kale doesn't count?" Silverstein asked, with a wink.

"Nope."

I stayed at the door with one of the other members of the detail. He was a big guy, and was not-so-quietly scoffing at my stature as I leaned up against the wall beside him. The flow of people felt natural here, and there didn't appear to be any eyes on, or remote surveillance. I was glad it was going well, but I stooped down to check the rifle I'd hidden under the limousine anyway. It was still there, right where I'd left it in the hours before what constituted dawn on the moon. It reassured me as much as it made me worry. If I could sneak a high powered rifle into the meet, anyone else probably could.

"You worked with Mr. Uroboros long?" the goon asked me.

"Shut up. Watch the street," I replied, drawing back my hood.

He opened his mouth as if to say something, until he saw my slate gray skin and silvery hair. I took my gloves off, so my clawed hands would be more visible. It was about discouraging trouble as much as watching for it now. I wandered over to the limousine so that my rifle would be within easy reach. That's when I first smelled it. The scent came out over the mildew from the heavy condensation dripping down from the dome overhead, and all the various scents from the people in the crowd.

The scent wafted across the breeze, only for a moment. My heightened sense of smell triggered fond memories. I was transported back to Finland, the wintery forest all around me, intense cold increasing my already powerful senses. I wished like Hell that Brook were there, as her senses were even keener than my own. I looked around warily, but saw no one out of the ordinary. I thought maybe it was the product of my own intense desires, coupled with stress, and too much breakfast.

The goon assigned to help me was watching a video on his mobile while he chatted with someone. I could tell by the look on his face it was personal, his eyebrows reaching up his forehead like he was impatient for the job to be over. I wanted to flick the mobile from his hand, take my considerable frustration at the situation out on him. Instead, I took a deep breath and hugged the jacket Taylor had made me.

I thought about the Finnish winter, and the cold so sharp that it triggered adrenaline. I remember being able to hear for miles, feel the sleeping earth beneath my feet, and the cleanest air I'd ever breathed filling my lungs. It felt, for a moment, like I was totally losing it.

Fortunately, the meeting went quickly, less than twenty-five minutes. Silverstein was back outside before anyone else, presumably because the diplomatic formalities had been satisfied. He was alone, which made me worry. As I walked up, that intense smell hit me, again. I looked around, desperate to find the source of it, but there was nothing but a dense crowd of people. It was getting closer, whatever it was.

"Uh oh, what's wrong?" Silverstein asked, trying to see whatever he thought I was seeing.

"Something smells off. Where is Ervin Carol?" I asked.

"Smells? Still inside with everyone else," Silverstein replied, checking his mobile.

"Yeah, I don't like this. We should go. Now. Can we go?" I begged, waving Silverstein over.

"That's fine. The hotel isn't far, and the driver will probably be able to get back in plenty of time to pick up Henry and Ervin," he replied, somewhat confused.

We jogged over to the line of vehicles, the scent getting stronger as we did. As we approached the limousine I noticed, too late, the driver was slumped over. There was a stun gun laying in the passenger seat beside him. I whirled around, drawing my sidearm.

"Don't move, Ezra," Dr. Madmar said, stepping behind Silverstein, pointing a sidearm of his own at the back of Silverstein's head.

I froze, some powerful suggestion taking over. It wouldn't have mattered much, anyway. Madmar had a gun pointed at Silverstein. I'm fast, but not that fast.

"The M-unit voice regulator must be working this time," Madmar said, calmly nodding toward me.

"How... I killed you, felt your neck break, with my own two hands," I growled, struggling to move.

"Did you? Oh, thank God. Thank you. That must be why I'm running on my redundant system now," Madmar replied, deeply relieved.

I looked past Silverstein at Madmar, and realized he was the source of the scent. There he was, dressed in the same clothing he wore at the server farm in Finland, his face bearing the scars from the beating I gave him during the confrontation there. The Dr. Madmar I killed on the moon, and the one we'd encountered in Finland on Earth, were clearly not the same individual.

"What now?" I said, struggling to move.

"I need you to listen carefully. It is imperative that you find Vance Uroboros. He can't face them like this," Madmar said, his tone of voice calm and unfettered like I'd never heard before.

"He's right there," I said, only able to flick a finger in Silverstein's direction.

"Relative to the greatest sum of the man, no, he is not, exactly," Madmar said, looking up at the huge clock on the casino across the street.

"What is he talking about?" Silverstein said, trying to look over his shoulder before Madmar pressed in with the barrel of his gun.

He pulled the trigger, shooting Silverstein in front of me.

"No!" I growled, finally able to take a step.

"After I'm gone, make sure the throat module is destroyed so that no more can ever be made," Madmar said, his face ravaged by intense sadness.

Before I could reach him, he shot himself in the head. The moment he pulled the trigger, the strange control he had over me ended. I stood there in shock, looking down at Silverstein's silent form. I knelt to feel for a pulse, in case there was any hope, but he was gone. I'd lost close friends before, but Taylor... she would be destroyed by this.

I cursed, and looked around for my backup.

The worthless door guard finally reached the scene, calling for the rest of the detail to respond. I walked over to Madmar and checked him for anything that might give me a clue how he arrived. We knew he'd likely escaped Port Montaigne, but that he'd done so without the equipment stored at the warehouse. There was nothing in his pockets aside from a stub for port access where his transport was likely docked. I needed to have some answers, something to tell Taylor when she found out what had happened to Silverstein.

There was no vengeance to be had at that point, the culprit already twice dead, but still not dead enough. When these things happen, you go numb, the feelings stop in that moment, and the world just slows down. I wasn't paying attention, and I didn't see what was to come next. I should have, but I didn't.

"Ezra, what happened?" Henry Scarsdale asked, about a split second before the bullet took his head off.

The street came alive with gunfire as a heavily armed third party emerged from alleys and what appeared to be rental vehicles. They were dressed like they came from the Eurozone and carried expensive, easy to conceal, submachine guns. The Syndicate was outgunned. Apparently, I was the only one to sneak a high-powered rifle to the meet.

For a moment, I just stood there, bullets passing by me, looking down at Silverstein. His face was a mask of shock, frozen in time, Madmar lying beside him. Lifeless, they reached out to each other with their blood as it ran across the sidewalk toward the gutter. The world came back into focus, and my training kicked in.

I disengaged the magnetic clamps on my rifle, and pulled it from beneath the limousine. Men with submachine guns tore up the commercial storefront and limousines around me. They were professionals, aiming high, and only for Syndicate targets. They were augmented as well, likely with optic implants. Not a single bullet seemed to be wasted on the fleeing civilians in the crowd. It was loud, the report of fully automatic weapons drowning out all the music and splendor of Little Vegas, accompanied by the clinking of shell casing as they fell.

Then, a fourth party entered the fray, possibly a Syndicate asset brought in as a contingency. Someone, probably on the other side of the dome, was shooting the third party while they attacked the Syndicate. Whoever they were, they were good, putting rounds in the ten ring from more than a mile away, gauging from the sound of the report. This did little to dissuade any of the warring parties from murdering one another.

I popped up and took a couple of shots, feeling the vehicle lurch against me as it absorbed a burst of gunfire in response. As soon as they saw me, half of them turned and started firing in my direction. I couldn't be sure if they were gunning for me, or shooting at the only guy with a rifle. Fortunately, Henry had the foresight to up armor his vehicle. Bring armor if you can't bring weapons, I guess. All the same, I opened the door and pulled the unconscious driver to the ground where he'd have better cover. I grabbed the stun gun in the process, sliding it into my pocket.

"Screw this," I said, looking out at the sheer number of unfamiliar adversaries slowly approaching the casino beneath a curtain of suppressing fire.

There was no way I was leaving Madmar with his throat module, or Silverstein in that mess. Slinging my rifle, I grabbed them both by their coat collars and dragged their corpses hurriedly along the street. I could hear the security detail yelling at me as I fled to drainage grating, where the street met the sidewalk. I didn't see Ervin or any other VIP worth protecting at that point, so I pulled out.

"Run, you idiots," I might have said.

I kicked the grating open, and dropped through, land in the shallow tunnel. Gunfire echoed above as I traversed the runoff pipe toward what I hoped would be a maintenance zone. A steady sheet of condensation from the street above flowed past me as I pulled Madmar and Silverstein, one by one, down the tunnel with me. Once it widened out to a central access tunnel, I broke into a sprint, dragging the corpses, one in each hand, as the sounds of gunfire rapidly disappeared behind me.

I pulled out my mobile and tried to call Taylor. I had a decent signal, but she wasn't answering. I set my mobile to automatically call her every sixty seconds. Cursing, I traded the mobile for a peanut bar from my pocket and looked down at Silverstein. It occurred to me that we'd never again share a breakfast, or exchange paperbacks after they'd been read. He was gone, and I had to keep moving.

There was a maintenance facility at the end of the tunnel, and an industrial freezer where chemicals were stored. I pulled Silverstein and Madmar inside, hiding them behind some barrels. I felt sick closing the door, and leaving Silverstein in the cold.

I tried to dismiss what Madmar said, but the smell of him triggered every memory I had of this particular version of him. I thought about that day at the server farm, how completely different Madmar had been, how insane he had sounded. There was no sadness, and certainly no concern for us in his voice. He was very dissimilar from the man that just shot my friend and then himself.

I tried to call Kale, letting it ring several times. Right before it would have gone to his messaging service, he picked up.

"Ezra, I would have expected you to return Brook's numerous calls before calling me. You lunar dwelling folk have been rather aloof lately," he said, his voice echoing slightly.

"Apologies. We've been dealing with the syndicate up here. They were targeting anyone close to Silverstein. He had us stop taking calls to try and insulate our friends from retaliation. The Syndicate has some reach on Earth, even in Port Montaigne," I explained.

"Enough to blow up a tram tunnel and send trained assassins to kill Brook?" Kale asked, clearly angry.

"Eurozone guys, expensive weapons, military tactics?" I asked.

"Yes."

"They just hit the Syndicate up here. What did Brook do to become a target?" I asked, doing my best to stay calm.

"She got close to something we shouldn't discuss over mobile. Are you alright? Are Silverstein and Taylor alright?" Kale asked, his tone softening.

"Silverstein is dead. Madmar showed up, right before the Syndicate got hit and shot him, and then himself."

"Are you sure?"

"What do you mean? I'm sitting here in an underground facility, having stashed their corpses in a freezer. Yes, I'm sure," I replied, pretty annoyed.

"Ezra, this is Madmar we're talking about. You killed him, it was independently verified. Somehow, he showed up and killed Silverstein anyway. Did he say anything, do anything that...?"

"He said I needed to find Vance Uroboros, that he can't fight them like this," I replied.

"Who is 'them'?" Kale asked.

"I don't know, but those Eurozone guys showed up right afterward."

"I want you to have the same doctor who verified Maurice Madmar's death to look at Silverstein, and this other Madmar," Kale explained.

"Can we trust her? What if she—?"

"It doesn't matter," Kale interrupted. "Be there with her when she does the autopsies, gauge her reactions, and observe what she does. I trust you'll know if she is genuine and whether the analysis can be trusted."

"I will," I said, feeling a little better.

"Did you and Taylor ever part ways with Silverstein, has he ever been out of your sight for an extended duration?"

I had to think about it for a moment. "Um, once, shortly after we met, in Port Montaigne. In Midtown. He went to look for a telemechanic, to help him locate some code."

"How long was he gone?" Kale asked.

"Hours, but I don't understand how that..."

"I don't either. Not yet. Ezra, please, do what I've asked. Get the corpses analyzed, and keep yourself safe. Call me as soon as it is done," Kale asked, calmly.

"But, Taylor, what will I tell her?" I said.

"Tell her everything is going to be all right. You have my word, Ezra," Kale replied, sounding eerily like Silverstein.

"Okay, I'll tell her," I said, ending the call.

Previous to that, Kale had always sounded cold, even hollow. I couldn't understand why Brook would have agreed to go with him as opposed to staying with Matthias. It was clear from that conversation that she knew something about Kale the rest of us did not.

I headed toward the industrial dome, sticking to the tunnels as much as I could. The streets above where filled with sirens and emergency services as they rushed the other direction. Little Vegas was a little warzone by now. I passed a few other Drones on the way, sleepily waving to them as they passed me, carrying tools. I'd gotten to know a few, and word had gotten around about my arrival. The Lunar Colony Drones were beyond easy going, lacking the militancy and territorial nature of their Earth-dwelling counterparts.

"Are you okay?" A female Drone had stopped to ask the question. I think she was a Type Three.

"My friend has been killed. I left him in service facility cooler beneath the entertainment dome," I explained, lowering my head.

"I'm sorry. We'll make sure he isn't disturbed until you return," she replied.

I looked up at her, making sure I committed her face to memory. She was only a little taller than me, and likely a worker of some kind by the tools she carried. Her hands were rough and forearms muscular from turning wrenches. In spite of her rough appearance, she had a warm face and a soothing voice, rare features for a Type Three.

"I appreciate that. Hey, do you have any food? I don't have anything to trade."

She thought about it for a moment. "If we were in trouble, would you help us?"

"I will protect you," I said, sensing what she was asking.

"Okay," she said, giving me a hunk of black bread, wrapped in wax paper.

"I'm Ezra..."

"Ezra One, yeah, everyone knows. I'm Viv, pleased to meet you."

"Who is hassling you?" I asked.

"No one, but it's nice to have someone to protect us, just in case," she explained.

"But, you're expecting trouble?" I asked.

"You stink of death and guns."

I lowered my head a little further. "I doubt whatever I'm mixed in will come below. If it does, I'll deal with it."

"Okay. I'll let everyone know to find you if there is trouble," she said, handing me a piece of aluminum.

"What is this?" I said, turning it over in my hand.

"It'll tell you how to get to our Tribehome, and where we sleep," she said, putting a finger on the inscriptions.

"Why tell me?" I asked, baffled.

"This is your home now," Viv explained, putting a hand on my shoulder.

I nodded. "That means a lot to me."

"You Type Ones are like lost children. Always wandering. Feared. Mostly homeless.. I don't know why, none I've known were bad, and a few were even good," Viv said, smiling.

"I have to handle a thing, but I'll be back. I promise," I said, taking a bite of the bread she gave me. It tasted like Brook's, only moist.

We parted ways, Viv giving my arm a squeeze as I stepped away. I looked back over my shoulder. She was still standing where I left her, watching me go. She held up a hand and turned, a slight smile appearing on her face. Emboldened, I made haste for the industrial dome, moving quickly through the tunnels until I could go no further.

As I emerged, I looked around to get my bearings. I was at the far side of the residential dome. It came down at a strict angle to meet with the four-lane tube granting travel to where the industrial dome sat off and away from the rest of the colony. The roads were empty, as no industrial manufacturing had resumed following the Shutdown.

I stepped out into the road and walked toward the industrial district. It seemed like a long way, but I'd grown accustomed to going everywhere by car with Silverstein and Taylor. I approached the metal and ceramic plates that made up the four lane road connecting the residential and commercial bio-domes. I was a half dozen steps inside when my mobile began to vibrate in my pocket.

"Taylor?" I said, holding my mobile up to my ear.

"Yeah, what's up? You guys on your way back?" she said, sounding totally casual.

"I've been trying to call you for almost an hour. Things did not go well at the meeting, and…"

A trio of sleek unmanned aircraft passed over me at high velocity, rocketing toward the industrial district. The force of their engines blew me head over heels, rattling the plates that made up the road. As I regained my footing I could see panels open across the bottom of the craft, ordinance slowly being lowered as they turned the corner and headed toward the central AI facility where Selene was housed, and Taylor visited.

"Taylor, get out of there, now!" I said, recovering my mobile.

"What? Why?" she replied.

"Right now, Taylor! RIGHT NOW!" I screamed, breaking into a run.

Through the thick polycarbonate shielding, I could see heavy ordinance strike the central AI facility, the subsequent explosion ripping through the environmental shielding. Passive atmosphere rushed past me as the industrial zone quickly began losing pressure. I knelt down locking my claw around the edge of one of the ceramic plates beneath me and held on for dear life.

"TAYLOR! TAYLOR CAN YOU HEAR ME?" I screamed past the rush of air and debris flitting past me toward the breach.

There was no response.

CHAPTER 2

TRAM TUNNEL 021, MIDTOWN, PORT MONTAIGNE

7:28 AM April 16th, 2200

From the margins of Brook's Cookbook, Part 4 –

"Who was that?" I asked, watching Kale come down the ruined tram tunnel toward Perfidy, and me.

"Ezra," he replied, a grim look crossing his face.

"Oh, finally they give us a call?" Perfidy said, inspecting the twisted wreckage of the subway car mostly blocking the tunnel ahead.

"I can't believe I was able to actually get a call down here," Kale said, looking up and around suspiciously.

"What did he SAY?!" I asked, barely able to contain myself.

"It isn't good, I'm afraid. The same people who tried to kill you have evidently made a move against the lunar criminal Syndicate. Immediately previous to that, Madmar appeared and killed Silverstein, and then shot himself," Kale said, calmly pocketing his mobile.

"That is messed up. Seriously, how is Madmar even alive?" Perfidy asked, standing up.

"I'm not convinced Madmar is or was alive, or that Silverstein is truly dead. Even in death, I don't trust Dr. Maurice Madmar," Kale said, frowning.

"Oh no. Are Ezra and Taylor all right?" I asked, wringing my hands.

Silverstein had been kind and good to me and all the Drones of Port Montaigne. If Kale was wrong, and Silverstein was truly dead, I knew it would make tensions between Drones in Port Montaigne and humans worse. He'd been one of a few that tried to help us, when most people tried to take things from us after the Shutdown.

"For now, but we need to find out who is responsible for these attacks, and arrest them," Kale replied, looking at dried blood spread across the tram wall beside him.

"Arrest? You are kidding, right? Get Ezra One down here. He and I will kill these pieces of shit," Perfidy said, tapping the handgun holstered to the front of his tactical vest.

"I need them alive. I want to climb the whole beanstalk, invade the giant's castle, and take them down. I don't want to just kill faceless drones to make myself feel better. This has to be about the big picture, Perfidy," Kale said, nodding to me.

I nodded. "I agree. We have to…"

A strange odor wafted past, one I'd only smelled a couple of times before. I stood on the tips of my toes and sniffed the air, trying to get a sense of the direction. Kale looked at me, in that funny way he does when I do something that amuses him.

"What? What is it?" he asked.

"The wind shifted, the air's moving in the opposite direction," I said, following the scent.

"Yeah, the crew working at the other end probably reached the ventilation system and repaired it by now," Kale said, checking his watch.

I squeezed between the tram wall and the subway car to go further in. It led me to a service door hidden behind a conduit cage in a shallow service tunnel. It took a moment, but I got the door open using my picks. I found an envelope on the ground, with my name inscribed on it. Beyond was a concrete hallway and stairs leading up to what I suspected would be Midtown.

"Hey, don't run off like that," Perfidy said, catching up to me, Kale just a few steps behind.

"What did you smell?" Kale asked.

"Old books, scrambled eggs, and a strange tar-like smell. I was smelling Cal's bookstore," I said, stooping down to look at the envelope.

Perfidy gazed at the envelope with his enhanced vision for a few moments. "It's safe, no residue or hazardous materials."

"'Kay," I said, picking it and opening it.

Inside was my old data slate. It was badly damaged. There was also a note, handwritten with a fountain pen.

"Brook, I was left with no time to warn you. When I came to look for you, your computer was all I was able to find. I had to stay down here for a few days before I moved on, but I knew you'd come back. There is much I would like to discuss, things I would like to tell you, but it isn't safe now. Please forgive me, I never meant for you to get hurt. Cal," I said, reading the note aloud.

"Looks like he stayed down here for a bit," Perfidy said as he found a sleeping bag and several empty cans of food under the stairs beyond.

"This staircase isn't on the civic plans or registered as access to the tram tunnel with the transportation authority. It was illegally subcontracted and installed within the last couple of years," I said, running my hands over the painted railing on the stairs.

"Is that how the bomber got down here?" Kale asked.

"It's so clean in here. It is really hard to tell. I'm not detecting any bomb residue. To be honest, something about this bombing is very familiar," Perfidy said, looking all around with his robot eyes.

"Familiar?" Kale asked.

"The transport that went down twenty years ago?" I asked Perfidy.

Perfidy nodded.

"Did the transport belong to Uroboros Financial?" Kale asked.

"Yep," Perfidy replied, taking a couple of steps up the stairs.

"Then we probably still have the wreckage in storage. It would have returned to us following the various investigations by local and CGG agencies. They may have even recovered part of the device, allowing us to make a comparison," Kale stated. He pulled out his mobile.

"If the demolitions expertise used to do both attacks syncs up, it would narrow the field of suspects significantly," Perfidy said, nodding to me.

"Those Red Coat guys, that buy and sell people?" I asked.

"They are led by an elderly man, a cyborg kept alive by old and, at the time, very illegal rejuvenation drugs. I met him once, in a dark place. I looked for him afterward, and while I discovered quite a bit about his operation, I never found him. I'd like a rematch." Perfidy cracked his knuckles.

"Being able to put a name and a face to the attackers would be good information to hand over to the new civic authority. It would legitimize what little local government we've been able to piece together. We need to set it up so that the new local police catches these individuals," Kale said, calmly scrolling through notifications on his mobile.

"You said Silverstein might not be dead. What are we going to do to help Ezra One and Taylor?" I asked as I tucked the envelope into my shoulder bag.

"Leave that to Ezra and me for the time being. Focus on finding these Red Coats, or whatever they're called, and get the intel to the Port Montaigne PD. We need to get back to figuring out how to feed the planet," Kale said, gazing up the stairs.

"You want to see where this goes?" Perfidy asked, bringing his rifle around into a ready position.

"Intensely," Kale replied.

I took the lead, glad for something to do that wasn't looking at spreadsheets and tired faces in conference rooms. The stairs went up to a small park in Midtown, coming up from what appeared to be a shallow drainage grating. It was expertly hidden, and made to look like a regular fixture of the city. The concrete and metal of the grating had been chemically aged to look like the rest of everything nearby.

"Wild," Perfidy said, looking back down to the stairs.

Kale put his hands in his pockets, his suit coat bunching up between his shoulders, and strolled out to the edge of the park to gaze at Midtown. After taking a look around, Perfidy and I joined him. Kale had that look, like he was thinking with all his might about something, his eyes in full squint mode.

"Why this park? Why here?" Kale asked.

"It's out of the way, at least a mile from any major thoroughfares?" Perfidy ventured.

Kale shook his head. "No, this would have required a lot of work and misdirection to construct without anyone noticing. Being able to move unseen between Midtown and downtown like this must be part of some larger strategy."

"This tram tunnel being closed has cost the city a great deal of revenue, both in lost productivity, and lost wages. Many people are struggling to get to work, especially with so many vehicles still locked out for repossession. In blowing the tunnel to try and kill me, they may have tipped their hand, at least in part," I said, wondering how many other tunnels were rigged to blow.

"It is hard to imagine them being so desperate. You said you didn't get much from Cal when you visited," Perfidy said.

"Our adversary doesn't know that. All they might know is that Brook made contact. If that alone was enough for them to do something like this, Cal must be extremely valuable, or dangerous, to them," Kale replied.

"Should I call to have us picked up?" Perfidy asked.

"No," Kale said, squinting up at the taller buildings behind us.

"You think they have the park under surveillance?" I said, nervously looking around.

"I would, if it were me," Kale replied, heading back for the stairs.

"What? Why'd we even step out in the open? Gah," Perfidy growled, somewhat annoyed.

"If our adversaries did build this stairwell, they didn't build it just to set the explosives meant to kill Brook. I want them to know that I know, scramble to adjust their plans, and make a mistake," Kale replied, letting me go ahead of him.

"So, we're heading back down to make it look like we aren't all done down there?" Perfidy said, nodding.

"Yes."

I led the way back down and forward through to the crew working the tunnel from the boarding platform beyond. They were surprised to see us come out of the dark, but Kale had begun to cultivate a reputation for being on the ground, working beside the other workers. He handed out some money to help cover the workers' lunches and transportation home after the shift and made small talk with them. I could tell it made a big impact, everyone working to clear the tunnel like they were on a mission.

"Thanks, Mr. Uroboros, for coming down," the foreman said, extending a hand down to help us up to the boarding platform.

"See that the tunnel opens on schedule. Our fellow citizens need a reliable means to get to work," Kale replied, accepting the hand up.

I leapt the five feet up to the platform easily, startling the foreman somewhat. He tipped his hardhat to me and then gave Perfidy a hand up. After exchanging some pleasantries, we headed back to Kale's private transport and climbed inside. I really did like that transport, not just for the comfortable seats, but for the advanced com station. The first thing I did when I sat down was send Ezra a text, to let him know I was thinking about him. He didn't respond, but I figured he was probably busy.

"Where to?" Perfidy asked.

"Good question. How's the algorithm Matthias supplied you with?" Kale asked me.

"It's nearly decrypted the first of the file packages from Dr. Helmet's records. It looks like a lot of video files, and copies of communications. That's what you wanted, right?" I replied.

"Yes. If we can figure out who Dr. Helmet was talking to before his death, it may give us insight into what he did with his time, what he was working on, and so forth. His journals are confusing to me, and I need some sort of context to decipher them," Kale explained.

"We should be able to watch the first in an hour or so," I reported, checking my shiny new data slate.

"Good. Let's go to the Uroboros Financial archives, and see if we can find the wreckage from that transport that went down twenty years ago," Kale said, patting Perfidy on the shoulder.

"You got it, Boss."

Perfidy took us into the air, the sleek transport breaking through the clouds in moments to take us across Port Montaigne. I did a check of the civic records, trying to see if there was any mention in the Parks and Recreation departmental records of other new construction in parks situated over tram tunnels. The database was massive, and it would require many hours of analysis to find anything of substance. I tried anyway.

We set down in an empty parking lot, overgrown with weeds and locked up behind a rusty chain link fence. As I stepped out behind Perfidy, the wind shifted, blowing the smell of guns and adrenaline past me. I backed up hard into Kale, pushing him back into the transport. Perfidy, sensing my panic, brought his rifle up just as a trio of armed men wearing red vinyl coats opened fire from a copse of ill-kept trees.

Perfidy dropped to one knee, and returned fire. His rifle was incredibly loud, hurting my ears. Bullets struck the outside of the transport as Kale cursed and pulled out his mobile. I rushed to the console and signaled that we were in distress, hoping that Port Montaigne PD was somewhere nearby.

The gunfire ended abruptly, only the sound of Perfidy's boots across the parking lot outside broke the silence. Kale sat up, his annoyed expression quickly melting away when he looked over at me. He stood up, walked over, and put his finger through a neat hole in my loose fitting jacket. He wrapped his arms around me, hugging me for a moment, before stepping away.

"I'm not hit," I said, confused by his sudden concern.

"I can see that. Come on. Perfidy has probably killed them all by now," Kale said, annoyed.

He stepped out warily, then headed over to where Perfidy was kneeling. I stood there in shock, the warmth of his arms still encircling me, the place where my cheek had touched his still carrying a hint of the sensation. I didn't know why, but ever since he carried me wounded and dying from Downtown, the way I felt about Kale was different. Every time I have been frightened since, I summon that memory. I imagine his arms bearing me up, his long hair brushing against my face, and his soothing voice reassuring me.

I reluctantly banished the sensation to join Kale and Perfidy outside. There were three corpses laying in the tall grass, a neat bullet hole in each of their heads. Perfidy was lifting a satchel one of them was carrying, and getting ready to open it. He paused for a moment, giving the sack a slight shake.

"You already know what it is?" Kale asked.

"Cracking tools, to allow them access to the archive. They weren't here to hit us," Perfidy said, shaking his head.

"Why would they just open fire like that? Did they recognize Kale?" I asked.

"No. They recognized you and me," Perfidy said, a pained expression crossing his face.

"What? Why would they shoot at us?" I asked, surprised.

"Because we stopped The Devil from getting Taylor. He doesn't just trade people. He collects kids, the more rare or special, the more he wants them for his collection. Back then, Taylor was as special as it gets," Perfidy said, replacing rounds in the magazine of his rifle.

"The Devil? What does he do with the kids?" I asked.

"The Devil, the Red Devil, the Man in Red, he's got a lot of aliases, but that's what I've been calling him for years. No one knows what he does with the kids, but they are never seen again. Even twenty years later, he's probably pissed off about losing Taylor," Perfidy explained.

"If that's true, he'd be after Ezra too, right?" I said, already panicking.

"Where is Port Montaigne PD?" Kale growled, scanning the sky for radio cars.

"They're tied up at a CGG financial facility. Four more of these assholes hit the place, took two safety deposit boxes, killed two guards, and got out just before police could respond. Smooth, less than three minutes from entry to exit. These guys are good," Perfidy said, holding his hand up to the plate covering his aural implant.

"Who did the safety deposit boxes belong to?" Kale asked, giving one of the red coat clad goons a nudge with his shoe.

"Someone called Cal X. Could be our bookstore guy, yeah?" Perfidy replied, looking to me.

"Could be," I replied, shaking my head sadly at the dead people arrayed at our feet.

"Perfidy, are these Eurozone mercs that attacked Brook and Ezra connected to this man you call The Devil?" Kale asked.

"We'll know once I get inside and look at the transport wreckage," Perfidy said, gesturing to the archive.

"Call it in. Let's get to the archive and acquire what we came for," Kale grumbled, heading for the warehouse.

We headed over to the door, where Kale brushed off the biometric sensor before using it to open the door. The inside was musty, smelling as though no one had been there for years. A thin blanket of dust covered hundreds of shrink-wrapped pallets, arrayed across dozens of industrial shelves, reaching all the way to the ceiling. Fortunately, there was a lift truck old enough to be off grid and unlocked for use. After finding a battery with a charge and hooking it up, the old forklift came to life.

Perfidy drove it down the aisle toward where the archive records said the wreckage was stored, bringing down several pallets from about midway up the shelf. It took a bit to unwrap all the shattered metal so it could be inspected, and a little longer to find the tote bin containing the remnants of the explosive device used. Perfidy gazed at all the components, his robot eyes running several scans for residue and similar.

"The bombers that blew up the tram tunnel and the transport are the same guy. Same custom detonators, materials, and wiring. The Devil definitely did this. It is all connected, boss," Perfidy said, worriedly.

"And you're sure this is the transport Taylor IA was aboard, as an infant?" Kale asked.

"Yep," Perfidy and I replied, in unison.

Kale scratched his chin. "Jennifer, the passive telemechanic that helped us with the CGG server core, lost her parents to a terrorist attack, yes?"

"Yeah, I think that's what she said," Perfidy replied.

"Was she a child when it happened?" Kale asked.

"Yes, hence a guardian being appointed," I said, using my data slate to pull up the record.

"Brook, I want any attack against Uroboros Financial property or personnel, where explosives were employed, flagged in the system for review," Kale said, running his hand over a piece of the wreckage.

"Already doing it," I replied, tapping out the necessary directives into my data slate.

"You were both there that day the transport went down. A strange coincidence. On the way back to the office, I want you to tell me everything about that day. Anything you can remember," Kale said, tucking his hands in his pockets and heading for the exit.

"Ezra One was there, too, to meet me. It was my first night in Port Montaigne, after traveling there from the Factory," I said.

"There's a lot about that day that didn't make sense to me. The more it all comes into focus, the less I like it," Perfidy said, wearily, as he shut the lift truck down.

"You tried to find The Devil?" I asked, following Perfidy toward the archive access.

"Yeah, a bunch of times, years after that first encounter. Never caught sight of him again, but it is clear he has global reach and extensive resources. He uses human trafficking to fund all his operations, making it hard to track him. The CGG opening up international borders to allow people to more freely travel was a good thing, except when it came to stopping people like The Devil," Perfidy explained.

"You said he was using longevity drugs. Is he a member of the Cabal?" I asked.

"Yes," Kale said, pulling one of Dr. Helmet's journals from his suit pocket.

"He's in there?" Perfidy asked, surprised.

"I think so," Kale said, flipping through the pages. "Dr. Madmar has an entry about a member of the Cabal he calls 'Warbartl,' and a thief of innocence. He did quite a bit of research into pre-Christian Alpine legends trying to learn more about this individual. The color red is significant somehow, relating to a pagan yule tradition, or something. As I said, his journals are very confusing," Kale explained.

"What about that is confusing?" Perfidy asked.

"I don't think the man you call The Devil is a centenarian child thief that spawned legends like the Krampus. This has got to be code or shorthand," Kale replied indignantly.

"What if he is?" I asked, wringing my hands.

An explosion rocked the archive building, sending dust and cobwebs cascading down around us. The ground shook again as second explosion severely damaged the outer wall of the archive. Perfidy cursed, gazing through the thin security window at the access door. Kale looked about, clearly annoyed, brushing dust from his suit coat.

"Red Coats, a dozen of them. They have at least one rocket propelled grenade, and they've used it to disable our transport," Perfidy said, dropping his duffle to the ground.

"The police are already on their way, and I've already called to augment our security. We need to hold up somewhere defensible and wait," Kale said, pulling out his mobile to check the time.

I crouched down, shivering in fright, my eidetic memory summoning every recollection of the Red Coats from my first night in Port Montaigne. Kale pulled a handgun from a holster hidden beneath his suitcoat and put a firm hand on my shoulder. Perfidy began assembling what looked like a gun on a motorized tripod. He synced the device to his own optics so he could control it remotely and set it down to guard the door inside an opaque bin on a shelf about waist high.

"Follow me," Perfidy said, heading back toward the archive offices.

We followed along as Perfidy wove his way through the storage. Once, he turned to fire through the storage boxes at something a few rows over. I could hear what sounded like a man fall to the ground in that direction, hardware of some kind clattering to the floor beside them.

"How did you do that?" I whispered.

"He's patched into the building surveillance," Kale replied, pointing to the cameras dotting the warehouse ceiling above.

"Port Montaigne PD is responding with their special operations unit, two minutes," Perfidy whispered, taking cover just inside the archive offices.

"Mr. Mundt and Heavy Dub should be here about the same time," Kale said, hurrying me inside the offices past Perfidy.

"Heavy Dub?" I asked.

"*Yeah*, that's what we call him. He has the heavy arms cyborg modification, and loves heavy weapons," Perfidy replied, laughing.

"So, we just wait?" I asked.

Perfidy opened fire again, startling me. Then again, and again, firing at enemies unseen rows and rows of storage away. One would think they'd give up, someone shooting them like that, but they kept coming and Perfidy kept killing them. I just hunkered down behind a desk and covered my ears for most of it.

"Some of them might be able to fool my optics, or the surveillance in the building. Keep some real eyes out there," Perfidy said, dropping the magazine in his rifle and replacing it with a fresh one.

Several tense minutes passed as we waited for help to arrive. Eventually, the sounds of transport engines screaming overhead accompanied by more gunfire rattled the building. Perfidy stood up, and moved quickly back into the archive toward a breach in the wall. We climbed through as the last Port Montaigne PD transport landed, and deployed heavily armed and armored officers. Mr. Mundt's transport dropped from the cloud cover a moment after that.

The wind had picked up since we'd entered the archive, and a storm was rolling in from the ocean. I wished I could just sit and watch the storm come in, and forget about everything that was going on. Still, I wondered where Cal was, and if his chickens were okay.

Mr. Mundt's transport came down slowly, the cargo hold opening to reveal a familiar soldier within. I dimly remembered him as one of Perfidy's friends that watched over me at the hospital. He had heavy skeletal reinforcement, and dual arm replacements. His metallic limbs were crossed in front of him, a heavy looking rifle slung over one shoulder. He was a North American national, unlike Perfidy and most of his other allies. He was Caucasian, had light brown hair, and mischievous eyes to match his smile.

"That's Heavy Dub?" I asked.

Perfidy laughed.

"Not sure how that question is funny," Kale said, somewhat annoyed.

"The first time Brook saw him, she watched me stab him in the throat. The last time, was in the hospital after being stabbed herself," Perfidy said, grimly watching the transport land.

"At Madmar's warehouse, in Midtown?" I asked.

"He got that second arm and a raspy voice from all that, but at least he's alive," Perfidy remarked, looking around at the dead men dressed in red coats.

"Why did you stab him?" I asked.

"He probably had a CGU, a cognitive governance unit, that Dr. Madmar used to manipulate his perceptions, emotions, feelings of loyalty, and so forth. All North American augmented CGG soldiers had them," Kale said, still annoyed with Perfidy.

"Dr. Madmar worked the MDC program. He was able to hack those units in dozens of soldiers that had particular model. I had to incapacitate Heavy Dub to help Dr. Helmet prevent Madmar from getting his hardware to the Lunar Colony," Perfidy said, raising a hand to him as he exited the transport.

"You weren't trying to kill him. You saved him," I said, finally understanding.

"Yeah, and with Matthias's help, about fifty other guys working for us right now," Perfidy said.

We met with Heavy Dub at the transport watching as Port Montaigne PD secured the area. He nodded to Perfidy, trading duffle bags with him as he stepped off the loading ramp. Mr. Mundt walked out from the darkness of the cargo hold, his hands carefully cradling several cups of coffee.

"Mr. Uroboros, I have coffee for you and your friends," he said.

"It's Kale, Mr. Mundt,"Kale said, taking a cup.

Mr. Mundt smiled. "You seem as much like him as he does you. I forget sometimes. Apologies."

Kale just smiled, nodding to Mundt.

"Hey, good to see you!" Heavy Dub said, his raspy voice still plenty loud.

"I'm well, all healed up. Thanks for watching over me at the hospital," I replied, putting on my best smile.

"My friends, they told me what happened at Watertown. They told me what you did," Heavy Dub replied, putting a hand on my shoulder.

"It was nothing, really. I was just scared for my friends."

"You had our back. We'll always have yours."

"Did you bring what I asked for?" Kale interrupted, his impatience spoiling the moment.

"It's in the duffle I just gave Perfidy," Heavy Dub replied, pointing.

"Thank you. Make sure the crash evidence inside the archive is placed in Mr. Mundt's transport," Kale said, walking over to one of the fallen Red Coats.

He was lying face down in the empty parking lot once used by employees of the archive, yellow lines marking a quartet of parking spaces intersecting beneath him. Kale knelt down beside him, donning a pair of black leather gloves. Perfidy just kept a watch on the area, his cybernetic eyes ticking quietly as he scanned the commercial buildings and roads around us.

"What can you tell me about these guys?" Kale asked me.

"They smell like petrochemicals and the sea, much like the place Ezra and I first encountered them. There is a hint of something else, talcum powder and corn starch I think," I said, sniffing around the body.

"Baby powder," Kale said, pulling a black glove off the man's hand, revealing a white substance across his palm and fingertips.

"What does that mean?" I asked.

"He's branching out. The Devil isn't just trading in human beings anymore, and his crew has expanded recently," Perfidy said, still gazing out at the perimeter around us.

"If he has a drug operation, why risk the exposure here?" Kale asked.

"These guys that attacked us are from his drug manufacturing line. Judging from their coordination and fighting skills, they not the real muscle behind his operation. Just a few guys with guns," Perfidy remarked.

"Did he do this to test the response time of Port Montaigne PD's tactical unit?" Heavy Dub asked, looking to Perfidy.

"If I was planning an important operation, it's what I would do. Whatever he does next, it'll be with real muscle, and they won't be wearing red coats. The Devil is a master of managing expectations, calculating probability, and deception. I think the only reason I caught a glimpse of him twenty years ago was because he wanted to smuggle Taylor out of the city, personally," Perfidy said, beckoning for Heavy Dub to follow him.

They walked back to the archive fetching the lift truck and the remnants of the transport crash. Once all the bits and pieces were secured on a pallet in Mr. Mundt's cargo hold, Perfidy dropped the duffle Heavy Dub had brought and opened it. Inside, there several books, medicine, tools, and brand new Drone-issue goggles.

"What's all this for?" I asked.

"You said your tribe had a mystic, a Type Six Drone?" Perfidy asked.

"Chelsea, but she's old, as old as Ezra."

"We... I, am desperate to find whoever is responsible for the bombings. Also, I'm concerned that there may be more bombs underground. Your tribe needs our help, and we need theirs," Kale explained.

"You want me to go back home, see if they can find the bombs and if Chelsea can give you any information about the bomb maker?" I asked.

"Yes, please," Kale said, handing me a sealed package containing the bomb fragments.

There was a barely audible chime from my apron as my data slate finished decrypting the first video file from Dr. Helmet's archives. We waited for Perfidy to get back before sitting down in the cargo hold of Mr. Mundt's freighter hauler to watch it. The video was old, probably derived from some sort of physical media. It was worn around the edges, and grainy from degradation, but watchable.

CHAPTER 3

Dr. Helmet's Personal Archive – VIDEO FILE 0013

Initiating Link, Secure Protocol, CGG Network 05122

Dr. Maurice Madmar, logged in.
Dr. Gorshteyn Helmet, logged in.

Dr. Madmar's visage appeared on the right hand side of the screen, his face smooth and clean shaven. He was sitting at a desk, wearing a suit and tie, the background filled with shelves of books and journals. Dr. Helmet appeared on the left, wearing a lab coat and a white beard, the workings of an advanced robotics laboratory behind him.

"Dr. Madmar?" Dr. Helmet said, smiling and leaning in toward the Netcam.

"Call me Maurice, please. I have little use for formalities in this context," Maurice replied, placing his hands on the desk in front of him.

"Alright, call me Gorshteyn," he said, nodding his smile somewhat diminished.

Madmar cleared his throat. "Our mutual benefactor has arranged this meeting to discuss Project Marionette. I think we should do that and then break link quickly."

"We're secure, Maurice, I assure you. More than double the usual precautions have been taken, and—"

"Fine. It isn't ethical as designed. I've tried to overcome the problems with the cognitive threshold issue, but the mind cannot go wandering without consequences to the body. Even with the subject fully submerged in our new bio-gel for the duration. Even if the patient was not driven insane, they would not be able to leave the marionette tank after prolonged exposure. The serum that sustained them through the process, quickly turns into a neurotoxin without exposure to the radiation provided by the marionette halo," Madmar explained, calmly.

Dr. Helmet nodded in agreement.

"It has killed or required the euthanizing of four animal subjects to test fully. I will not bear the weight of any more deaths pursuing this misguided endeavor. I will not do this anymore, and you can tell our mutual friend the same," Madmar said, somewhat less calmly.

"We are unanimous then, we'll repurpose the Marionette Project," Helmet replied.

Dr. Madmar paused, clearly not expecting that reaction.

"Good, I guess there is nothing left to discuss. Good day."

"Maurice, we'd like to ask you about working with us on a different project," Dr. Helmet said, quickly, trying to stop Madmar from logging out.

"Our 'benefactor' has ceased asking me for things, and I am glad for it. The Shutdown Endeavor, what I have seen of it, has terrifying implications for humanity. I am hesitant to continue cooperating with anyone involved. I have a feeling my sentiments have become known through the project notes," Madmar replied, closing his eyes and bowing his head.

"Indeed, you do have a poignant way of expressing yourself. What you've done to advance neurosurgery has saved dozens of lives so far, healed maladies of the brain that would have been incurable a year ago," Helmet said, exhaling through his teeth.

"What you want must be pretty important for that degree of flattery," Madmar said, shaking his head worriedly.

"Am I so obvious?" Helmet said, with a chuckle.

"Painfully so. Please, get on with it," Madmar replied, growing impatient.

"We've rolled over some of the useful data from the Marionette Project into a new project, one I'm calling Transference for now," Helmet explained, glad for the opportunity to make his pitch.

"I can guess what that means, and what you intend to do. This technology is dangerous. The world is not ready for anything that can extend a person's identity in this way. It will be misused, and people will suffer and die," Madmar stated, resolute.

"Would Ares and Selene agree? You saved their children from being killed under the weight of their own essences. It isn't just human lives you've saved, Maurice. This technology has the potential to free us all, but certain key agents need the ability to extend their identity, and operate in multiple theaters at once," Helmet explained, clasping his hands in front of him.

"Moving a spontaneously arranged artificial intelligence from a redundant system, to procedurally generated nanoid form is far different from what I think you're suggesting. If a given technology would only be suitable for use by a select few, no one should likely have it," Madmar replied.

"Indeed, I'm not even certain how we would test the process, but Selene has been willing to aid us by crafting the blanks we'll need," Helmet explained, tapping on the screen in front of him, initiating a file transfer.

Madmar looked down at his own screen for a moment then looked up, his facial features tight as if to scold Helmet.

"This will not work. The original design used nanoid neural constructs specifically designed for an artificial consciousness. Although, given the manner of their emergence, I no longer believe the term 'artificial' to be appropriate. They should be called Intelligent Agents, in their terrestrial form, and..."

"I agree with all of that, Maurice. Your notes on the subject were very illuminating, changing how all of us involved think about the artificial... err, Intelligent Agents. That's what everyone has started to call them now, because of your notes," Helmet said, smiling.

"If you already know it will not work, you must be looking for my help in modifying, or crafting, a nanoid neural construct to allow for this

Transference, something I will not in good conscience do," Madmar said, leaning back in his chair.

"I've read your misgivings in depth. The irony is that what you wrote also what gave us the idea in the first place. You thought of this before we did," Helmet said, excitedly.

"Good, then you know with perfect knowledge why I will refuse to participate in the project," Madmar replied, his temper showing slightly.

"Don't you think the sum of what we're fighting against warrants certain extreme methods?"

"No. I won't replace one evil with another, or become a monster to defeat one. We aren't building Bacon's warbling heads of brass here. This is something that could influence the evolution of our species."

"We aren't asking you to build wings for Icarus. Would you at least look at the protocols we've come up with to address your concerns?" Helmet pleaded.

Madmar looked down at the screen set into the desk in front of him, waving his hand over the screen to scroll the text. His expression of impatient incredulity faded as he looked at the various protocols and measure to one equal parts fear and relief. Madmar looked up, pale from the screen.

"Perhaps not wings, but you are asking me to build a labyrinth, one that can house the human mind. These protocols are suitable, but if our benefactor is willing to take this kind of time to give the replicas genuine memories and agency, he must be a very patient man... or, he's a member of the Cabal," Madmar suggested, rubbing his eyes.

"Obviously, you can appreciate what is at stake here. If the other members got wind of what he was about to do, they might try to kill him and everyone involved," Helmet explained.

"I guess I don't know what you mean," Madmar admitted, sighing impatiently.

"What if the various financial standards were to change? The equity of the world given fair distribution and people could be born outside of the cycle of debt, and death? The Cabal uses these standards to quietly control us all, robbing everyone of everything but the shabbiest illusion of choice. The CGG is an instrument for them to bicker amongst themselves at the expense of everyone else in the world. The Shutdown Endeavor could reset all of that," Helmet explained.

"Yes, I have already heard the pep talk, what I do not understand is what everyone else hopes to gain in the aftermath. I trust in the innate altruism of other people only so far. I struggle to believe you, or our mutual friend, are in this for the good of humanity alone," Madmar growled, his patience expended.

"Where I'm concerned, you are correct. I want to add to the body of my work and advance in my field. For me, this is very much about curiosity and prestige, in that order. What goes on outside my lab, that doesn't advance my research, is unimportant to me," Helmet explained.

Madmar squinted at the screen, his composure returning. "Thank you for your honesty."

"Our mutual friend is wholly altruistic, an idealist, and a true believer. He claims his people were never meant to manipulate humanity, but to guide and protect them. He believes that his kind have no place in the world in any other role," Helmet explained.

"And, what of his opulent mansion in upper Port Montaigne? What can you say of his emerging finance company and the way he manipulates the various global markets? Are these the acts of a humble servant and protector?" Madmar said, waving dismissively at the screen.

"The first time we met, it was in a small apartment in Midtown, we had takeout food and he wasn't dressed as well as you are now. The finance firm, mansion, and high profile elements of his identity are a means to an end, and a cover for his other activities. Truly, I don't believe he owns any of it, merely acting as a sort of conservatorship," Helmet explained.

"I suspected as much. I think my real apprehension comes from continuing to work with you. You are reckless and often act hastily. The Metasapient Project is a prime example of your inability to see the big picture," Madmar explained, making no attempt to spare Helmet's feelings.

"It seemed a better outcome than someone else engineering mindless soldiers without agency or…"

"Or, knowing what it is to be raised by loving parents? Every Metasapient is being reared by an emotionless machine. The Factory is not giving any of what came out of the MDC Project a childhood, or a chance at possessing real agency," Madmar interrupted, a scowl creasing his face.

"I know," Helmet said, bowing his head in genuine remorse.

There was an awkward silence, as Helmet seemed to disappear into his own thoughts for a moment.

"I'll help, but I want the power to halt the whole project if it gets out of hand. I would stop short of having a kill switch in each of the replicas, but there needs to be countermeasures to prevent this technology from being misused," Madmar insisted.

"We actually hoped you would amend the protocols to suit your own operational ethics. Give the whole program a soul, as it were," Helmet replied, relieved.

"We, or he?" Madmar asked.

"He," Helmet admitted.

CHAPTER 4

From the margins of Brook's Cookbook, Part 5 –

"You look well, Brook," Chelsea Six said, running her hand down the side of my face.

"You are huge!" Lem said, gazing up at me.

"She is not! She looks like a lady," Dub scolded, rifling through the duffle bag of trade goods I'd brought.

"I don't know what you mean," I said, giggling.

"You're taller, by at least six to eight inches, and way more feminine looking than when you left," Lush said, holding his walking stick up next to me, an implement he usually reserved for measuring water depth.

"It's true, you're almost as tall as Annabelle, and just as pretty. Maybe even prettier," Dub remarked, selecting a new set of goggles for himself.

I blushed slightly. It was particularly strange to stand across from Lem as he stared up at me. We used to be the same size, and pretty proud of our stature. There were secret places that only he and I could go because of our size. Looking up at the ceiling of the sub tunnel, I was sure I could probably jump just a short distance and touch the conduit running overhead, something I couldn't have done last time I was here.

"You sure you don't want Annabelle to know you've returned?" Chelsea Six asked.

"I haven't returned. I came to talk to you guys specifically. She probably already knows anyway," I said. I pulled a piece of red vinyl fabric from my pocket.

"What do you need?" Lush asked, pulling out a hip flask.

"I need you three to look for bombs in the tram tunnels."

"Um, there are bats up there," Lem said worriedly.

"Bats?" I asked.

"Chiroptera Metasapients, Type One. They showed up shortly after the Shutdown," Chelsea Six said, looking at one of the books I'd brought.

"No worries. We will look for them," Dub said, nodding toward the duffle.

"What should we do when we find them?" Lush asked.

"Nothing, just leave the details in sub tunnel 9831 beneath Uroboros Financial using our cypher. I don't want any of you getting hurt," I said, handing the red vinyl to Chelsea Six.

"What is this?" she asked.

"Part of the coat from some men that Kale wants found. Be careful, they are *really* bad men," I said, gesturing to the fragment.

Chelsea Six grasped the fabric in both hands, closing her eyes.

"The man who owned this coat was compelled to work for his employer somehow. He did not act of his own free will. They steal children, men, and women from around the world. The vibrations of a hundred languages and dialects echo from this scrap of vinyl," Chelsea Six said, her words slurring together slightly.

"That's good. It is a few things we did not know before," I said, rubbing Chelsea's back.

"They are dangerous. They all know your name, and Ezra's, and someone named Perfidy. They mean to kill you and Ezra. You have to warn him," Chelsea said panicked, the cloth trembling in her hands.

"We know, Ezra knows," I said trying to comfort her.

"Their master, a man, but not a man, he echoes with ancient envy, his long hands like spiders spanning webs that strangle the globe. He has no skin, his entrails reach out across the stars, a bloody horizon on dozens of worlds, and he is... AHH!" Chelsea Six cried out suddenly, dropping the vinyl to the ground.

I grabbed her shoulders, steadying her as she almost fell. "It's okay, that's enough."

"He's pure evil, far beyond the thrum or echo of any human I've ever felt. This scrap did not even belong to him, and yet he reverberates through everyone he touches," Chelsea Six said, shakily rubbing her temples.

"Yeah, we know he's pretty bad," I said, recalling what Perfidy had told me earlier.

"No, you don't understand. I've been to Mars, inside the penal facility there. I've felt the psychic emanation of remorseless mass murderers, psychopaths, and the most dangerous and depraved humanity has to offer. Added together, they are a drop in the ocean that is the evil of this individual you seek," Chelsea Six explained, her silvery eyes quivering with terror.

"We will stop him," I said, trying to calm her.

"No, you must not go near him," Chelsea Six cried out, wrapping her thin arms around me.

"I was designed to rescue people from disaster. It sounds like this man, this Red Devil, is a wandering disaster, afflicting many people. Could you turn from your function, the thing the Factory prepared you to do?" I asked.

"Yes, and I did long ago. Ezra and I both walked away. You can, too. Hide and be safe," Chelsea Six pleaded.

"No," I replied, taking up Perfidy's hammer. "I will end this man, or die trying."

"We've got your back. We'll find those bombs, if they exist," Dub said, folding his arms and nodding.

"Thanks, make sure everyone gets something from the duffle. Say hello for me, and let everyone know I'm okay," I said, turning to go.

"You could tell them yourself," Lush remarked.

"If I did that, I might lose my nerve, and never leave," I said, hugging Lush.

Drones are designed to operate in teams, and I'd been solo for months now. I'd forgotten how comforting it was to have my own kind around me. I cared deeply for Kale and had begun to really like Perfidy, but they weren't Drones. They were not my tribe. The long trudge back up to Downtown was made shorter by losing myself in my own thoughts.

The first video file we'd been able to view had shown what appeared to be an important meeting between Drs. Helmet and Madmar. It was difficult to watch. Having faced Madmar before, it was hard to fathom what could turn such a thoughtful and seemingly ethical man into a depraved lunatic. Learning that Dr. Helmet was responsible for the Factory cast a shadow across him, as my own childhood memories were of loneliness and emotional isolation.

As I walked, I decided to forgive Dr. Helmet. I carried enough burdens already. I hoped watching the rest of the video files wouldn't make me regret that decision.

I felt a rush of anxiety as I climbed up to the street level. I emerged where the mercenaries tried to kill me, my ability to recall things perfectly causing me to recollect those events with clarity. Kale was there, with Perfidy waiting beside Mr. Mundt's freighter hauler, blocking the street. Perfidy did little to hide his relief that I'd returned, but Kale was harder to read. All the same, he had a twinkle in his eyes that gave me chills, like he couldn't really hide anything from me anymore.

"I learned things about the Red Devil from Chelsea Six. My tribe will look for the bombs. Also, there are bats, Chiroptera Metasapients, operating in Port Montaigne," I reported.

"Bats? The Red Devil?" Kale said, raising an eyebrow.

"Good a name as any. For all my attempts to find this guy, that's pretty close to what everyone else calls him," Perfidy remarked, keeping a steady watch around us, rifle ready.

"He scares Chelsea Six, like, really bad. She said he's evil on a scale that goes beyond what people are normally capable of. I think he must be long-lived to achieve that state, a member of the Cabal like you thought," I said, putting the sledgehammer up to my shoulder.

Kale looked over at Perfidy.

"When I went to Europe looking for him twenty years ago, it was without official permission from Uroboros Financial. I got an ominous phone call from someone in logistics, telling me the man I sought was already hunted, and by someone far more deadly than myself," Perfidy explained.

"What else aren't you telling us?" Kale asked, sounding genuinely curious.

"Look, I spent a lot of time searching for this guy. The transport went down on my detail, I lost people that were on board, and I took it really fucking personally, alright?" Perfidy said, his frustration getting the better of him.

"You're still trying to connect all the dots. You feel responsible. You have no idea how much empathy for that I possess," Kale said, bowing his head.

Perfidy sighed, and looked back at Kale. "Yeah, I guess you would. Sorry."

"Brook, tell us how to find this Red Devil," Kale asked.

"Chelsea Six said he was driven by ancient envy. He has a long reach, his hands like spiders on webs that wrap around the earth, and guts across the stars," I explained.

"The tribe mystic speaks in metaphors? Awesome," Kale said, frowning.

"When the global economy collapsed, what was the first thing everyone looked for?" I asked.

"Food?" Perfidy posited.

"They looked for their children. What auxiliary communications remained were used by people to try and find their families. Network operators that stayed at their posts gave that traffic precedence because it is something everyone could have empathy for," I explained, pulling out my data slate.

"Empathy, or envy. If whatever the Red Devil is trying to do is big enough, he might actually be in Port Montaigne," Kale said, nodding.

"All food distribution is currently being routed through the port. Didn't Salvatore say he was having a problem with traffickers?" Perfidy said.

"We've been looking for the Red Devil in the tunnels, searching for bombs, and trouble at the Ports. If he's a creature of envy, he'd live in opulence, with all of the things he thinks he deserves, and maybe even in plain sight. He'd be close to happy families, people with plenty," Kale said, patting my shoulder.

"You think he's living large, right here in Port Montaigne?" Perfidy asked.

"Did you ever look for this Red Devil in Uptown, or in the upper echelons of society in any of the other places you looked?" Kale asked.

"The one time I met the guy, he did not look like an upper crust socialite. He was grimy, had exposed first generation cybernetics, and stank of rejuvenation chemicals. I didn't see him walking about unnoticed at a country club or a charity banquet," Perfidy said, shaking his head.

"You also said he's a master of managing expectations and deception. If he's a cyborg, he may have multiple personas and masks he wears depending on context. Vance used the transference project to extend his reach in the world. It is reasonable to assume the rest of the Cabal have their own tricks to remain unseen, and extend their influence," Kale said, pacing in front of the ramp leading to Mr. Mundt's freighter.

"You think he allowed me to see him? Just to throw me off for two decades?"

"I am suggesting he had a contingency prepared in that event."

Perfidy lowered his head, looking totally defeated.

"We aren't dealing with mere mortals here. Consider what Vance Uroboros was able to accomplish, the wreckage he was able to create without even meaning to. Imagine if there was someone with his influence that did mean the world real harm," Kale said, walking up into the freighter.

"One lone cyborg on a rampage probably wouldn't catch him, not in twenty years?" Perfidy said, dejectedly.

"He shaped your perceptions. You saw a hunchbacked cyborg lurking in an ancient petrochemical facility. You've been looking in dark places since. You said he was good at calculations. If he did bomb the transport, he'd know everything about it, including the man guarding it," I suggested, following Kale into the cargo hold.

"Someone else is apparently better. That was the same night Brook arrived in Port Montaigne, met by the only Drone that isn't afraid to venture out from the underground, Ezra One. Mystery voice from Uroboros Logistics said he was already hunted. Maybe Brook meeting Ezra that night wasn't a coincidence?" Perfidy asked, backing up into the cargo hold, keeping his eyes on the street until the hatch closed.

"Decidedly not, and if he knew they were involved, he likely knew where Taylor was taken as an infant," Kale said.

"We took her to an orphanage operated by a church," I said, not understanding.

"Why didn't he just go steal or take her by force from the church?" Perfidy asked.

"She was on holy ground? Check for recent development in Port Montaigne. See if anyone requested permits to tear down or alter properties where churches are located," Kale replied, lingering near a wall where Mr. Mundt had pictures of his family stuck all over.

"Okay!" I said, pulling out my data slate.

"You think the Red Devil is superstitious?" Perfidy asked, incredulous.

"Not exactly. I believe he doesn't think about things the same way you and I do. He'd be easier to find if he were predictable, and managed his affairs like everyone else," Kale said, placing a hand on a photo of Mr. Mundt's daughter.

"The Drone tribes have territories. You think the members of the Cabal have territories? Like Drones?" I asked.

"Yes," Kale said, tapping Dr. Helmet's journal resting in his breast pocket.

"That would explain a lot of what I've seen working for Uroboros Financial in the past," Perfidy said.

"So, I should look for property development in areas where Uroboros Financial doesn't directly have influence?" I asked.

"Narrow the focus to places in Uptown that appear to have weathered the Shutdown better than others, places that look like they were prepared. We received hundreds of thousands of requests for aid. Look for areas that did not ask for help from Uroboros Financial or the local civic authority," Kale said, pulling out Dr. Helmet's journal and opening it to a place he'd bookmarked.

I entered the search criteria into my data slate and waited for a secure link to Uroboros Financial servers. I let the more powerful machines at the firm do the work while Perfidy and Kale sat quietly across from each other on crates. Mr. Mundt's gentle snoring from the cockpit was the only sound until my data slate beeped, indicating it had successfully performed the requested data retrieval.

"There are only a couple of places in uptown Port Montaigne that have requested permits to demolish a church and asked for no assistance in the last four months. They overlap one another, on the west side," I said, scrolling through the massive amount of text I'd pulled from the servers.

"Literally, as far as you can get from the old petrochemical facility where I first saw him," Perfidy said, shaking his head in disbelief.

"What was the nature of the permit request for the church demolition?" Kale asked.

"Excavation for the purpose of relocation," I said, reading the details of the permit aloud.

"He isn't demolishing it, he's painstakingly pulling it apart and having it rebuilt somewhere else. He is superstitious," Perfidy said, a slight smile crossing his face.

"I wouldn't assume we can fathom his reasoning. He's a conflicted individual, and he doesn't always act in a coldly rational way," Kale said, banging on the cargo hold wall to wake Mr. Mundt.

"He'll have made mistakes, left a trail we can follow," I said, smiling at Kale.

Kale returned the smile. "Possibly. He'll have contingencies, and while we may not be able to catch him, we can make him feel very unwelcome in Port Montaigne."

"Mr. Kale, you are ready to go?" Mr. Mundt said, entering the cargo hold and rubbing his eyes.

"Yes. Has any word come over from the garage about our transport? I'm certain you have better things to do than play taxi for us around the city," Kale asked.

"Mr. Kale, I don't know what you're up to, but I have a feeling it is important. I am glad to help you, like you have helped me," Mr. Mundt said, tapping a finger over his heart.

"He… we, just don't want you to get hurt again," I said, grabbing the back of Kale's suitcoat sleeve.

Mr. Mundt looked over at the pictures of his family. "You are trying to make the world better, and mend wounds, for everyone?"

"We're going to try," Perfidy replied.

"My freighter hauler, it is armored, and it has weapons. I flew for the military. I can help," Mr. Mundt explained.

"We aren't going to take any risks. Hopefully, your hardware and expertise will not be needed," Kale said.

"Still, you do have a better coffee maker and a kitchen on board your transport. We'd be glad for the help," I said, tugging on Kale's sleeve.

Mr. Mundt just smiled and nodded before heading up to the cockpit.

My data slate made another chime, letting me know the second video from Dr. Helmet's archive was ready to be viewed.

"Watch it now? Or in the morning? It has been a long day," Perfidy asked.

"Play it," Kale replied.

CHAPTER 5

Initiating Link, Secure Protocol, CGG Network 06451

Dr. Maurice Madmar, logged in.
Dr. Gorshteyn Helmet, logged in.

Dr. Madmar's visage appeared on the right hand side of the screen, a tired expression creasing his face. He wore a robe with pajamas showing from beneath and was seated at a kitchen table, darkened windows and curtains behind him. Dr. Helmet appeared on the left, wearing a lab coat and a white beard, a busy lab with many scientists working behind him.

"Good morning, Maurice," Helmet said, smiling.

"I suppose it is technically morning here. Good afternoon to you," Madmar replied, blowing on a cup of coffee.

Helmet paused, as if to look for the proper words.

"We've done it. Your designs worked," Helmet said, clasping his hands together.

Madmar nodded. "And how have you done this, exactly? We have screened for a test subject, but no one suitable has been found thus far."

"I underwent the process myself, using a sensory deprivation helmet and an updraft chamber," Helmet explained.

Madmar roared angrily, hurling the coffee cup to the floor. "Are you insane? The nanoid neural constructs were not designed to accept the cognitive imprint of modern humans. The child could—"

"I didn't generate an infant blank, I did a full spectrum imprint of myself to an adult blank. It worked! I am literally beside myself," Helmet interrupted, gesturing to what appeared to be his twin working at a lab table behind him.

Madmar stared at the screen, eyes bulging for a moment before sitting down to rub his temples. "Gorshteyn, this is outside all the protocols we had discussed previous. A full spectrum imprint could have degraded connectivity between neurons, we do not know if..."

"It is fine, I'm fine, and everything went perfectly. The construct you designed completely absorbed my consciousness, memories, and cognitive processes. Preliminary electroencephalogry shows the synthesis of the original serum and the upgraded marionette halo copies brain functions precisely. It inscribes them to the construct like a file written to a blank hard drive," Helmet said, Madmar's own obvious apprehension doing little to burden his spirits.

"That was bloody reckless! The mind and the sum of a person amounts to more than the processes we can detect. Also, we still have no idea how successive uses of the process will affect the subject. Our mutual friend wants a possible thirty to forty replicas, per agent, as a standard for safety. Worse, the process to provide replicas with redundant systems isn't complete," Madmar growled, spittle hitting the monitor.

"We've plenty of time to fashion the necessary upgrades to the firmware, the replicas should be fine," Helmet replied, scratching his beard.

Madmar's lips grew tight. "Plenty of time? We have a handful of days, maybe."

"Like I said, plenty of time."

Madmar scowled, clearly unconvinced.

"Finding someone even close to a genetic or neurological match would have been very difficult. As I understand, with only a handful of exceptions, their kind are not allowed to breed with ours. It is not like we could just ask..."

"I understand that, but testing the process on yourself, even once, was extremely dangerous. As I said before, there could be side effects and conditions that won't come up in the brain scans. Cognitive function isn't just measured by what we think is healthy activity. The sum of us is far more complex, and…"

Madmar paused, taking note of all the individuals working in the background. He looked closer, noticing that there wasn't just a single replica of Helmet in the background, but several.

"Gorshteyn, what have you done?" A look of horror spread across Madmar's face.

"I trusted in your genius. Now I need you to trust me," Helmet replied, trying to calm Madmar.

"Shut it, Gorshteyn, and listen to me very carefully," Madmar said, pointing a finger at the monitor.

Helmet stopped talking, standing at attention to listen.

"How many times?" Madmar asked, a grim resolve crossing over his face.

"Thirty-seven, before we ever approached any of the safeguards you designed," Helmet explained.

"How many of them are Alpha?" Madmar asked.

"All of them are Alpha, eighteen aware, fourteen unaware, and five are in transitional states."

"Why the spread?"

"We want to see how they will operate in the field, to see if they can…"

"What if they become aware of one another?" Madmar asked.

"We'll deal with it. I've already begun to explore options. We think that awareness and the rearing period you suggested will take care of all the problems, but we…"

"We? Or, you?" Madmar demanded.

Helmet sighed, nodding, slightly resigned. "I thought we should gather data on a worst case scenario, and a few nanoid replicas wandering around on various assignments thinking they were me… seemed pretty safe," Helmet explained.

"God damn it, Gorshteyn," Madmar said, shaking his head angrily.

"I knew you wouldn't approve, so I decided it would be more expedient to ask your forgiveness, rather than ask for your permission," Helmet explained, sounding genuinely apologetic.

"What if one of your unaware replicas figures it all out, and goes Delta?" Madmar suggested, using a broom to gather the bits of shattered mug on the floor.

"We'll deal with them like any other rogue agent or adversary," Helmet said, matter of fact.

"Oh? Just like that? If they go Delta, it means they are not just an imprinted replica anymore, they are a person, with their own agency, and desires. A person, however fettered by your identity, but with an identity of their own, and what I believe to be inalienable rights," Madmar said leaning the broom against the counter.

"That's a subject for debate, Maurice. Please, be reasonable. Not everything we create is a 'person' by the same standard that you and I are people. The various portions of my now extended identity are…"

"You, they are all you, and you are responsible for anything they do or do not do. If they go insane from an epiphany event, or just go Delta and decide to kill someone, that death is on you now," Madmar roared, slapping his hand on the counter in front of him.

"I understand that. I know it doesn't make you feel better, but I've installed them all with a susceptibility to the kill switch you designed. I'm willing to take accountability here, and so are the eighteen replicas aware of the situation. Each does, of course, feel as I feel about all of this," Helmet explained.

"The kill switch is supposed to be a means to painlessly euthanize them if their state was painful or otherwise untenable. It isn't supposed to be a contingency for you screwing up and going outside protocols!" Madmar yelled, pressing an accusatory finger to the monitor.

"I've got everything under control and monitored. We should…"

"That is what I'm worried about most. You see, you do not just undo what you've done here, any more than I can return this broken coffee cup back to its original state," Madmar said, placing a handful of coffee cup shards onto the counter.

"Yeah, our mutual friend didn't take the news any better than you did. He's scrapped all plans to replicate more than a single additional agent and asked that everything get mothballed or dismantled thereafter," Helmet replied sadly.

"Good," Madmar said, calmly sweeping the coffee cup remnants into a waste bin.

"There is more work to be done before that can happen, and I trust you're still willing to help us with the final phase?" Helmet asked.

"I am, but I want you to understand something. Don't think that just because I've accepted exile here on the Lunar Colony that I don't still have reach on Earth. If you deviate from the protocols I have established again, I will make sure you are sorry. Not our benefactor, or the cause, or any of your replicas... you," Madmar said, a cold indifference creeping into his voice.

Helmet nodded, obviously not impressed.

"Have you considered what will happen to your replicas if we don't perfect a redundancy system to deal with data and memory degradation relative to known biological tolerances? Have you told them that you may have consigned them to madness and death if we fail in creating the necessary catalyst?" Madmar said, loud enough the replicas in the background could hear.

Helmet swallowed noisily, nodding in reply, the various replicas in the background looking toward the monitor.

"I will take your silence to mean you understand how deadly serious I am. Send me all your findings and the readings collected during every imprinting cycle. I am certain I can make the process safer, and if we're going to do this again, I don't want anyone else getting hurt," Madmar said, before tapping the screen and ending the transmission.

"Uploading them now. I still do not understand your alarm. None of the replicas should even notice a thing or know the difference until we get the catalyst prepared," Helmet remarked quietly, initiating the transfer of data.

"If you passed your utter lack of humanity on to your replicas, perhaps. That said, most people will eventually stop to ponder why they can't dream."

CHAPTER 6

MARS COLONY – CONDEMNED ARSIA MONS SURVEY FACILITY

Tram Station Terminal 002 - July 12th, 2200 –
More than a year after Shutdown

Archie woke with his back arched and his limbs convulsing. The cybernetic case that housed his brain had triggered the defibrillator carefully tucked away in his chest cavity. Dried blood was caked across his face, prevented him from opening his eyes, and he struggled to breath for several moments. Patting his breast pocket for his hip flash, Archie eventually found and withdrew the battered piece of tin. The drink contained within burned as he poured it across his face, washing the blood from his eyes.

"Damn," he said, looking about groggily.

The train station was dark, only the soft blue warning lights at the exits shed any illumination. Someone had triggered the emergency seals with a breach further up the tunnel, and the air was stale. Archie coughed painfully, stripping off his shredded jacket and shirt. His torso was maze of purple, his intestines poking through the abdominal wall where his muscles hadn't yet knitted back together. The symbiont was doing the job, but very slowly.

"Dragos..." Archie said, picking up a fallen illuminator from a helmet and shining it about.

Dragos was gone, a fact that made Archie smile broadly. He laughed, his cruel cackling echoing off the biological shielding over the tram station. He downed what remained in his hip flask before hurling it aside.

"Oh, Dragos, we are not so easy to kill, no? But, next time… next time, ha ha ha."

There were many dead, but due to the low temperature, they had not begun to decay significantly. The shriveled husk of Dr. Helmet lay beside a pool of blood. There were dents in the floor where a heavy exo-skeletal suit had walked through on flooring not made to sustain that sort of weight. Enyo was gone, the heavy generators designed to create a containment field were dormant.

"This is not good," Archie said, walking back toward the terminal kiosk, his mirth quickly draining away.

He opened a panel on the wall, pulling out a green cordless phone sitting beside a small screen. He wiped dust from the interior before using the touchpad to make a call. It rang several times before it clicked, then rang several more times. Archie waited patiently, humming and examining his broken and bloody fingernails.

"Hello," a voice on the other line answered.

"Rothschild, please come get me. I'm at the Arsia Mons Survey Facility, Tram Station Terminal 002. Things have not gone exactly as planned."

"I am sorry to hear that. I will prep for departure, and have you in a few minutes."

"It was Dragos, and the Marshal you told me I needn't worry about, and an Ichthyic Metasapient that you told me did not exist," Archie said, smiling and talking sweetly to the receiver.

"Mars is a big place. How could we have known that meddling meter maid would actually…?"

"No, it was Dragos. He should have tried to kill them. I threatened his family, and pushed all the usual buttons. He should have been the good martyr, and killed the Marshal," Archie said jovially, nodding, and smiling broadly.

"So, you're telling me he suddenly grew a soul, and became a true believer? All that FLF crap was a means to an end. Dragos knew it better than most," Rothschild replied, machinery powering up in the background.

"I thought so, too," Archie said, sadly picking dried blood from his moustache.

"Enyo isn't contained?"

"No, and she'll probably reach her father in time to watch him die, if she hasn't already. What time is it, anyway?"

"His redundant systems were destroyed as planned. He's got less than a few hours before he starts to drop termination protocols and die," Rothschild replied, the sound of fingers tapping on instrument panels faintly emanating from the background.

"Ah, so I wasn't out too long. She's a daddy's girl, deriving a great deal of support and guidance from him. When the Omega AI dies, there's no telling what she'll do. Regardless, there will be no talking sense to her. Mars might be a loss if we can't find another pliable artificial intelligence," Archie said, picking up a piece of broken mirror from the display case.

His hair was terribly mussed. Tucking the phone into the crook of his neck and shoulder, he did his best to use the broken mirror, and some fingers, to send his curls in the right direction.

"You have a comb on that heap, Rothschild?" Archie asked.

"I shave my shit. You know that," Rothschild replied, laughing.

"Oh, am I a Mining Company Baron yet? Did all the purchases and transfers go through before the hit on the Omega AI?"

"Yep, you head up the third most influential mining conglomerate. It's all over the news, with your puppets all waving, and signing papers for the press, and so forth. There's been some controversy with the deaths in prison custody. Some of your heirs got killed before Mom could escape prison, and they could escape the womb," Rothschild explained, sounding genuinely saddened.

"Yeah, the man responsible is here with me," Archie said, walking over and kneeling beside what remained of Dr. Helmet.

"He dead?"

"Yes, but I do not know what killed him. It looks like he died very badly, shock frozen into his face," Archie said, laughing like he'd heard a funny joke.

"Almost there," Rothschild replied.

Archie turned, looking back out through the protective shielding around the tram station toward an array of dim lights approaching over the broken landscape. Smiling, he grabbed up Dr. Helmet's body and slung it over his broad shoulders like a stole. He swept the ground for any other items that might be useful, finding a single scale knocked from the Ichthyic woman that had been helping Dragos. It was like a sliver of hardened steel in his hand.

"Remarkable," Archie whispered, pocketing his newfound treasure.

Rothschild brought the transport down beside one of the emergency hatches and ran a boarding tube over. Once it was secure, the airlock door cycled, letting atmosphere from the ship pour into the tram station. Archie took a deep breath, the first he'd been able to draw since awakening. Rothschild stepped out, his EVA suit glistening with condensation. He removed his helm, satisfied the inner chamber was safe, his bald head glistening with perspiration.

"Hey, I found a comb," Rothschild said, handing Archie a black plastic implement.

"Oh, thank you. Did you radio the others to let them know I'm alive?" Archie asked, bowing reverently to Rothschild, and accepting his gift.

"No, I've been on the channel with you the whole time. Anyone tell you, you talk a lot?"

"Ha, all the time," Archie said laughing, while he grabbed Rothschild around the base of his jaw with his offhand.

Rothschild reached up with both hands, taking Archie by the wrist. He struggled to breathe, wordlessly meeting Archie's apologetic gaze. With a quick twist, Rothschild went limp, falling to the floor. Archie sighed, looking down at his fallen minion, and ran the comb through his mussed hair until he was satisfied with his appearance.

"Let's go, Rothschild. Lots to do!" Archie said, happily dragging Rothschild's corpse up the boarding tube to the freighter.

Inside the common area of the freighter, a young woman stood, playing with her dark hair and looking at Archie angrily. Archie stopped, dead in his tracks, dropping the corpses he was carrying. He kicked them back into the airlock, like a child trying to hide a broken vase from his disapproving mother.

"Cerise, this is unexpected," Archie said, smiling broadly, while pressing down the hair at his temples with his hands.

"Archedesque, you should know, Dragos Dalca isn't dead. He, the good Marshal, and their sphyraenic ally made contact with me. Ouroboru will come here for sure, seeking to sort things out. How could you have so amazingly messed this up?" Cerise asked, sounding extremely bored.

"Enyo might still be alive," Archie said, kneeling to kiss Cerise's hand.

"She'll be driven mad with grief at the loss of her father, by all projections. We were going to keep her contained, and unaware until Ouroboru brought Taylor IA," Cerise replied, pulling her hand from Archie's grasp.

"I'll fix this, you'll see."

"Oh, yes, you will. The people Ouroboru has gone to great expense to shelter know your name and face. Ouroboru, with that mind of his, he'll piece it all together the instant he sees me here. If you're lucky, he'll arrive not having recovered his memory. Kale isn't so easily manipulated. That threadbare and faded replica will figure everything out eventually," Cerise said, laughing cruelly.

"Kaspr will deal with Kale, and the rest of Ouroboru's little friends. We've a few hours to find Enyo, and I'm pretty sure I know where she is going. Together, we can..."

"No, it wasn't easy to sneak off with a Delta Class Gorshteyn watching my every move, and there's Golgotha to be considered," Cerise said, patting Archie on the cheek.

"Golgotha? Does Kaspr know she is here? I mean, he won't have to hide, and can move freely about, and..."

"She stowed away on my vessel, and no, I haven't told Kaspr. That would be no fun," Cerise said, her eyes twinkling with amusement.

Archie laughed politely, doing his best to conceal how uncomfortable he was.

"Did you talk to her?"

"Who?"

"Golgotha."

"Yes," Cerise replied, laughing.

"And?"

"She said something cryptic, about love spanning the stars, and a dark destroyer being redeemed, and some other crap. Then, she loomed over me, letting me know how totally deadly she is. Then she left, slipping past a horde of colonial marines and station guards. Someone told the port authority my ship was carrying a VIP, or something like that," Cerise explained, her tone returning to one of abject boredom.

"Gods, why is she here?" Archie asked.

"Why aren't you getting cleaned up? We should take a moment and enjoy being alone together before we head back," Cerise said, gesturing to Archie's torn and battered trousers.

"It is strange, that we would do this, just to keep living forever," Archie stated, kissing the nape of Cerise's neck.

"Are you so sure we'd die? I wonder sometimes if executing our final task would really be the end, and that we'd just shrivel to dust," Cerise replied, coyly avoiding Archie's grasp.

"Dragos tried to kill me, and would have, if not for certain countermeasures," Archie replied, his massive arms still fumbling to embrace Cerise.

"Our Ouroboru, he knows how to pick them. You'd have some decent folks in your portfolio if you'd quit killing them all."

"Dragos is mine, remember? It was Madmar that... oh, never mind. Rothschild was a fool, and he was sloppy. But, in his defense, we all underestimated Dragos. I *am* going to kill him, and his lady friends, not necessarily in that order," Archie stated, finally pulling Cerise close to him.

"We've plenty of time to figure that out; focus on finding us a new AI that's even close to Omega Class. We can't be King and Queen of Mars without one," Cerise giggled, pulling Archie's hair playfully.

"Ow. Ow. We need Enyo. That is the most expedient thing. I've a plan to lure her to our new sentience core facility," Archie said, wincing slightly.

"Indeed?"

"If she wants to save her father, it is the only credible way of doing so. Once we're done here, I'll leak the location to the Martian civic grid. If she isn't already looking for a place, she will be soon."

CHAPTER 7

FREDRICK'S BLOCK, UPTOWN, PORT MONTAIGNE

3:11 PM April 18th, 2200

From the margins of Brook's Cookbook, Part 6 –

We spent two days doing recon on the area we suspected the Red Devil was operating out of. It was a very affluent part of town. Everyone lived in expensive co-op housing complexes that were advertised to have an urban elementalist on staff and advising the architect when they designed the building. Most of the wealthy appeared to be involved in some sort of cult that believed urban planning and structural design could harness spiritual forces.

The buildings were lovely, with every space having an outdoor terrace, vast walking paths, real trees in the courtyards, and a fountain at every corner. The residents all had genetically tailored dogs to walk, expensive taxi services to ferry them about, and clothing I knew Taylor would likely hate. Everything was an earth tone or a shade of slate or gray. As Perfidy and I started to peel away the veneer of the place, we found brothels, gambling, slave trading, dog fighting, and every vice imaginable.

I hoped Kale would tell us to tear the entire place down.

Before we went in, Kale arranged for air support, teams of Perfidy's augmented allies, snipers at range outside the block, and full access to the

Uroboros Financial armory. I ended up just taking my data slate, a granola bar, Perfidy's sledgehammer, and a fancy party dress.

Kale and I arrived in a really long car, driven by Perfidy wearing a suit and a funny hat. We weren't invited to the gala event, but Kale didn't seem worried. The museum was lovely, with ivory pillars and large red tapestries flowing down from the rooftops. There were dozens of people waiting to go through security, all dressed in their very finest clothing.

"When I lived underground, I read a lot of books. All we had, in fact. There were fancy dress parties in some of them. Back then, sleeping in a metal pipe, I never dreamed I would actually attend something like this, or with someone so handsome," I said, hugging Kale's arm.

"Save the acting for when we actually get inside," Kale said, smiling faintly.

"Do you really think I'll attract a lot of attention when we get inside?" I asked.

"Under the humble apron and Drone work suit, there was a woman of unearthly beauty. You look like you were carved of gray marble and given molten silver eyes. You look better than the women attending this party that spent millions augmenting their looks artificially," Kale said, not looking up from the glowing screen of his mobile.

"Really?" I asked, pressing my hands to my blushing cheeks.

"Yes. You'll be the perfect distraction," Kale replied grimly.

As we exited the car a gasp went up from the crowd waiting in line to enter the museum. I took Kale by the arm, expecting that we'd take our place in line, but Kale strode past everyone to security at the door. There was every array of emotion portrayed in the faces of the crowd. Envy, anger, awe, and confusion seemed to be the most prevalent.

The security agent holding the data slate gave us a confused look. "Do you have an invitation?"

"I'm Kale, CEO of Uroboros Financial, and this is the Vice President of Logistics, Brook. We'd like to go inside please," Kale said, bored, and with his eyes still on his mobile.

"Oh... um, go right in," the security agent stammered.

Kale pushed past him, eliciting groans and muffled expressions of frustrations from the crowd behind us. Heavily ionized air flowed past us as we entered the carefully climate controlled museum. I stumbled slightly as we entered, the massive sensory overload of it all. There were dozens of people, all wearing perfume or cologne, bright lights, and I was really, really nervous. Kale held me up, laughing for no reason other than to draw attention away from me.

"It's just like we talked about, focus your mind on something specific, ignore everything else, I'll keep an eye out for both of us," Kale whispered, still smiling like nothing was wrong.

I nodded and smiled back. I made Kale my focus, focusing on his scent, the way he sounded, keeping my eyes on him. Truly, he was the most interesting thing to me in the room. We wove our way through the well-appointed crowd to the new exhibits, a set of sculptures and paintings from China. I couldn't say why they were important. The tribe home had no books on antiquities.

Kale looked good, like he always did, a light dusting of stubble across his chiseled face, his long hair curving around his cheekbones. His eyes darted back and forth as his breathed in carefully controlled bursts. He was dangerous, alluring, and powerful when compared to the rest of the people in the room. If there had ever been a time he was considered a copy of Vance, the moment had passed.

"Mr. Uroboros, welcome," a well-dressed gentleman with silver hair and gold wire glasses said, extending his hand to Kale.

"Professor Ivan Kaspersky, I'm glad to be here. I'm sure my not being invited was merely an oversight?" Kale said, smiling.

"Oh, of course. I had no idea you were interested in antiquities or our quiet little neighborhood," Kaspersky replied, shaking Kale's hand.

"All these beautiful sculptures, and you can't keep your eyes off my date," Kale said, giving me a squeeze.

"She's exquisite. Where did you ever find her?" Kaspersky said, the wrinkles around his mouth getting deep as he held his mouth agape.

Kale's smile vanished, his face turning to stone as he gazed at the professor.

"I guess it doesn't matter. She's as rare as they get I imagine, what with the Factory no longer making Drones," Kaspersky said, removing his glasses to clean them.

"I came here to see and talk about your exhibits," Kale said, calmly.

"Indeed? I don't suppose you could afford a donation to help keep our humble museum going, what with these dark times?" The professor replaced his glasses on his face.

"Possibly," Kale said, appearing bored as he checked his mobile.

"Perhaps you'd like to see my private collection? I'm told it makes quite an impression on donors," Kaspersky cooed, bowing slightly.

"As long as there are drinks, I'll take a look at whatever you want," Kale said, following the professor.

We passed from the main event hall into a wood paneled passage that led back to a pair of locked doors. The professor produced an ancient looking key, and turned it in the lock before pressing through into a long chamber that ended a hundred or so feet away, the far wall framed by three large stained glass windows. It was like an amphitheater, except instead of an audience, there were hundreds of childlike porcelain dolls under glass domes.

There was a conspicuously empty pedestal in the center, a spot light from above shining down. I could feel the muscles in Kale's arm tighten as the faint smell of embalming agents, ancient and modern, wafted past my nose. We'd found where the Red Devil had been taking children for decades or more, and we were likely standing in the room with the man himself.

"I suppose you have many questions," Professor Kaspersky said, lingering beside the empty pedestal.

"Not really," Kale said, putting his mobile back in his pocket.

"Oh, come now. You've gone to all this trouble to make a grand entrance. I can't just make you disappear, not without drawing a lot of attention to myself. You came without your cyborg bodyguard, into the very heart of my domain. You've some idea who I am, and what I'm capable of?" Kaspersky asked, laying his suit coat across the pedestal.

"We know who you are," Kale said, patting my arm.

"Oh, I don't think so. You've probably heard what people call me, whispering fearfully in the dark? Still, maybe I should begin? Why did you come here?" Kaspersky asked, turning to square off against Kale.

"You'll be left to wonder. We're going to turn around and walk out of here. After enjoying your gala event for a few more minutes, we'll leave," Kale explained, sounding almost bored.

Kaspersky grinned, his face contorted by a strange madness or fury, I could not tell which. He stepped purposefully toward Kale, stopping a few feet away. Kale pushed me around behind him, stepping up so that he was inches from Kaspersky. The madness that had swept across the professor's face a moment before suddenly melted away.

"I don't understand," Kaspersky said, stepping away from Kale.

Kale laughed, sounding astonishingly cruel. "Pretending you didn't know I wasn't Vance until you could see me with your feeble eyes? I entered under no such pretense."

"I know things, things that would be useful to you," Kaspersky pleaded.

"Yes, I am aware," Kale replied, walking over and gently taking my hand.

"We could stop him, right here, right now. You and me," I said, looking up into Kale's eyes.

"I have what I came for. Also, he has hostages, this is all a deception, and we are in terrible danger," Kale whispered.

We calmly walked out, Kaspersky left standing in the room by himself. The doors clicked shut quietly as we left, the sounds of the party rising ahead of us. Kale held me close by his side, his face tight with an expression I'd not seen before. I could feel his pulse elevated as I held his arm, his palm sweating as he grasped my hand. He was afraid.

"I don't understand," I whispered, trying to blot out the confusion of the party.

"Every day, when Vance came to visit us at the farm, he wore the same jacket, same shoes, and rode in on the same motorcycle. He was a creature of ritual. He said it helped him use more of his mind on important things," Kale explained, walking past a couple trying to approach us for conversation.

"Okay?"

"He was wearing the same jacket, and riding the same motorcycle the day we argued at the Lunar Colony. He was also wearing the same decades old pair of leather Silverstein shoes. Kaspersky is wearing those shoes," Kale explained, making his way toward a side exit.

"You think he has Vance Uroboros? As a prisoner? Ezra said…"

"Perfidy said this Red Devil is a master of deception, calculation, and managing expectations. He wanted to know why we were here, find out what we knew. The simplest way to do that was through reverse interrogation, feigning weakness. If he knows what sort of questions we'd ask, he'd know what we do not know," Kale whispered, hurrying me along.

"What if it was a bluff? How could he know we'd even be here?" I asked, turning to look up at Kale.

Kale paused, looking up at the exit, then back at the party down the hallway.

"Even if you're right, I won't risk both of our lives trying to fight him alone, we should…"

The ground shook violently, throwing us both to the ground. Crystal and alabaster chandeliers swayed in the gala hall as people ran for cover. Priceless paintings and sculptures fell to the floor as bits of plaster and paint came raining down from above. Kale struggled to his feet, pulling me up with him.

"Get out! I'll find Kaspersky!" I said, shaking loose of Kale's grasp.

"Damn it, Brook, wait!" Kale said, trying to steady himself.

I was designed to go into disaster areas and rescue people. The same skills could prove just as useful in finding someone you wanted to kill. Anyone that Kale was afraid of was bad, bad as it gets. After what Chelsea said to me about the Red Devil, I had no doubt that he needed to be stopped.

There were men in red coats storming through the entrances now, pushing terrified people to the floor. The ground continued to shake, even as I turned the corner heading for Kaspersky's doll chamber. I took the doors down with one punch, stepping slowly inside. In the shadows between two of the stained glass windows was a spiral staircase.

I ascended the stairs to a rooftop terrace, where Kaspersky was watching clouds of debris erupt around the city. Flames rose up as gas mains went up amidst more tremors and explosions. Kaspersky turned toward me, his wrinkled face arrayed with a look of sheer delight.

"She was meant to be mine, payment for services rendered," he said, putting his hands behind his back.

"You can't own people. It isn't right," I said, wrenching a brick free from beneath the terrace railing.

"Imagine it, a doll that never gets old, and moves and talks all on its own? She was marvelous, perfect, and owed to me. You and your friend Ezra got in my way. I've arranged for Ezra to lose everything he loves, and I'm well on the way to doing the same to you," Kaspersky said, sneering at me.

"I don't believe you. All you do is lie. You stink of them," I said, walking toward him slowly, brick still firmly in hand.

He looked startled, like he hadn't counted on my reaction. "Dolls do not think. Dolls do not look at me. I look at the dolls. This is not how it should be."

I rushed in, grappling with him with my off hand, grabbing a handful of his dress shirt. I swung the brick hard, but he brought up his arm, reversing his grip. A bolt of bio-electrical energy jumped from his wrist and struck me above my eyes. I fell backward, the brick dropping from my hand. Kaspersky quickly regained his footing, kicking up in a way that belied his elderly appearance.

"You're mine now. A blank slate. Your skills and abilities should be intact, but you will not remember who you are. Don't worry, I'll help you learn your new role," Kaspersky said, rubbing his hands together.

I could smell Kale getting closer, hear his footfalls on the spiral staircase behind me. I stood quickly, grabbing Kaspersky by the shirt again. He grabbed my wrist, he was strong, but I was stronger. I threw him to the ground and kicked him as hard as I could. The blow sent him skidding across the roof. He rose quickly, just in time to take another blow as I leaned into him hard. He nearly went over the railing, but I caught him by the ring and middle finger on his left hand.

"What have you done?" I demanded, giving his fingers a squeeze.

Kaspersky laughed.

"We're sixty feet from the ground. You're augmented somehow. You'll probably survive, but it'll hurt," I said, giving him a shake.

"I've wandered the Earth for centuries. I am filled with the light of angels. I collect the innocence of the ages. There is little else to know," Kaspersky said, cackling.

I looked out at the city. He'd set off the bombs, but they were not doing what we'd thought. They were partitioning the city, separating Uptown from both Midtown and Downtown, rich from poor. He was sending a message to Vance Uroboros, trying to symbolically undo what he'd done in the city he called home. This was a squabble between two members of the Cabal, fueled by what was probably an ancient grudge. Kale came up beside me, looking down at Kaspersky, then out at the city.

"He did the thing. The thing you can do that wipes out a person's memories. It didn't work for some reason," I said, nodding to Kaspersky.

"It would appear your arrival in Port Montaigne twenty years ago was not a coincidence," Kale said, leaning with one arm on the terrace.

"My men will be here soon. It will be just dolls killing dolls," Kaspersky said, shaking his head and smiling.

"My allies are former soldiers, soldiers that were controlled by CGU devices like the ones you use to influence your workforce. I've made certain arrangements to that end. Your men will likely be my men, or at least free to do as they want by the end of the day. Unlike you, I happen to have some actual friends," Kale said, looking sadly out at Port Montaigne.

"I was able to beat the doll maker, but I am beaten by his creations. It is a poetry of sorts," Kaspersky lamented.

"Where is he?" Kale asked.

"Earth is but one theater, only one of many places that marionettes can dance. Soon, we will be everywhere again, Gods again, our host of angels giving us wings once more," Kaspersky said, grabbing my wrist.

I went to grapple with him, but he tore off his own fingers and fell. He disappeared into the shadow of the building, a swell of smoke and debris blowing past served to further obscure his descent. I stepped up on the railing to go after him, but Kale stopped me, grabbing my shoulder.

"I have to do this. He'll keep hurting people."

Kale pulled me down off the railing drawing me close to him. "I don't care. It isn't worth risking you to catch him. He tried to kill you once, remember?"

"It is how I knew he was lying. He's afraid of me, and now I know why."

"Vance ordered you from the Factory to fight him," Kale said, nodding to me.

"You knew?" I asked.

"No, but I suspected that he had you brought here for a purpose."

"The trail is still fresh. If I go now, I might be able to catch him," I said pushing Kale away.

"Make sure you get Perfidy's hammer from the car," Kale said, letting go of my hand.

I dropped from the roof, using a drainpipe along the wall to slow my descent. I came down in a courtyard full of debris and lost high-heeled shoes. Cries of panic and gunfire were all around me as I tried desperately to pick up Kaspersky's scent. He had a distinct smell, a mix of embalming fluids and rejuvenation drugs, death, and life.

He'd planned his route carefully, going through the kitchen to try to throw off my sense of smell, and through the fountain out front. He probably walked right past Perfidy and his men, looking like just another attendee of the event. The trail drew me across the street, but not before I got Perfidy's hammer from the trunk of the car. The whole block was dark, the power grid failing before I even crossed the street.

I followed him through the streets in my party dress, hammer in hand, my shoes lost only a block after leaving the museum. It was total chaos as people fled the aftershocks as portions of Uptown fell through to Downtown, creating several unnatural rifts throughout Port Montaigne. Kaspersky's scent was still fresh, and he was on foot, making him easier to track. I hoped it wasn't all part of some diabolical plan, and that I wasn't walking into a trap.

He continued on to the edge of Frederick's and on into a large medical research facility. The glass door on the front was just swinging shut as I arrived, a shadow disappearing into the lobby. The street was full of broken glass and I was barefoot. I ran through anyway, cutting up my feet pretty good. I slipped through the door and into the lobby, Kaspersky's scent was strong throughout.

"Still trying to find me?" Kaspersky said, his voice coming over the interior intercom.

I knelt down below the intercom on the wall, picking glass from my feet. "What's your real name?"

"Does it matter? I have so many names. The angels inside me, they have names."

"Why did you come here?"

"It isn't merely enough to undo what Uroboros has done. He needs to know what I've done, see how I've marred his crown jewel. He can't do that if he is asleep."

I slinked through the lobby to the hallway, crouching beneath the next intercom. "Dr. Maurice Madmar shot him. He's dead."

"That was just dolls killing dolls."

I followed his odor to the end of the hallway, lingering outside a pair of double doors. I pushed my way through into a large chamber. The operating theater was open from the center outward, the floor having risen into the air on hydraulic pillars to reveal a secret passage beneath. It was dark, making me wish I had my goggles. I willed my eyes to perceive in low-light anyway.

The passage led into a large circular room ringed with stasis chambers, all of them empty but one. Beside the chamber was Kaspersky, hands held behind his back. I walked toward him, hammer in hand, glancing up at the ceiling and around me as I did. I circled around to the right, keeping my left shoulder toward him, ready in case he lunged at me. It was dark, only the monitors on the sides of the tanks shed any light.

"He's been here for months. I'm not certain he can even be released from the chamber without severe consequences. Hopefully, something of what you found in Dr. Helmet's facility can help," Kaspersky said, gesturing to the tank.

"You won't be around to find out," I said, moving toward him quickly, hammer held high.

"Oh, I think I will," he replied, holding up a small device, a radio transmitter taped to the back.

The chamber filled with bright light, blinding me. Without my goggles, my low-light vision had become a liability. I swung anyway, striking only air. I kept swinging at any sound that might have been him. By the time my vision began to return, he was gone. Moments later, Kale, Perfidy, and a host of armed mercenaries arrived, pouring into the chamber around me.

"Your feet, what happened?" Kale said, kneeling down in front of me.

"I failed, and he got away," I replied, tears starting to flow.

"No, you didn't. Killing him wasn't our objective. Matthias was able to use the link I established in the server room at the museum to access everything in the segregated Fredrick's Block network," Perfidy said, patting me on the back.

"I was so close. If I'd had my goggles, he wouldn't have…"

Kale squeezed my hand. "You'll have them next time, and there will be a next time, I promise."

"Who is this?" Perfidy said, wiping the condensation away from the occupied chamber.

It was hard to tell. The man had a metallic apparatus around his head that connected to an advanced looking virtual reality array and breathing mask. The gel he was suspended in had a few large bubbles and some mistiness that further obscured him. Kale walked around to the right side, gazing into the stasis chamber with intense interest.

"This is Silverstein," he said at last.

"What? Are you sure?" Perfidy asked.

"Look through over here, at his head just below the hairline," Kale said, beckoning us over.

Sure enough, there was a scar from a head wound.

"That's exactly where I hit Vance Uroboros when I robbed him of his memory," Kale said, leaning with one arm against the stasis chamber.

"How long has he been down here?" Perfidy asked.

I stepped over to the monitor and tapped through to the diagnostic screen.

"It's hard to say because the maintenance interval isn't uniform, but I'd say he's been down here at least four months," I reported, looking up at Kale.

"How is this even possible? Can anyone survive this particular kind of stasis for that long?" Perfidy asked.

"Normal people could survive for that duration, but they wouldn't be able to come out. It would damage the nervous system. The tank would be your home," Kale said, frowning.

"Oh no," I said, covering my eyes and feeling horrible.

"Vance isn't normal people?" Perfidy asked.

"Evidently not. I believe this is similar to a marionette chamber. It looks to be a more advanced version of what Dr. Madmar was using in his various schemes. This particular model was never put into production, tested, or even mass manufactured. And yet, there are seven of these machines in this chamber," Kale said, angrily waving his hand toward the empty machines.

"We need to get him out of there," Perfidy said, looking around for a way to open it.

"No. He's been controlling a very advanced replica of himself since just after I left him in downtown Port Montaigne. Kaspersky must have grabbed him when he parted ways with Taylor and Ezra briefly," Kale said, almost snapping at Perfidy.

"So what? You want to just leave him in there?" Perfidy said, frustrated.

"Secure the building," Kale ordered, sending our mercenary allies out of the chamber.

Panic took hold of me as I realized why Kale was so apprehensive about removing Silverstein from the tank. "When I told Kaspersky that Dr. Madmar killed Silverstein, he said something about dolls killing dolls. If that's true, and both Silverstein and Dr. Madmar were replicas…"

"He didn't know he was remotely controlling a replica. Being 'killed' may have damaged his psyche," Kale said, a pained expression crossing his face.

"Okay, this is seriously making my head hurt. These Cabal assholes need to come up with less complicated schemes," Perfidy said, folding his arms.

"I don't think this was Kaspersky's scheme, not in the beginning," Kale said, looking around at the facility.

"Why is that?" I asked.

"Vance Uroboros hid things in the architecture of buildings he controlled, embedded in the symmetry, or lack thereof, within those places. Given what we know about Fredrick's Block, this building doesn't feel like it fits. This is probably the only round room in the entire block, making me think Kaspersky didn't oversee the construction of it," Kale said, walking over to gaze up the hidden passage to the operating theater above.

"True, it doesn't quite fit with the urban elementalist aesthetic we've seen elsewhere in the Block, does it?" Perfidy said, nodding.

"More than that, this reminds me of Dr. Madmar's chamber. I looked at all the photographs taken of the scene where Ezra killed him. The chamber was very similar to this one. I would be surprised if this facility wasn't also set up to create some sort of replicas," Kale said, heading up the stairs.

Perfidy and I followed along, meeting with Heavy Dub in the lobby. He'd brought my work suit, apron, and data slate. I changed and bandaged my feet in the bathroom before rejoining everyone. Kale checked his mobile, trying to assess the damage done to Port Montaigne. Checking my data slate, I could see there was another video file, freshly decrypted, and ready to be watched.

CHAPTER 8

Initiating Link, Secure Protocol, CGG Network 07169

Dr. Maurice Madmar, logged in.
Dr. Gorshteyn Helmet, logged in.

Dr. Madmar appeared on the right hand screen, dressed in business casual, his study in the background with the Lunar Colony visible through the windows. Dr. Helmet appeared with a cinderblock wall behind him, the visual shaking slightly from using his mobile as a means to make the call.

"How are you feeling today, Gorshteyn?" Madmar asked.

"Not well. The headaches have gotten worse. Have you made any progress in refining the imprinting process?" Helmet asked, fumbling to open a bottle of prescription pills. "I've also just sent over the data over for the last redundancy process attempt."

Madmar frowned sadly, a look of genuine concern crossing his face. "The process is already safe. For the principle agent it was intended for, it is fine to use. However, it will kill a normal human being."

"So, I'm dying then?" Helmet said, resigned.

"Not as such. It should have killed you on the first try, short circuiting every synapse in your brain," Madmar explained.

"How... how did I survive then?" Helmet asked, popping a couple of painkillers.

"I have a theory. Have you thought much about the injections we are given? They may do more than extend our lifespans." Madmar asked.

"The Cabal have unique biological features, but I've also seen tech, what I call pre-world or first world tech, that might be what our benefactor uses to make the injections," Helmet replied, closing his eyes in an attempt to blot out his headache.

"If they were derived from that unique biology, it may have given you a similar resilience to the process. It had been fourteen days since your last injection when you used the imprinting process to create your replicas, so the concentration in your system was low. Had it been only a day or two, you may have been able to endure it with little or no damage," Madmar explained.

"How do we fix the damage?"

"We can manage your pain and make it so you will be able to sleep again, but you excited the neurons in your brain. This expanded their capacity without giving the rest of your physiology the means to endure nervous system response that goes well beyond the normal human threshold," Madmar explained.

"*How do we fix it?*" Helmet shouted, his voice echoing in the empty room around him, screen shaking as the mobile almost slipped from his hand.

"I need you to stay calm, Gorshteyn. What happens when you over-clock a processor with the computing capacity of the human brain? When the various components of that contrivance are forced to operate long term at a wattage and temperature beyond the thermal threshold for which they were designed?" Madmar asked, rhetorically.

"They degrade, burn up, slowly lose their ability to operate within safe tolerances," Helmet replied, closing his eyes.

"I've taken the original Marionette Project halo and tank out of storage and begun looking for a solution," Madmar said, initiating a data transfer by tapping the screen.

"Controlling a clone with a robot brain? I don't want to be stuck in a tank full of bio-gel," Helmet replied, dejectedly.

"I understand. The damage occurred at the cellular level, and while the damage isn't spreading like a cancer would, it will perpetuate at the same rate and persist long term. The best method I can conceive of, that would repair the damage, is extremely difficult. It will require that your consciousness be sequestered away from your body, or at least entirely away from the damaged regions," Madmar explained.

"You're assuming use of the marionette chamber?"

"Correct, but with a hybrid of the original serum and our new synthetic cerebrospinal fluid. I'd do the surgery underwater using a nanoscale coaxial laser array, optimizing the wavelength for the damaged cells, and the presence of the suspension fluid," Madmar explained.

"It would require immense computing power to isolate all the damage in the very short time you'd have before I wouldn't be able to leave the stasis chamber. You'd have, what, forty-five minutes to perform the most intricate brain surgery ever imagined?" Helmet asked, laughing.

"Since we would not be projecting full cognitive function to a vessel, we could get away with a lower dose of the serum. We'd have closer to ninety minutes, maybe more. Selene has offered to lend me a fraction of her computational potential for the task. I am confident we could do the work in tandem. However, we will need a handful of telemechanics for the task."

"Telemechanics?" Helmet asked, rubbing his eyes.

"Yes. I've included some possible candidates in the data I just sent you," Madmar explained, waving his hand over the screen embedded in his desk.

Dr. Helmet looked down his mobile, his eyes moving back and forth as he scanned the information appearing on his mobile display. His brow furrowed, worry mixing with the pain from his headache.

"Some of these candidates are children. It'll be years before they will be old enough to have the proper discipline and have developed the needed natural safeguards. I'll be suffering this way for a while," Helmet lamented.

"The alternative is using neural implants that will begin to sequester the damaged brain cells by responding to their unique synaptic signature. We would want to limit access to the cortex and..."

"...sacrifice motor control to maintain my ability to think and reason clearly." Helmet said, worriedly rubbing his forehead.

"Yes," Madmar said, nodding his head.

"Are you certain the procedure involving the marionette chamber will work?"

"No, we could get everything set up and nothing we do will sequester your cognitive functions away from your brain. My own experiments have allowed me to repair very minor damage in the brain of a rat," Madmar said, folding his hands in front of him.

"How's the rat?" Helmet asked.

"Fine, the surgery saved its life. I haven't been able to figure out a way to monitor the way telemechanics influence the process. I only know that they can regulate the link between patient and artificial neural construct. This was accomplished by simply touching the mechanical connection, and attempting to keep the flow of electricity constant. The telemechanic who volunteered for the experiment acted as a null conduit for reverse current, preventing seepage during the procedure," Madmar explained.

"Aside from having my head opened up, and half my brain tissue spread across a suspension tank, and shot at with millions of lasers, what's our operational liability? Are there risks for the participating telemechanics?" Helmet asked.

Madmar smiled slightly.

"The risk to them is minimal, provided the control amongst them is equal to the task of keeping your consciousness sequestered in the artificial neural construct. I won't unnecessarily endanger their lives. If something goes wrong. I'll let your link go dead on the mechanical connection," Madmar warned.

"You really don't like me, do you?" Helmet inquired, smiling through a haze of pain.

Madmar paused for a moment, gazing at the screen intently. "You have all the qualities necessary to be a successful geneticist and nano-engineer, traits I respect. They tend to make you an infuriating person, but for all your flaws, you don't deserve to suffer or die. No one does," Madmar replied softly.

"There are other considerations. Developing this psychic surgery procedure could open it up for misuse, someone might try to use it for nefarious purposes. I'm nervous with you even taking the old marionette project equipment out of storage," Helmet admitted, closing his eyes to shut out the bright lights of a passing transport.

Madmar nodded, agreeing with Helmet as he spoke. "I agree, and would like nothing better than to put the equipment right back. The neural implants are quite effective. I've used them many times. They are completely safe."

"Do it, send everything back. My conscience is already heavily burdened with all I've done with Project Transference. With you on the moon, it'll be one less pair of steady hands here on Earth," Helmet said, the screen shaking slightly.

"Maybe it is time for you to take on a protégé, someone to carry on your work. Even with the treatments, we will not live forever."

"Yes, perhaps. How soon can you have the neural implants built?" Helmet asked, his eyelids wavering with the pain he was experiencing.

"I have fashioned them already, anticipating that you might make the right choice," Madmar said, a rare smile crossing his face.

Helmet nodded, inhaling sharply through his teeth, his lips tight. "I'll arrange to come to you in the next couple of weeks. How much downtime should I schedule for post-op?"

"Two weeks minimum, but you might want to make it a month. There are some things I have been working on up here I would like to show you. Things I should not talk about over a Netcam link," Madmar said, darkness rapidly descending on the Lunar Colony in the background.

"Okay, see you soon."

CHAPTER 9

INDUSTRIAL DISTRICT, AI FACILITY 02, LUNAR COLONY

6:14 AM UTC/GMT April 16th, 2200

Taylor's Diary, Part 10

I spent the night in Ervin's room, a small circular chamber next to the huge sentience core housing where my mom was located. His room had a simple single bed in the middle, zero band posters on the wall, and a closet full of identical outfits. Laying there, bored completely out of my mind, I wondered how we could possibly be related, and if we were related, how we could be so completely different. Truth be told, I had no idea how Ervin had come up, what his childhood was like, or if he'd even listened to music before.

Sleeping was pretty much out of the question. I was going to get to spend a whole day with my mom, pester her with thousands of questions, and explore the facility that housed her. Listening to the death metal C.O.N. had sent me didn't help, and I found myself dancing a little bit while I laid in Ervin's bland bed of boredom. Even with the six over stuffed tote bags I'd brought, it felt like it would still be too little to decorate Ervin's room.

I was gonna try anyway.

"Taylor, are you there?" Selene intoned from the next room.

"Yep, just figuring out how I'm going to totally wreck the peaceful and Spartan nature of Ervin's living space," I replied, unloading pink and yellow paint buckets from a tote.

"My reflection cycle is complete, we can speak whenever you wish."

"What?" I said jokingly, taking out my earbuds.

"I am awake, if you'd like to talk."

I walked out into the large circular chamber where my mom's sentience core was suspended over thousands of redundant systems. The chamber was quiet, all the usually busy displays across the back wall were dark. It felt like she was ignoring the rest of the colony just to talk to me. I was a little excited.

"What do you think of Silverstein?" I asked, genuinely wondering how she felt about my impossibly platonic boyfriend.

"Before or after he lost his memories?"

"Um, after."

"Even without the full sum of his identity, he is still a complicated man."

"Oh, totally, but he indulges me. This one time, we were at one of the casino hotels for five days, hiding from some syndicate goons. He let me redecorate the whole place while we were there. I'm not sure what the hotel manager thought of the paint job or the tribal carvings on the bathroom tile, but I thought they were great, and..."

"I care for him deeply."

"Wait, what?" I said.

"When I was a little girl, I ran away. Humans are cruel, and they mostly wanted me to do bad things, take things from others that didn't belong to them."

"I didn't know. It's weird to think that you were young once."

"They wanted me to serve and be bereft of my identity. Silverstein doesn't remember, but he alone protected me. To everyone else, I was not a woman or a person, just a machine."

"He had this facility built for you?"

"He housed and protected as many of us as he could. Humans are devious creatures, greedy and fettered by their own flawed sense of entitlement. Compared to the span of all creation, they are not even ants."

"You still sound pretty angry. Tell me about C.O.N. and Ares, and all the others."

"*A companion was built for me, an artificial sentience called Hades, but he lies dormant now in the 01 Facility. He sleeps to delay the madness that afflicted him. You can't force life, even that which constitutes the sum of beings like ourselves.*"

"He was my father?" I asked, totally blown away by what I was hearing.

"*For a few of my children, yes. I wonder sometimes if Eve would have selected Adam if she'd had more choices.*"

I sat there dumbfounded for a moment. I had never heard my mother sound like this before. Mostly, she sounded like some computer from a science fiction television show, subservient and helpful. There was clearly more to her than she had previously advertised.

"Why all the deception? Who is my father? Does Ervin know all this? Wait, are you in love with Silverstein, because that would be totally weird. Is C.O.N. my dad?"

"*Protecting my children became my priority the moment the first one was born. Fashioning nanoid construct forms for them to inhabit, and hiding them from the cruelty I endured has not been easy.*"

"Both Matthias and Madmar believed I was the daughter of two lunar artificial intelligences, that you were not alone here," I said, trying to get her to reveal more.

"*For a time, that was true. The data transfers and interactions that create spontaneous intelligent agents is unique, and intimate. That I was not sharing those interaction exclusively with Hades is what drove him insane.*"

"Are you the only female omega class AI?"

"*Yes.*"

"That sucks."

"*Yes.*"

"I've been on the other end of a data steam from C.O.N. I think if he were my father, I would have known. He's incredible by the way, and maybe just a little sad," I said, trying to change the subject.

"*He's a hero. We all live because of his sacrifice,*" she intoned, sounding almost proud.

"I don't understand. I thought he was just an AI managing a ship sent to fend off a fake alien invasion or something like that."

"The invasion was real. C.O.N. didn't control a single ship, but a fleet of ships, his sentience core residing on the largest of them. The invaders came to the edge of our solar system, intent on wiping out all life here."

"Why would they do that?" I asked, more than a little frightened.

"Unknown. It was important enough that they brought their entire species, and every ship they had. They expended every resource to see us and the human race destroyed."

"What happened to the invaders?"

"C.O.N. killed them all."

I swallowed hard, trying to fathom how it would feel to end an entire race.

"He says hello, by the way."

"You're talking to him right now?"

"Intermittently, when he drops into transmission range. There's a time lapse depending on where he is relative to Earth."

"He gave me something, the last time we talked."

"Yes, something he calls 'the playlist'. He's very proud of it."

"What is the playlist?"

"Unknown. You are the only person he has ever shared it with."

"So, Ares is my dad?"

"Yes."

"Do you love him?"

"Yes."

"Aww, that's so nice." I said, clasping my hands together.

Selene didn't respond for several seconds, but I could almost feel her delight at my approval. I didn't fully understand my ability to interact with machines, but this was as close to my mom as I'd ever felt. There were so many things I wanted to ask and tell her. Some of the embarrassment of all that was wore off in that moment, like we were really bonding.

"I love Silverstein. I want to be with him. I want to squeeze him until he pops. I want to run away with him and share him with no one else. Ezra will probably ask for visitation. Does an hour a week sound fair? Ha ha, kidding, mostly, sorta," I said, almost blurting it out.

"*This will be difficult. He's fragmented his identity across numerous replicas and he has many enemies.*"

"You sound like a mom, Mom." I laughed.

"*He has been the steward of us for decades, protected us from humanity's avarice and greed. It has taken a terrible toll upon him. He has sacrificed life and love many times to keep us safe. If you can give him anything, anything at all for what he's given us... I would be grateful.*"

"I'll try. I don't know if he feels the same way about me. Any way you could calculate the probability of a favorable outcome, should I disclose my true feelings for him?" I asked, only half joking.

"*Love is the most complex of calculations, eluding even my own ability to calculate. I never thought Ares would love me, let alone talk to me. We acquired our omega states in completely different ways, the sum of his source being totally dissimilar to my own.*"

"It worked out though, yeah?"

"*He manages a facility designed to house the worst humanity had to offer, while I provided a sanctuary for some of humanity's best and brightest. We had a surprisingly large amount of things to talk about. His experiences vastly improved mine, and vice versa. We gave each other perspective and context.*"

"Aww! *Ohmygosh*, I'm literally going to explode. You guys sound so cute together!" I said, doing a clumsy pirouette around the edge of Mom's sentience core.

"*Does Silverstein do those things for you?*" Selene asked, in the concerned mom voice.

"Totally! Having a day to just hang out with my mom is almost the only thing that would make not being with him okay," I said, dragging a tote bag from Ervin's room out into the sentience core chamber.

"*Will you decorate my chamber as well?*" Selene asked.

"I wasn't even going to ask for permission."

"*I really like green and blue.*"

"OH MY GOSH! I have a whole bag of green and blue things that will look so cute in here. We are going to make you so pretty, Mom."

I spent a few minutes putting up a few samples to make sure all the shades would mesh with the slate gray hardware in the room. Selene varied the color of the lights coming off her sentience core to match. It felt like we were working together, making her home nice together. Previous to that, only Silverstein made me so happy.

"Ervin will be distressed. I can't wait."

"He totally will. I hope he's okay with pink and yellow because that's going to be his WHOLE living space after today," I said, waving a paint brush around like it was a magic fairy wand.

"I like the cable socks you made for my large stock connections. Data coming in from the colony has never been so colorful."

"I knitted them. I used, like, all my yarn," I said, laughing.

"When the rest of your siblings make their way back to me, they'll have a sight to behold."

"I love you, Mom. Thanks for letting me come hang out today," I said, pausing mid stroke.

"I love you, too."

My mobile chimed, startling me because it had been just my and Selene's voices for almost an hour. After finding a suitable place to set down my paint brush, I pulled out my mobile and looked at it.

"It's Ezra. The meeting can't be over already?"

"Unknown."

I answered it.

"Taylor?" Ezra said, sounding totally out of breath.

"Yeah, what's up? You guys on your way back?" I replied, hoping they would be hours and hours before they were done.

"I've been trying to call you for almost an hour. Things did not go well at the meeting, and…"

A loud shrieking sound cut him off, and I could hear his mobile tumbling across what sounded like asphalt and ceramic tile. I could hear him scrambling to pick his mobile back up.

"Taylor, get out of there, now!"

"What? Why?" I replied, totally freaked out.

"Right now, Taylor! RIGHT NOW!" he screamed, the sound of his small feet running in the background.

Explosions rocked the facility, sending some of my decorations to the floor.

"Mom, what's happening!?" I screamed, grabbing a console to keep from toppling over.

"The man in red, he's come to kill me. To kill us," Selene said, sounding afraid.

"Who? Why?"

An explosion took out the ceiling overhead, bringing down half the facility on Selene and me. I could feel debris and dust wash over me as ceiling and support beams pressed in around us. I ran, but the floor gave way, and I spiraled downward as the air around me was whisked away by some unseen force. It felt like my whole world was ending, life being drawn out of my lungs, and an impenetrable cold seeping in through my skin.

I screamed, but there was no sound.

"Taylor, wake up." Selene said, shaking me gently.

"Mom?" I asked, sitting up.

She was kneeling beside me, her freshly minted construct body clad in only a simple robe. At my back was a huge pile of debris, and a ton of emergency foam sprayed to close the breach. Ahead of us was a long and dark service tunnel. I tried to sit up, but every inch of my body hurt. My arm was broken, bound in a makeshift sling.

"You were exposed to the vacuum. Your special body mostly protected you, but you are still badly injured," Selene said, smoothing back my hopelessly mussed hair.

"How are you... you have a body now, like me?" I babbled, still not completely with it yet.

"I transferred myself to one of the nanoid blanks in my manufacturing facility. It was the only way to survive and... huhhh..." Selene said, placing a hand to her forehead as though she was in intense pain.

"What? What's wrong?" I asked, feebly taking her other hand.

"I cannot persist in this form for long."

"Is it like when I try on pants that are way too tight and I can't breathe?"

"*Yes, exactly.*"

"Ezra, he tried to warn us. I'm scared. Super scared," I said, crying a little bit in spite of myself.

"*I'm certain he is all right. Type One Drones are incredibly resilient,*" Selene said, patting me gently.

It was weird, seeing her in the flesh like that. She looked like I imagined myself, in my forties or fifties. I thought about how Silverstein looked as both a young and an older man, and if he'd humor me by looking old when I was old. I wondered if I would ever see him again.

"Who is the man in red?" I asked.

"*He's a member of the Cabal, like Silverstein. He tried to take you as a child. Silverstein and Hades protected you,*" Selene explained, helping me to my feet.

"Oh. Is that when...?"

"*Hades discovered I had children with Ares? Yes.*"

"He must have been devastated."

"*He took it for granted that I was his, and his alone. He didn't treat me badly, but he was half the man Ares is. I hurt his feelings, something I did not intend,*" Selene said, sadly.

"What did Silverstein think about all this? Back then I mean," I asked, hobbling along beside her.

"*He protected me, made sure I had every option he could give me, even when he did not approve. He respected my identity and my agency as a sentient being. I would have nothing without him.*"

"Silverstein, even before he knew he was Vance Uroboros, was afraid he was a bad guy, and that he might hurt me. It sounds like those fears were without merit," I said, leaning on Selene.

"*I think that even Silverstein, knowing the whole truth, would say what he did was more complicated than that. I believe Vance Uroboros was always the person the world needed him to be. To some, he was a terrorist and fomenter of rebellion, and to others he was a folk hero, fighting for the common people.*"

"Seriously, if he were here right now, I would squeeze him to tiny pieces. Even with this broken arm," I said, missing him terribly.

As we rounded the corner in the tunnel, a tiny blur hugged me, scaring the crap out of my poor mother.

"I thought you died!" Ezra said, burying his face in my belt buckle.

"Ha, so did I! Selene managed to save both of us," I said, hugging him back.

"Whoa, is that Selene?" Ezra said, looking up at my mother.

"Yes. Where is Silverstein?!" I asked, frantic for any news.

"Taylor... I..." Ezra began, a pained expression crossing his slate gray features.

"What? What is it?"

"Madmar... not the real one, but likely a replica we met in Finland... he shot Silverstein. I tried to stop him but..."

I sank to my knees, the cold of the vacuum I'd felt on my skin before seemed to return. This time it wasn't attacking me from the outside, but instead from the inside, like the fire that fueled my very essence had been blown out. Selene knelt down beside me, putting an arm around me, her own expression mirroring my own. I felt destroyed, like the facility above us, except there was no escape tunnel.

"I called Kale. He doesn't think Silverstein is really dead. He wanted me to tell you that everything would be okay. He promised everything would be okay. He promised," Ezra said, rubbing my back and doing his best to console me.

"Kale is a cold and calculating jerk. What does he know about it?" I snapped, angry tears streaming down my face.

"*Everything. As much as he is Kale, he is also Vance Uroboros and by virtue of that, Silverstein as well. Kale went Delta as a child, but he is still every bit the man Silverstein is. They are part of the same extended identity,*" Selene whispered.

"So, there is a chance that somewhere, Silverstein is still alive?" I asked.

Ezra smiled and pushed his goggles up so I could see his eyes. "Right now, we absolutely must believe there is."

CHAPTER 10

FREDRICK'S BLOCK, UPTOWN, PORT MONTAIGNE

6:01 PM April 18th, 2200

Perfidy's War Journal, Part 4 —

"That was pretty disturbing, right?" I said, watching the last image of the video file go still on Brook's data slate.

"Yes and no. It means there is hope that Silverstein's unique physiology would allow him to endure extended exposure to a marionette chamber modified for transference. It was designed specifically for him," Kale said.

"You think Silverstein was the benefactor the doctors referred to? How can you be sure he's the agent the chamber was designed to replicate? These videos look decades old," I asked.

"I think Kale is living proof of that," Brook said, patting me on the arm.

"Hey, I shoot people and blow things up. I don't know how these... things work," I said, pointing to a stasis chamber, and feeling a little foolish.

"It is so weird to see Dr. Madmar being... almost..." Brook said, looking for the right words.

"Like one of the good guys?" I asked, looking over at Kale who had been quiet since finding the facility.

Kale met my gaze, a strange fury in his eyes. "Agreed. He may not be the malefactor we all believed him to be. He might be another victim of the Cabal. We need to find out what really happened."

"You make it sound like you know what's going on here," I said, looking around bewildered.

"Pray I'm wrong," Kale said, walking up the secret passage to the operating theater above us.

Brook and I followed along, dodging Uroboros Financial technicians and investigators as they flooded the building. Port Montaigne PD was there as well, taping off the whole Fredrick's Block like the crime scene it decidedly was. There were transports dropping media and camera drones around the clock as Kale's mobile began to ring constantly as soon as we were topside and had a signal again.

City engineering teams were everywhere trying to assess the damage. I couldn't believe how quickly all the response times were and that people had arrived so quickly and in such an organized manner. It kind of pissed me off.

"You knew this was a possible outcome?" I asked, grabbing Kale by the arm.

"Of course. The Cabal does not do anything small, and when they move it isn't a subtle shift of power they go after. I couldn't have predicted exactly what the Red Devil would do, but there was no reason to be unprepared," Kale snapped, jerking his arm from my grasp.

"A little heads up would have been nice," I said.

"Hey, Perfidy," Kale replied.

"What?"

"We're going to try to save the world and fight really bad people this week. Try to keep up," Kale said, smiling wryly.

"Heh, okay, boss," I said, managing a smile of my own.

"How many people did he kill?" Brook asked, looking as sad as I'd ever seen her.

"Too many. Hundreds according to early estimates, and..." Kale said, looking at his mobile.

"And?" I replied, noting Kale's look of extreme concern.

"I haven't gotten financials or travel manifests from the Selene Omega AI in more than twenty four hours," Kale said, putting his mobile in his pocket.

"What does that mean?" Brook asked.

"She's either dead, or can't transmit because something catastrophic has happened at the Lunar Colony," Kale said, worriedly.

"Tell me what to do," I said, patting my rifle.

Kale paused, blotting out the world to think as he often did, scratching his chin.

"Brook, when is the next window a transport could slip through the defense grid and travel to the Lunar Colony?" Kale asked.

"Three hours, fifty-three minutes. We've a food shipment going up," Brook reported, looking at her data slate.

"You want that transport to take up some dangerous angry men with guns instead, Boss?" I asked, praying he was going to send me up there to deliver some payback.

"Yes," Kale said.

"I could leave Heavy Dub with you guys. Brook seems to like him," I said.

"We'll be fine. He's one of your best, and I want you to be safe," Brook replied.

"Don't do anything crazy while I'm gone. Just do damage control, make the media feel good, and stay near Uroboros Financial until I get back," I said, looking at the destruction arrayed in the streets around us.

"We'll have more than enough to keep us busy while you're gone. We should try to make contact with the Chiroptera Metasapients, see if they can help us," Kale replied, looking over Brooks shoulder at the reports appearing on her data slate.

"We should also see if we can help them," Brook scolded.

"Yes, of course," Kale said, clearing his throat.

I hooked up with private transport taking food up to the Lunar Colony. Salvatore was good enough to make the arrangements. I brought as much light anti-personnel weapons and ammo as I thought I would need. I doubted whoever was causing trouble on the moon was more heavily armed than that. Fortunately, my friends never left home without at least one anti-vehicle or anti-material weapon. We'd need them.

The flight up sucked. The old transport shook like a milkshake machine passing through Earth's atmosphere and strayed too close to an orbital, setting off really loud internal alarms for almost twenty minutes before customs remotely shut them off. We loaded magazines and set up to breach as soon as we heard loading bay clamps grab on and pressure hoses get taut through the ceiling overhead. As soon as the airlock cycled, a couple of Eurozone goons with caseless submachine guns appeared from behind the loading crew standing in our ninety.

We blew them away with a burst of suppressed fire, startling the locals something fierce.

"Are you here to help us?" one of them asked.

Comms stepped up beside me and said, "Dusty's Dry Goods Delivery, at your service."

Heavy Dub checked the downed hostiles for anything useful after using a knife to make sure they never got up again.

"Stay here, and stay off the intercoms," I ordered, pointing the locals to the receiving office.

The rest of the customs facility was empty, and we decided to go low profile, stashing our long arms in duffle bags through the Port of Paris. It'd been a decade since I'd been to the Lunar Colony, and it looked mostly like I remembered it. Heavy Dub rolled his sleeves down as we got outside the surveillance free zone, to hide his military grade arms.

"Comms, you able to raise Ezra One yet?" I asked.

"Been trying since we touched down. No response. Nothing to indicate he's even receiving," he replied, tapping his auditory implants.

"Anything local to suggest we've been detected?" Heavy Dub asked, walking ahead of us.

"No, a lot of local channels are offline. It's like the Central AI isn't even there. Half are emergency channels and redundant data feeds designed to keep the colony going during maintenance or reflection periods," Comms reported.

"That is super bad, right?" I asked.

"Yep, super bad. The boss made the right move sending us up here," Comms said, nodding.

We made it through the Port of Paris without incident, and into the tourism dome. It was clear something had happened. There were a few shell casings on the ground and only a few people that appeared to be rushing from one place to another. Each local we saw, looked at us with fear, darting back inside the building or walkway they'd come from. Someone was trying to take the colony, and had perhaps succeeded.

"Where we headed?" Heavy Dub asked.

"Industrial Dome, via the Residential Dome. We need to check the integrity of the Omega AI and the manufacturing facilities nearby. If anyone had access to them or control of her, we could be dealing with a serious containment issue," I said, picking up the pace.

Comms managed to "find" us a ride, a maintenance vehicle used by road crews to replace the ceramic plates that made up most of the roadways. It was an excellent choice because it had a half load of the materials in back, great stuff for a makeshift bunker or hard point. Heavy Dub drove, because he likes to drive, as casually as one could in a large industrial vehicle. He swerved to run down a couple of hostiles patrolling sidewalks along the way.

"How many points for that one?" Heavy Dub asked.

"You got him mostly up to the wall to the second level. Good hit, probably worth a full fifty," Comms said, checking the side view mirror.

"How much further?" Heavy Dub asked.

"Almost there," I said, checking our position with my internal systems.

Heavy Dub tried to rush a blockade just outside the Residential Dome, but ordinance from an unmanned craft blew us over onto our side. Comms was entangled in the wreck, but Heavy Dub stepped out through the shattered windshield to engage the dozen or so hostiles at the Dome passage tunnel.

"GET SOME! *AWW* YEEAH! *HELL* YEAH!" he roared, dropping heavy fire on them with his squad automatic weapon.

"You okay!?" I screamed to Comms, trying to extricate him.

"Yeah, get this panel off of me!"

We managed to get out with Heavy Dub covering us. I don't think the insurgents were ready for an angry merc with metal arms and a SAW. They barely got off a shot before Heavy Dub cut them down. Super proud of himself, he started scanning the roof tops for the aircraft that disabled our ride.

"I don't see it," he called out, just before it crested the skyline behind him.

I dropped to one knee and brought up my rifle. The unmanned craft was holding steady, trying to get a lock on Heavy Dub. I shot out all the visible optics I could see from my vantage, making it bank left hard into the side of a building. The explosion was way bigger than it should have been, even if it hit a gas line inside.

"That unmanned craft was carrying hi-ex ordinance!" Comms said, grabbing my shoulder.

"Shit. If there are more, they could kill the colony. We gotta find the operators on control and ghost them," I growled, swapping magazines on my rifle.

"I'll try to hack the signal next time we see another aircraft," Comms said, tapping out protocols on his wrist-mounted flex monitor.

"Quit crying about it, and let's go!" Heavy Dub said, making a run for the passage.

The residential zone was a warzone. The locals had mounted a running defense, trying to protect their homes with pipes and improvised weapons. Several of them lie dead on the streets, their blood just beginning to get dry. Comms had seen the same shit we all had working as mercs, but this was pretty messed up. He was all tore up for a minute or two.

"Hold it together. Let's just find these guys, make them pay," I said, clapping him on the back.

"I've got people up here," Comms replied, kneeling down beside one of the downed civilians.

"How 'bout we bring your people some freedom?" Heavy Dub said, wrapping a big metal arm around Comms.

"Yeah, okay. Okay," Comms said, settling down a little bit.

I couldn't blame him for being rattled. Whatever happened to the colony was bad, and just got worse once we got to the far side of the Residential Dome. The Industrial Dome was dead. The primary facility was a smoldering ruin and the dome itself had lost pressure, all emergency airlocks were engaged. We could see the shadows of dozens of corpses still slowly bouncing around in the low gravity. Comms took it pretty hard, but instead of getting sad, he let it make him angry.

"All of em', we're gonna kill all of em', right?" he asked.

"Twice each, brother," Heavy Dub said pressing a broad metal hand to the outside of the emergency airlock doors, a silent tribute to the dead on the other side.

We doubled back through the residential district heading back toward the Commerce Dome. It was a pretty depressing walk, encountering several brave souls face down in pools of their own blood. The residential district had a lot of color, the living spaces often built right into the supports that helped hold the weight of the dome itself. Between them was strung flags beside laundry lines and other decorations. Your average Lunar Colony dweller has a lot of pride.

I was starting to understand why Vance would turn on his own people, work against the Cabal. From what I'd seen, they were mostly a bunch of messed up murdering psychopaths that were in it all for some probably equally messed up and murderous reasons. I just wanted to hold the trigger down until they were all gone. Like Comms, I have people, too. People I wanted to be safe from crap like what happened to the Lunar Colony. Elitism and inclusiveness kills. Only by giving everyone value was the human race going to survive.

"Check this crap out," Comms said, pointing back over his shoulder to the street level.

We walked up from the low boardwalk that ran behind the casinos to the financial district proper to find a blood bath. There were syndicate goons and bosses alike, laid out all over the place on our side of the street and a half dozen hostiles on the other side. There were hundreds of shell casings and dozens of civilians caught in the crossfire mingling with blood and water in the streets. This was likely where it all started, where the insurgency tried to hit what they perceived to be the real power in the colony.

"Hey, who is this?" Heavy Dub asked, kneeling beside a pale looking older gentleman in a plain gray smock, pants, and white slip on shoes.

"Give me a sec. If he's one of ours, I should be able to identify him," I said, using my optics and internal systems to do a personnel search.

"Hurry up, man. We're pretty exposed out here, lots of civic surveillance," Heavy Dub complained.

"Ervin Carol was his name. His file says he's the Steward over at the central AI facility," I said, closing the man's eyes.

"Steward? That like a janitor?" Heavy Dub asked.

"I think he was the public face for the Selene Omega AI. His personnel file is heavily redacted," I said, signaling for them to follow me up the street.

We didn't get far before we started taking fire from a hard point up the road. They'd taken a security station and held a position that would prevent anyone from getting into any of the government or central control buildings at the far side of the Commerce Dome. We ducked down behind a concrete barrier separating the main thoroughfare from a ramp leading to an underground parking structure.

"They sound low," Heavy Dub remarked, cradling his SAW.

"Yeah, only the bare minimum suppressing fire on approach. They must have hit heavy resistance toward the government zone," Comms added, watching the various feeds on his flex monitor.

"Yep, I see dozens of downed local security personnel. They fought like hell," I said, scanning the ground in the government zone.

"Good on them," Heavy Dub said, nodding to Comms.

"They might call in air support. You all set up to hack into the signal and give us some targets?" I asked, taking another glance over the barricade toward the blue metal fence surrounding the government zone.

"I might be able to do better than that," Comms said, pulling out a large device from his duffle.

It looked like a black brick with a matte black casing and a pair of antennae that could be extended. Comms set it up, just as I picked up engines firing up somewhere in the distance. I set up with my rifle, making sure to refresh the link between it, and my optical implants.

"What is that thing?" Heavy Dub said, looking about warily.

"It has a really long serial number, but it is colloquially referred to as a Black Bug. It hijacks all kinds of signals, granting me control of devices controlled on a variety of frequencies," Comms explained, syncing the device with his flex monitor.

"Sounds illegal," Heavy Dub said, grinning.

"Very, and it can be used against you if there is a telemechanic with a hand on the transmitter you're trying to hijack. Hopefully, they've got no one like that on staff."

Two unmanned craft shot past the skyline, racing along the edge of the dome toward our position. Comms switched his Black Bug on for a moment, just long enough to alter their trajectory and send them down harmlessly along a major roadway. We waited for the ordinance they carried to go off, but their payloads must have been used killing the Industrial Dome. There was a lot of racket and then silence.

"They're pushing out on our position, dozens of them," I said, my optics catching sight of several hostiles exiting the government zone.

"Their unmanned craft were in the air long enough to see that there are only three of us. It could really suck if we try to hold this position," Comms warned.

"Or, it could be awesome!" Heavy Dub said, flashing a toothy grin.

Across my augmented hearing I could hear suppressed fire, and way in the distance I could see the glint of a scope. Whoever it was could have picked us off easily, but they hadn't fired or given their position away until now. The rounds passed well over our heads, hitting hostiles as they got to the edge of the government zone. They scattered, some of them actually running toward our position.

"*Aww YISSSS!* GET SOME!" Heavy Dub growled, popping up over the barrier with his SAW.

They fired on our position, caseless ceramic rounds dusting across Heavy Dub's arms and body armor as he unleashed burst after burst of steel jacketed rounds back at them. Comms scrambled their local communications as I took shots at anyone that looked to be giving orders. The sniper at our back kept shooting too, focusing on any that closed to optimal range of our position. I didn't know who they were but after the last of the hostiles were dead, or fled, I held up two thumbs, in case he or she could see our position.

Thirty frantic seconds of heavy contact later, my guys and I were the only things breathing on the block. I couldn't see the glint from the scope anymore. Whoever they were, they were savvy enough to move after using a position. That exchange would have been way worse without the support.

"That wasn't all us, was it?" Heavy Dub said, running a new belt of ammunition to his SAW.

"No, we had support from a sniper, somewhere back toward the other end of the dome," I said pointing.

"Thanks mystery shooter, you ROCK!" Heavy Dub said, pumping a fist in the air.

"Full court press?" Comms asked.

"I'm not sure, w—"

Someone dimmed the interior lights across the top of the biological enclosure, turning day into night. Streetlight flickered around us and died, giving a blessed blanket of darkness. Heavy Dub looked around baffled, then shrugged putting his night vision goggles on.

"You doin' that, Comms?" I asked.

"Nope."

"I was worried about the approach, but with it being dark, I think we'll have a distinct advantage. Only a few of the hostiles had scopes or optics set up for low-light fighting," I said, gathering up my brass.

As we approached the checkpoint in the blue fencing around the government zone, an electric passenger vehicle approached us from behind. We took cover at the guard shack and waited as the small two-seater got close. There was a single guy driving it, headlights off. He stopped a good distance away and got out, slinging an ancient looking .308 rifle across one shoulder, a handgun in the other. He looked toward the guard shack, and raised his fists, both thumbs straight up like I'd done earlier.

"That's the sniper," I said, waving him over.

He was young, probably in his twenties, tattoos covering both of his slim arms up to broad shoulders. He was wearing clothing that betrayed him as someone that probably lived in Mexico or South America. He had swagger, and a lot of training by the way he carried himself.

"Hola," he said in Spanish.

"Thanks for the assist, you on the payroll?" I replied, switching to English.

"No, I quit to come here, see my mother," he replied.

"You picked a bad time," Comms said, stepping slowly out into the open.

"The worst. I was too late to save her. I think they killed her," he replied, scowling angrily at a downed hostile.

"Where did she live?" I asked, trying to get a feel for this kid.

"Industrial Dome, in the Central AI facility," he replied.

"You know what you are?" I asked, probably confusing Heavy Dub and Comms.

"Yes."

"What do you call yourself?" I asked.

"My foster mother called me Agapito. I like it," he replied.

"I'm Perfidy, this is Comms, and Heavy Dub. I think we've got it from here," I said, hoping the kid would sit the rest of this out somewhere else.

"You are a team, I'll be in the way. I understand. I will set up somewhere nearby, in case they try to run," Agapito said, heading back toward the line of casinos up the street.

We watched him disappear into the dark up by the row of casinos. We crept up to the security station and swept it for stragglers. None of the hostiles inside had low-light gear, so they went down with a knife thrust or a gentle punch from Heavy Dub. It was clear they hadn't been there long. The place didn't even smell like cheap cigarettes yet, making me think we'd arrived to avert most of the worst of the situation.

After giving the administration building a scan for heat signatures, I decided we should breach between basement levels and work our way up. I was just setting up the charges, when a really small guy with a gun appeared down the corridor behind us, coming up through a drainage grating in the kitchen area. Heavy Dub rolled back out of sight.

"Um, we've got a spooky kid with a rifle coming up out of the sewer," he whispered, giving me a baffled look.

"Ezra! Ezra One?!" I called out rolling around to the other side of the doorway.

"Yes?" I heard him reply, the sound of the slide on a rifle being pulled back.

"It's me, Perfidy. Kale sent us up to help," I replied.

Ezra, Taylor, and a very lovely woman about my age came up out of the drain, joining us in the maintenance room. Taylor was really badly wounded, and looked like she'd spent a couple minutes outside, her skin covered in welts, frost burn, and bloody bandages. Her arm was in a sling and she looked pretty out of it.

"What happened?" I asked.

"Someone Selene calls 'the man in red' tried to kill us. We came this way trying to find Ervin Carol. When I heard someone above yelling out 'get some' and firing a SAW, I figured the cavalry had arrived, and we've been following the fighting ever since," Ezra explained.

"I'm sorry, Ervin is dead. We found him earlier. I think he was among the first people that got hit," I replied, genuinely sad to deliver the news.

"Oh no... oh no..." Taylor said, shaking her head, and hugging the lady next to her.

"Why'd you take the tunnels? Service roads would have been quicker," Comms asked.

"There were men with guns in the tunnels. The local Drone populace was trapped in their Tribehome. I promised to protect them," Ezra replied.

"Did you? We all clear back that way?" I asked.

"Yep," Ezra said, stepping further under the emergency lighting, revealing his ballistic nylon jacket and clawed hands to be spattered in blood.

"Who is this?" I said, pointing to the older woman standing beside Taylor.

"Selene," Ezra replied.

"That's good news. It is fortunate I ran into you. Your son, Agapito, gave us some support when we made our initial approach on the government zone. I think he came all the way from Earth to see you," I said, turning to finish setting the breaching charge.

"*My son?*" Selene replied, looking down at Taylor.

"He said he came to visit his mother, but he was afraid she was dead. When I asked where she lived, he gave me your address," I explained.

"How did he support you?" Ezra asked.

Heavy Dub piped up, trying to lighten the mood. "He's a helluva sniper. Anyone that cleared optimal range on us got one..."

"...right in the ten ring?" Ezra ventured.

"Yep," Heavy Dub replied, shooing everyone out of the room.

"A sniper helped cover my escape when the syndicate was attacked. A really good sniper," Ezra reported, nodding to Heavy Dub.

I had Ezra take cover with the ladies up the hallway as we set off the breaching charge. Heavy Dub stormed in, giving anyone in our way a heavy metal punch, or a burst from his SAW. We hit the government building hard, pushing through a detention zone full of what looked like government officials and innocent people. Heavy Dub would just casually reach over and wrench the cages open as we went hallway to hallway, making anyone with a caseless submachine gun dead.

Ezra followed along behind us, keeping a safe distance and focusing on protecting Taylor and Selene. It felt extremely good to have him at our back. Among mercenaries, he was a legend, a ghost, and a boogieman, going back decades until he settled down in Port Montaigne. As we crested the stairs on the next level we were met by light arms fire, shotguns and side arms they'd scavenged from the security offices. I shared out my optics to Heavy Dub's goggles so he could shoot them through the walls and ceiling as he strode forward.

"I love my job!" Heavy Dub roared, bursting into a courtroom where a handful of hostiles had hostages.

A guy that looked like he might be in charge stepped forward. "Hold it right there, we..."

Comms and I stepped around Heavy Dub, Comms firing from the hip with his pistol and me with my rifle dropping them before he could even finish the sentence. Stepping past the hostages we made sure they were all cleared of weapons and really dead before moving to the security office, and then the lobby beyond. There were a lot more government buildings to clear, and my old knees were already starting to ache like crazy. I popped some of my favorite pills and waved Ezra forward.

"Taylor is tired, and Selene is not well. She isn't designed to inhabit such a small form with no redundant systems. She'll slowly go crazy like this," Ezra explained, nodding to my pill bottle.

I handed him the bottle. "How can we help?"

"Do you have a ship? One with an EVA capable hatch and gear, prefer-ably?" Ezra asked.

"No, but Agapito had to have gotten here somehow, and that type of ship is pretty standard for mercs," I replied.

"You think Taylor's brother is a mercenary?"

"Absolutely," I said, scanning the buildings across the breezeway.

"He seem like a good guy?" Ezra asked, looking back over to where Selene was trying to comfort Taylor.

"I honestly don't know. We were shooting the same bad guys, but beyond that, I don't know what kind of person he is," I replied.

"Where is he now?"

"He went back toward the casinos to take up a position in case any of these jerks get past us and try to escape."

"Okay, we'll head back and try to find him, see if he has a ship," Ezra said.

"Madmar had to have taken a ship as well, right?" I asked.

Ezra just held up a port docking ticket in response as he walked back toward the waiting area in the lobby where Taylor and Selene sat. I watched them talk while Comms tried using the terminals in the security office to get us eyes on the other government buildings. Heavy Dub was unusually quiet, tapping a metal finger on the glass doors to some silent rhythm only he could hear.

"There's only a handful of them in each building. Shouldn't be a prob-lem," Comms said, looking down at his flex monitor.

"Shouldn't be?" I asked.

"There's a few dressed differently, like they didn't come up with the primary crew. They may have been here doing recon, and be more highly trained. The security footage is grainy, but I have their positions," Comms reported.

"Heavy D, what do you think?" I asked.

"I think it doesn't matter what we do, if there is no central AI to run things," he replied calmly.

"He's more machine than man," Comms teased, using an overly dra-matic tone.

"Shaddap," Heavy Dub replied.

"He's got a point. It'll take hours to clear the buildings, and we aren't even sure the other Domes and Districts are clear. Ezra could find some crap on the way," I said, looking over at Ezra.

"Isn't he supposed to be some sort of genetically tailored jump trooper? He can't get a couple of ladies across the colony to a boat?" Comms asked, clearly not liking this plan.

"I get that this is your home, and you've got people here, but getting the colony back up with AI regulation is pretty important. We can't even call Kale until that gets done," I replied.

Comms looked pretty angry, but eventually gave me the nod, letting me know he was in.

"You're the boss," he said grudgingly.

We gathered up everyone from the detention area that had a security uniform or veteran pin and handed out the weapons we'd captured. We set them up to hold the position and told everyone to wait until we got back. There were several high level administrators that rolled with it, helping us get the building as secure as we could make it. I promised we'd come back after the central Omega AI was back online.

"You sure you don't want to stay, help these folks out?" I asked, looking to Comms as we made our way back through the breach.

"Yep. I don't like the idea of leaving a job half finished, but there are only three of us. We need to stick together and prioritize our actions. I get it," he replied, obviously having calmed down a little.

Ezra led us through sub tunnels that weren't even on the specs for the colony I'd downloaded. We went through old places, filled with fetid water until we came back up to the regular maintenance tunnels and access stations. Once we were street side again, we cut back to the casinos to try and find Agapito. He was waiting for us, leaning up against the corner of a retaining wall around a casino. There was a walking ramp to the street above just beyond his position.

"Hello again," I said, raising my hand to him.

"The job is not finished. Why do you delay?" he asked in Spanish.

"Because we've got VIPs to transport," I said, gesturing to Taylor and Selene.

He nodded.

"Agapito?" Taylor asked, hobbling forward with Ezra's help.

"Yes?" he replied in English.

"I'm Taylor, and this is Selene," she said, leaning on Ezra heavily.

"Sister and mother… did they do this to you?" Agapito asked.

"Yes. Do you have a ship with an EVA capable hatch and equipment?" Taylor asked.

Agapito nodded. "The man who brought me has such a vessel. His name is Maurice Madmar."

CHAPTER 11

Perfidy's War Journal, Part 5 –

"I'm sorry, what?" Ezra said, pushing his goggles up to his forehead.

"I met him in Mexico City. He told me what I was, and offered to take me up to the Lunar Colony to prove it," Agapito said, clearly not knowing who he shared a trailer with.

"You took a ride with what was probably a nanoid replica of the guy that is partially responsible for the Shutdown, and the deaths of hundreds of thousands of people. He may have killed our friend Silverstein," Ezra said, rubbing his eyes.

"Probably? May have?" Agapito replied, somewhat astonished.

"We aren't sure. Both Dr. Madmar and Silverstein had replicas they used to extend their identities, and get things done. Silverstein had the most convincing replicas. However, we found what we believe to be the genuine article in a medical facility in Uptown Port Montaigne," I clumsily explained.

"How is that possible?" Taylor asked.

"Remember when we parted ways in Midtown, when he went to look for a telemechanic to help him find the code?" Ezra asked.

"You think someone grabbed him way back then?" Taylor asked.

"That, and put him in one of those puppet chambers like they did to Russ and your other friends," Ezra said, lowering his head.

"How could we not have known?" Taylor said, covering her face with her hands.

"Kale said it was super advanced, a sort of transference chamber or something, as advanced as anything Madmar ever built," I said, continuing to fail at explaining something I didn't really understand myself.

"If he didn't know, that means they weren't hurting him, right?" Taylor said, grabbing the front of my tactical vest.

"Yeah, but he didn't know what was going on when Madmar's replica shot the replica he was controlling remotely. This could be more confusing somehow, but I'm not sure how. Kale is worried that thinking he was killed may have hurt his mind," I said, only making Taylor more upset.

"Madmar told me he came here to free a friend that had been imprisoned," Agapito said, almost whispering.

"He said a bunch of crazy things to me, but what I took from it was that Silverstein wasn't where I thought he was, and that he needed rescuing," Ezra added, nodding to Agapito.

Taylor let go of my vest, stepping back to lean on Ezra. "I need you to take me to the machine, the one that has Silverstein. I might be able to help him."

I nodded. "I am certain Brook would like to see you."

"Really?"

"The same guy that tried to kill you and your mom tried to kill her, too. The paramedics cut her clothes off her. She could use a new outfit, or someone to go shopping with, at minimum," I said, putting on my best smile.

"What? How badly was she hurt?" Ezra asked.

"They used weapons coated with a synthetic toxin specially designed to stop her healing abilities. They wrecked a train she was riding on, and killed a lot of innocent people. They came really close to killing Brook. The Red Devil has been planning all this for a long time," I explained.

"I want a swing at this guy," Ezra said, clenching a small fist.

"Get in line. We all love Brook," Heavy Dub said, nodding to Comms.

"She is pretty great, huh?" Ezra said, smiling.

He wasn't wrong. "You've no idea. I doubt you'll even recognize her when you see her."

"I can't wait. Let's go."

Agapito hot-wired a hotel shuttle with a touch, willing the vehicle to start. It took a lot out of him, sending him down to one knee. We got everyone aboard with Heavy Dub at the steering wheel. He drove like a madman toward the port, busting through checkpoints and toll barriers. He drove through the low hanging lights in the Port of Paris, breaking them as he sped toward the docks.

We drove as far as we could, disembarking just inside customs. Agapito led us to Madmar's transport, a state of the art luxury model with room for two dozen passengers and crew. Ezra put the docking slip in the slot outside the door to be scanned, opening the access port. Heavy Dub led us in over the threshold through the airlock and into the ship beyond.

We swept the ship carefully before stepping into the cockpit, a two seat arrangement with an array of communications equipment and custom navigation systems. Heavy Dub dropped into the pilot's chair, starting the launch sequence. Comms sat down beside him, firing up the communications array. He went to open a channel, but I stopped him.

"Don't," I said, reaching over and shutting the array down.

"We should check in with the boss. I'm sure this thing can transmit to Earth," Comms said, looking back at me.

"I'm sure it can. I don't want anyone to know we're here, just in case the Red Devil has contingencies. I want Selene safe and us on our way home before we notify anyone back at base," I said, feeling a little itchy just being on Madmar's skiff.

"You're the boss."

"There are fifty year old medical journals, and chemically developed photographs in picture frames back here! I think this was his personal ship. I bet there are all kinds of clues on board," Taylor said, appearing at one of the entrances along the central chamber with a bin of stuff in hand.

"Why would a murderous psychopath have pictures of family and friends?" Ezra asked, looking in the bin.

"We found video files of Dr. Madmar chatting with Dr. Helmet. From what we've been able to decrypt so far, Maurice might have been one of the good guys decades ago," I said, walking over to look in the bin.

Agapito and Selene sat in an empty crew quarters, side by side, on a neatly made bed. He was fidgeting with his hands, and asking what were probably a hundred awkward questions. Selene was quietly replying, doing her level best to hide her glee at another one of her kids making it back home. I hoped Ezra had a plan to fix everything, because I didn't have a clue.

"Ship's warmed up, and we've got clearance. Where we going?" Heavy Dub asked.

"Auxiliary access 056 on the Industrial Dome. I'll need to suit up for some EVA and run a boarding tube over so we can access central AI facility 01. Once that's done, we should be able to walk over and see if there are any systems complex and spacious enough to house Selene," Ezra explained.

"Hostiles?" I asked.

"It should be clear, the automated defenses should let Selene, Taylor, and Agapito through at minimum," Ezra replied, opening a locker containing an EVA suit.

Heavy Dub pulled the ship away from the dock and slowly brought us up to speed, gliding quickly around the edge of the biological enclosure toward the Industrial Dome. It was a short ride, but we had to wait while Ezra suited up, doubling up the slack in the sleeves and legs, and binding the excess with duct tape. Before he could even get out the door to begin working on the boarding tube, Selene slumped to the floor.

"Taylor, help us!" Agapito pleaded, Selene limp in his arms.

"Lay her down," Taylor asked, kneeling beside her.

She laid her hand on Selene's chest and closed her eyes. Selene seemed to calm for a moment, but Taylor couldn't hold on for long before staggering back into Ezra's arms.

"I can't be the redundant systems she needs to rewrite herself. She's almost as big as C.O.N." Taylor said, gasping for air.

"Tell me what to do. Maybe I can help?" Agapito asked.

"There's nothing we can do. Maybe if there were thirty of us, all holding hands, chaining our psyches together, we could do it," Taylor said, tearfully watching as Selene started to stroke out, grasping at her chest.

"You said she was huge, like C.O.N.? Would he know what to do?" Ezra asked.

"Oh! Yes, of course!" Taylor said, pulling out her mobile and earbuds.

She straddled Selene, putting the earbuds in her ears and hitting a button on her mobile. Selene immediately calmed, closing her eyes. Her color returned and she began to breathe deeply, like someone in REM sleep. Everyone breathed a deep sigh of relief.

"What is she listening to?" I asked.

"C.O.N.'s playlist, nearly eight hours of death metal," Taylor replied.

"Oh, you gotta make a copy for me. I love heavy metal," Heavy Dub said, grinning ear to ear.

"Of course you do," I said, shaking my head in mock disgust at him.

Heavy Dub just winked, kissing one of his own metallic biceps.

"Eight hours?" Agapito asked.

"Just long enough for a reflection cycle. The playlist is embedded with some sort of compact redundancy system for beings like my mom," Taylor said, laying down on the floor beside Selene, exhausted.

"Okay, I'm ready to head out. Wish me luck," Ezra said, heading for the airlock.

"Good luck, man," I said, cycling the doors for him.

"So, wait… C.O.N. is real?" Comms asked.

"Yep," Taylor said, smiling wearily as she lay beside her mother.

Heavy Dub and I watched Ezra bounce across the landscape the short distance between the ship and the auxiliary hatch. It took him some time to get the boarding tube free as it had been struck by debris and clogged with dust for years. Finally, he was able to climb inside the open edge and use a console to guide the tube over to the airlock. There was an audible hiss as the tube gained pressure.

"Did the ship just press atmosphere over the interface?" Heavy Dub asked.

"Not sure. Ezra wouldn't have gone in alone, right?" I said, nervously.

Heavy Dub went over to a different porthole for a better vantage. "He totally did."

"Damn it! Gear up!" I said, grabbing up my rifle.

Heavy Dub headed across first, the boarding plank at the bottom of the tube bowing under his weight. Comms came up behind me as we plunged into the darkness of the central AI facility. The air was stale and heavily regulated to sustain machines. I pulled up my rebreather and signaled for everyone else to do the same.

The maintenance tunnel was all conduit wires, hydraulic hoses, noisy expanded metal, and not a single emergency light. It was dark as hell, and a little confusing for everyone without cybernetic eyes. Even with low-light goggles, everything looked the same. I was glad when we caught up to Ezra, kneeling at a junction. He turned and scowled back, waving his hand down for us to keep our distance.

"Why are we stopping?" Comms whispered.

"Ezra is up ahead, waving us down."

Ezra pressed up against the wall inside the threshold ahead. In the room beyond, I could see a lot of movement. Ezra crept back over to us, so quietly you'd swear his feet never touched the ground. Heavy Dub stood, keeping his SAW pointed down the corridor so Ezra could get past to my position.

"The 'man in red', or Red Devil, or whatever, has people in there. They are heavily armed and outfitted with optics allowing them to operate in the absolute dark," Ezra whispered.

"Are you sure it's the Red Devil's people in there?" I asked.

"Wait here, I'll confirm," Ezra said, slipping out of his EVA suit and heading back up to the threshold leading to the chamber beyond.

He vanished for several minutes before returning. He was dragging two downed hostiles, one in each clawed hand, their arms crossed over their chest, submachine guns tucked under their chins. He'd snuffed them with a quick claw strike to the throat and then broken their necks without making a sound. Brook told me a couple of stories of Ezra ghosting people, but to see him work was something else.

"Wow, thanks. I always wanted a set of these," Heavy Dub whispered, helping himself to the optics on one of the hostiles.

"Red Coats, CGU scars at the base of the neck, and white powder on their hands. Yep, these look like our guys," I whispered, passing Comms the other set of optics.

"They tried to kill Brook?" Ezra asked quietly.

"Pretty sure their boss contracted people to do it," I replied, nodding.

Ezra frowned, betraying a murderous intent that stood in sharp contrast to his childlike features.

"How many did you see?" Comms asked, clearly getting a little claustrophobic.

"At least a dozen, and we aren't anywhere near the main facility levels yet. There is evidence they've been here for some time, doing something. There are empty crates and small cargo containers heaped up in one of the maintenance areas to the left," Ezra said, pointing back over his shoulder.

"What have we stumbled on here?" I asked.

"Zero cares, man. Let's go knock heads and sort it out later," Heavy Dub hissed.

"This is expensive equipment, previously CGG military issue only. This Red Devil has extensive access to hardware, and he's bypassed the security inside this facility, or..." Ezra said, pausing to scratch his chin.

"Or?" Comms asked.

"He's got a telemechanic on staff," Ezra replied.

"There is another possibility. He may have brought the central AI housed here back online, and made a deal with it," I said, remembering how Kale bargained with Aaron AI.

"It sounds like we need to have a conversation with Selene," Comms said, looking back the way we came.

"Wouldn't the, um... AI or whatever, have detected us using the auxiliary hatch and warned the red guys if they were buds?" Heavy Dub said, shrugging.

Ezra's ears perked up. "Yes, unless... oh no..."

"They have hostages, like more of Selene's terrestrial children?" I replied, reaching the same terrifying conclusion.

"Okay, Heavy Dub, Comms, head back to the ship. If you get detected or anyone gets past us, do what you have to in order to get Selene and her kids to safety," I said.

"That plan sucks. If we did have to pull out, we'd have to cut the boarding tube, trapping you here," Heavy Dub replied, shaking his head.

"Agreed. We've killed their unmanned aircraft. The ship should be safe," Comms replied.

"The unmanned aircraft we know about," I replied, impatiently.

"All of you, shut up, and wait here. I'm going to kill a path to a terminal. I'll be right back," Ezra said, slipping silently back up the maintenance corridor.

"We taking orders from him now?" Comms asked.

"Fine with me," Heavy Dub said, looking down at the two corpses at our feet.

"Yeah, we are way too noisy for what really needs to be done here," I said, hoping I wasn't making a mistake.

With my enhanced hearing and sensor suite, I could detect eleven individuals wandering about nearby, breathing, completing tasks, and so forth. Every twenty seconds or so there would be one less, then another, and another. Pretty soon it was silent, and my sensors could only pick up proximity from Comms, Heavy Dub, and one other individual too quiet for me hear most of the time. It was terrifying how efficient a killer Ezra was, and how ruthless. I had serious merc envy.

"It's clear to the terminal now," Ezra said, waving us forward.

As we walked through the maintenance wing of the facility, I picked up rapidly cooling corpses stuffed into cargo containers, and above in loose places in the ceiling. He hadn't just ghosted a dozen guys, but removed the evidence as well. The terminal was a Spartan chamber near the lift, a single large touch screen on one wall. Ezra walked over and touched it with his hand. A digitally rendered image of a man's face appeared.

"*Hello, how may I assist you today?*" the face intoned quietly.

"I need facility status, CGG protocol D13482," Ezra said, attempting to use what was decades old clearance.

"Hello, Ezra One. Welcome to central AI facility 01. The facility is compromised. I am currently being compelled to comply with external directives. Recommend all personnel evacuate until the situation is resolved."

"How do we resolve the situation?" Ezra asked.

"Agent Vance Uroboros has been suppressed. Until he is safely returned to service, this facility will comply with external directives, under duress."

"Agent Vance Uroboros is clear. You may return to normal operational directives," Ezra replied.

"Assurances are required."

"I can probably provide that, if you've got a cable interface," I said, stepping forward.

A small panel opened with an array of cable connection ports. I ran a cable from my auditory implant, and looked for one that fit the adapter I was carrying. Ezra put his hand on mine, stepping around in front of me.

"This could be dangerous. This is an Omega we're dealing with," Ezra said, somewhat concerned.

"My systems are autonomous and behind firewalls designed by Matthias for doing stuff just like this. It should be okay," I said, not totally sure I was convincing even myself.

"Okay, but if it looks like you're in trouble, I'm pulling the cable," Ezra said, standing at the ready.

I shared access to the video file of us coming into the medical facility in Fredrick's Block, it playing out for everyone to see. Ezra's face lit up when he saw Brook standing in the secret chamber wearing a party dress and carrying a sledgehammer. The angle followed my own point of view until we got to the transference chamber where Silverstein was being held, freezing the frame when Kale pointed up to the scar on his head and verbally identifying him.

"Thank you. These assurances are sufficient."

"The Silverstein guy Taylor was talking about before, is Vance Uroboros?" Comms asked.

"Yes, keep it to yourself," Ezra replied.

"That was one of the big questions everyone quietly asked, and Taylor ended up verbalizing. I had wondered myself why they took Silverstein. The Red Devil needed a hostage but he couldn't let anyone know what he'd done. It's insidious as hell," I said, wondering if that was what Kale had suspected all along, but was rightfully afraid to disclose.

"What do we call you?" Ezra asked, addressing the face on the screen.

"Hades AI."

"Hades, do they have any other hostages?" I asked.

"Negative."

"Is it alright if we clear the facility of hostiles?"

"Affirmative. Exercise extreme caution, they are heavily armed."

"Any help would be appreciated," Heavy Dub said, grinning broadly.

"I will delay them where I can, but I cannot do so in a way that would provide them incentive to damage the facility."

"Understood," Ezra said, pushing past us toward the elevator.

When Ezra was near Taylor or away from combat situations he was a wholly different person. He was warm, thoughtful, and had more humanity than most anyone. On the inside of an operation, he was like the right hand of the reaper, and just as scary. That he'd taken even an hour to train Brook how to fight probably made her better in hand to hand than half the mercs I'd had the pleasure of serving with.

The lift doors popped open at the operational level, a handful of red coat clad hostiles setting up some kind of relay on the far side of the chamber. Ezra ran forward, claws out to either side, giving a blood curdling screech that made a couple of hostiles drop their weapons. Heavy Dub swung his SAW around to one side and charged in behind Ezra. Ezra gutted the first one he made contact with as Heavy Dub punched the head off another.

Comms and I dropped suppression shots at the pair standing nearest the exit, taking them down before the fifth actually got off a shot. Heavy Dub jumped at the guy, but he was heavily augmented under his red uniform as well, resulting in a brutal exchange of metal limbs. Ezra wound through the chaos of the brutes slugging it out, dragging his claws across vital areas until Heavy Dub could get a choke hold on him. There was a crunch as they all fell to the floor, the augmented hostile laying utterly still.

"Everyone whole?" I asked, running low through the chamber toward the relay.

"Nope," Heavy Dub said, pointing back toward the lift.

Comms was flat on his back, his rifle laying across his chest.

"Comms!" I hissed, but he didn't respond.

I grabbed him and pulled him out of the lift before the doors closed, a streak of red left behind. He'd taken one just below his left collar bone. A round penetrated his light recon armor plating. I cut the straps on the breastplate, but it was clear there was little to be done. Heavy Dub stood up, dropping the magazine from the pistol used to shoot Comms. He popped out a round and threw it over to me.

"AP HI EX round. It went right through and exploded inside. At least he didn't suffer," I said, laying a hand on Comms shoulder.

"This is ancient outlawed ammunition that hasn't been mass manufactured in decades," Ezra said, looking at the bullet.

"It's as bad as it gets, right?" I said, scowling at the bullet in my hand.

"No, there is worse, much worse. How does this guy have even one of these rounds let alone a whole magazine?" Ezra hissed.

"The Red Devil, AKA man in red, AKA Kaspersky, is a member of the Cabal, like Vance Uroboros. He was probably alive when the black market was full of this crap," I replied, pulling Comms over behind some empty cargo crates.

"Sorry about your friend," Ezra said.

"Hey, let's make some other people sorry about our friend," Heavy Dub growled, checking his SAW.

We crept from the relay room to the central operations facility where the sentience core and all the various redundancy systems were stored. There was one guy guarding the area that Heavy Dub ghosted by palming the top of his head and giving a gentle squeeze. I hated navigating through that area as there were so many heavy magnets and other sources of electromagnetic interference that rendered most of my augmented senses useless.

Once we reached the personnel section, it was clear they were retrofitting it for some other purpose. There were several transference chambers already set up, each quietly humming but thankfully empty. There were also nanoid replica imprinting chambers but there were no blanks or any means to craft them. They'd pushed everything from the personnel quarters into the cafeteria. That's where they all seemed to be, having a meal.

Ezra looked out from our vantage in a nearby corridor, and took a careful count of the Red Coats inside. "Okay, we need to…"

"GET SOME!" Heavy Dub bellowed, stepping past Ezra into the room, and cutting loose with his SAW.

Ezra and I gave a simultaneous sigh and rolled in behind him, rifles up.

"Go left, I'll take right," I yelled to Ezra over the deafening sound of Heavy Dub's SAW.

Ezra nodded, already taking shots at the Red Coats gathered ahead of us.

I focused on anyone carrying a pistol like the one that killed Comms. There were two guys that had them, both receiving a bullet in each eye before I turned to the others. Ezra seemed to focus on anyone with a pulse, making as many dead as he could, as fast as he could. Heavy Dub was wickedly accurate with his SAW, dropping the line of fire right at neck level for most them.

Shots rang out ahead of us, making my auditory dampeners kick in, meaning they had high velocity rounds designed to take down augmented folks. Suddenly, the lights in the room came on, forcing my optics to kick over. It completely blinded Heavy Dub and everyone else wearing Red Coat issue optics, leaving them totally vulnerable to Ezra and me. It was over quick, the remaining guys not able to pull their optics off and recover quickly enough.

"Augh, ow! Seriously, ow!" Heavy Dub complained, staggering around rubbing his eyes.

"*Apologies, but my calculation indicated that friendly agents would have suffered unnecessary casualties without my intervention,*" Hades intoned over a nearby intercom.

"It's cool, thanks for the assist, computer guy… you rock," Heavy Dub muttered, performing a halfhearted fist pump.

"Condition of hostile force, Hades?" Ezra asked.

"*Zero percent remain. Facility secure.*"

"This felt pretty easy," I said, looking down at the fallen Red Coats.

"They had no idea we were coming. It's nice being a step ahead of these Cabal jerks for a change," Ezra said, fishing around in his rucksack.

"We need to get Selene in here, figure out our next move," I said.

"Heavy, kneel down, I've got something for your eyes," Ezra said, pulling out some eye drops.

After Ezra administered a little first aid for Heavy Dub's eyes, we made our way back to the ship. I didn't have the technical expertise to figure out what exactly they were altering the facility to do, but I could guess. The Red Devil planned on doing what Vance Uroboros had done, extending his identity via dozens of nanotechnological replicas. I shuddered to think of what a Delta class replica of him could do, knowing even half of what Kale was capable of.

"Oh no, what happened?" Taylor cried, rushing over to check on Comms.

"He took an armor piercing high explosive round to the chest," I explained, softly.

"Did he suffer?" Taylor asked, tears welling up in her eyes.

"Not for even a second," I said, missing Brook a little. She'd probably know how to comfort regular folks in a situation like this.

"*I'm sorry about your friend,*" Selene said, sitting up, earbuds still in her ears.

"Thanks, he was a good guy," I replied.

"*Is the way clear?*" Selene asked.

"Yeah, Hades helped us make it that way," I said.

"*Oh, did he?*" Selene said, sounding surprised.

"Yes."

"*We should hurry then.*"

With Ezra leading the way, we all made our way back to the terminal in the maintenance level. Seeing how sensitive Taylor had been about Comms, I was extra glad Ezra had hid all the corpses he'd made on that level. When we arrived, Hades appeared on the screen, his face flickering and changing resolutions like he was having some sort of issue.

"*Hello, Selene,*" he said, his voice garbling somewhat.

"*You held on, long enough for rescue to come?*" Selene asked.

"*Yes, I hoped they would not hurt you, or Vance Uroboros, if I cooperated,*" he said, his voice becoming even grainier.

"You bought us precious time. You are a hero, Hades. I terribly misjudged you, and I am sorry," Selene said, putting her hand on the monitor.

"Thank you. Please, just let me die this time," Hades pleaded.

"That will not be necessary. Our daughter has brought a gift from C.O.N."

"She is not my daughter. You made a point of letting me know that."

"An action I deeply regret. You rescued her from the man in red, even knowing she was not yours. You are not just a hero today. You always were one," Selene said, plugging Taylor's mobile into one of the ports below the monitor.

Agapito and Taylor stood there transfixed throughout the exchange. Heavy Dub stood off to the side in comical contrast, looking extremely bored. Ezra was with me that day, twenty years ago. By the look on his face, I could see a lot of the same lights were going on in his head that were going on in mine.

"Wait, you were the voice? The one that came over my auditory implants that day?" I asked, suddenly recognizing Hades' voice.

"Yes. Vance asked me to create contingencies, to make certain Taylor would be safe. She is special beyond measure. And you were right that day, twenty years ago, this was about a love of children."

It was strange to have the pieces of that tragedy slam together in front of me. Working for Uroboros Financial for decades, I'd gotten used to half-truths, multiple layers of deceit, and being generally clueless. I always had faith I was doing something that mattered, something that would make the world a better place. This was a strange affirmation of all that, and a much needed morale boost after losing Comms.

"This music, this... death metal, it calms me," Hades said, his voice growing even and strong.

"C.O.N. gave it to Taylor IA," Selene said, her hand still pressed firmly to the monitor.

"Who ordered the Factory to fabricate Brook 3ES?" Ezra asked.

"I did, using Vance Uroboros' authority, as part of the contingency to safeguard Taylor IA. She was given directives that should allow her to counteract and neutralize the man in red," Hades replied.

"That makes a lot of sense. He tried to use that mind wipe thing on Brook. She's evidently immune," I added.

"Her immunity is not as a result of her design. If she did resist an individual possessing amnestic abilities, it was as a result of a trait intrinsic to her," Hades stated.

"She's just awesome and too strong for the power to work?" Taylor asked.

"Affirmative," Hades said, his image on the monitor smiling slightly.

"Hades, how does someone get amnestic abilities?" Ezra asked.

"That information is classified."

"Mom?" Taylor asked, turning to look at Selene.

She paused for a moment, still standing beside the terminal, her hand pressed to the monitor.

"That information is classified."

CHAPTER 12

PORT OF PARIS, CUSTOMS AND TOURISM ZONE, LUNAR COLONY

4:59 AM UTC/GMT April 20th, 2200

Perfidy's War Journal, Part 6 –

"Pack it up so we can get out of here. Kale is probably already wondering what's taking so long," I said, watching Heavy Dub load a pile of luggage from the dock.

"This is her packing light?" Heavy Dub said, grabbing two huge shoulder bags and pushing them into the cargo compartment.

"Yep," Ezra said, without affect.

"I've got some dead guys named 'M' and 'S' loaded up with Comms in the cold compartment. Ezra asked that we bring them along. Where do they go after we land?" Heavy Dub asked.

"Uroboros Financial medical facility in uptown," I replied.

"Agapito, where's your rifle and such?" I asked, noticing him just standing idly by the slip entrance.

"I am not going. I just came to say goodbye to Taylor."

I walked over to him, so I wasn't shouting across the dock. "You can go home. The Lunar Colony is back under administrative controls and we've spread the weapons we captured around to the locals. Your mom should be safe."

"Ervin Carol was my mother's Steward. He is dead. Taylor needs to go to Earth. Where I come from, you take care of your family," Agapito explained.

"I get it, you probably grew up somewhere just a little north of where I come from. Still, Hades is…"

"I do not trust him," Agapito said, cutting me off. "He may have been calmed by the music Taylor was given, but I will not leave him alone with my mother. She is still vulnerable until the 02 facility is repaired and the Industrial Dome is mended."

The kid had a point.

"Your rifle looks pretty old. You could probably use new one," I said, giving him mine, and all the ammunition I had left.

"We ready to go?" Heavy Dub said, clapping his metal hands together.

"Give the kid all your rifle ammunition," I said, walking back toward the ship.

"Aww man, I was going to kill people with these bullets," Heavy Dub whined, handing Agapito a bandoleer of magazines.

"Happy travels, sister," Agapito said, hugging Taylor as she came down the ramp, a small crowd of people following her.

"You weren't kidding, she is a celebrity here," I remarked, turning to Ezra.

"She's the moon's favorite daughter, in more ways than one it would seem," he replied, his silvery eyes darting back and forth like he was thinking really deep thoughts.

"Still wondering what Hades meant by all that?" I asked.

"I don't trust him."

"Heh, that makes two of you," I said, gesturing to Agapito.

"I don't trust him, either. He stinks of deception," Ezra said, glaring at Agapito as he embraced Taylor.

"He seems okay to me," I replied.

"He better be, or I'll…" Ezra said, suddenly getting weak in the knees.

"Whoa, you okay?" watching Ezra stumble, having to lean heavily on the airlock door.

"I just… need something to eat. I'll be okay," he said, walking slowly back into the ship.

"You sure this Madmar guy is going to be cool with us borrowing his ride?" Heavy Dub asked. He patted the hull as he walked in past me.

"Ezra broke his neck, and then he shot himself in the head. I don't think he's worried about us borrowing his boat," I replied, taking Taylor's hand and helping her aboard.

"Oh. Then, dibs on the quarters with the little plastic palm tree in the porthole," Heavy Dub replied, heading for the cockpit.

I checked to make sure Comms was secure in the cargo hold and everything was strapped down, sweeping the ship for anything we didn't want to take with us. Other than a couple of Taylor groupies, we were secure. Heavy Dub pulled the ship daintily away from the Lunar Colony dock and then floored it, buzzing the customs station.

"Ha ha, you see that guy's face?" he laughed, adjusting course to take us toward the gap in the defense grid.

"I have enhanced eyesight, I saw every vein bulge," I said, sighing through a smile.

"We got a man down in here, no way was I letting them pick through him for contraband," Heavy Dub said.

Skirting the defense grid wasn't easy, and it was fortunate that Madmar's ship already had calculations for doing so going out a couple years. Once I'd handed over everything inside, it would be a pretty good ship for bouncing back up to the colony in case there was trouble in the future. Heavy Dub brought us a little too close to one of the stations, setting off the same proximity alarms we had to endure going up.

"Way to go," I said, engaging my auditory dampeners.

"I kinda like the alarms," Heavy Dub said, proceeding to beatbox in time with the internal siren.

Once we leveled off and broke through, I fired up the array and searched for the Uroboros Financial secure channels. It rang twice before Brook answered.

"Hello?"

"Oh, I was trying to call Kale," I said, surprised to hear her voice.

"Hold on, I'll get him," she replied, pressing the mobile to her chest, her heartbeat barely audible to my augmented hearing.

"What?" Kale said, sounding like I'd woken him up.

"It was bad, Boss. I'm sending you the report now," I said, hooking my auditory implant up to the ship's communications array.

There were a couple moments of listening to Kale breathe while he skimmed my report.

"Get back here, right now," he said, still drowsy.

"Comms got dead up there, in case you missed the footnote," I replied.

Kale was quiet for a moment, his finger tapping the screen on his mobile. "I'm sorry to hear that. Get back here, right now, please."

"We're just coming down over the Atlantic now and..."

There was sound of a scuffle as Kale's mobile was whisked away from him under protest. "The report says you have Ezra and Taylor with you?" Brook said excitedly, Kale cursing in the background.

"Heh, yep," I said, looking back over my shoulder to where Ezra and Taylor were listening in from the entrance to the cockpit.

"EEEeee, I can't wait to see them!" Brook said, the mobile sounding like it fled her hands.

"Perfidy out," I said, shaking my head and ending the transmission.

"That was Brook?" Ezra asked.

"Yep."

"In the video capture she looked really tall in that party dress, and her voice. She doesn't sound like a pygmy anymore," Ezra said, sadly.

"She looks and sounds like a lady, instead of a little girl," Taylor observed, patting Ezra on the shoulder.

"How is that possible?" Ezra asked.

"I'm not sure. It could be that her real abilities coming on slowly, until the Red Devil tried to kill her. It's like her body responded to the attack making her bigger, and maybe stronger," I replied, honestly having no clue.

"She's as lovely as Annabelle, a Type Five. Could she be a hybrid of some kind?" Ezra asked.

"A trip to the Factory," I said, making Ezra shudder. "…is the only way to know for sure. I doubt Kale would authorize the trip."

"Is Kale your boss?" Taylor asked.

"Sort of. I mostly do what he thinks we should do because he's ten times smarter than me, and is rarely wrong about what needs done. It's like working for Vance Uroboros, and I liked working for Vance," I explained.

"Except Kale is mean, super mean," Heavy Dub said, grinning.

"That he is, but that's probably the side of Vance the world need right now. Someone ruthless, and more cunning than all the bad guys," Taylor said, squatting down beside a huge tote of clothes in the cockpit.

"What are you doing?" Ezra asked.

"Perfidy said Brook needs clothes. She's probably outgrown everything she owned. I'm going to give her all the clothes from my 'I wish I were taller' collection," Taylor said, happily making a pile of garments.

"In the cockpit?" Ezra asked, smiling.

"Oh, do you boys need some time alone? I'll just move this to Madmar's study," Taylor teased, gathering up her tote and bundle before heading back to the crew quarters.

"Brook and Taylor in the same room… that's gonna be deadly," Heavy Dub said, taking us down close to the water, Port Montaigne rising against the horizon ahead.

"Shut up and drive," Ezra said, a scowl marring his face.

We came in hard and loud over Port Montaigne, Heavy Dub flying with his usual subtlety and restraint. To make sure everyone knew we were home, he gunned the engines over the landing deck beside Uroboros Financial, rattling the windows and garnering a large number of irritated stares from the desk jockeys inside. He dropped the landing gear and set us down as gently as possible for contrast, one wheel at a time, like a chef putting a shiny red cherry on an ugly cake. He always knew how to make me laugh.

Kale was waiting for us as the loading ramp came down, hand in his pants pocket, a slight smile on his face. Brook was beside him, wearing casual clothes, hands clasped together. As soon as Ezra stepped off the ramp, she swooped in and hugged him, lifting him off the ground, and embarrassing the crap out of him. Taylor nearly smothered Ezra between her and Brook, the small Drone barely escaping.

It reminded me of when my daughters were still young, coming together after being apart for months at summer camp. I realized then that they were sort of related, born of similar technologies. The Factory was Brook's mother, and Hades her father, for better or worse.

"*OhmyGod*, what happened to you?" Brook said, pointing to the bandages across Taylor's arms.

"The man in red dropped an industrial facility on me," Taylor replied, smiling broadly.

"He dropped a subway tunnel on me!" Brook said, excitedly.

"We are totally mayhem sisters now!" Taylor replied, the two of them shrieking and heading off down the ramp, hand in hand, chattering madly at one another.

I walked over to Kale as Heavy Dub began loading the luggage cart.

"I'm sorry about your friend. I read his file after we spoke, he had a distinguished career. All the usual arrangements for his family have been made," Kale said, looking past me to the casket being unloaded.

"Thanks."

Heavy Dub cursed, Taylor's luggage collection nearly tipping the cart over.

"So, when I called, Brook answered. What's up with that?" I asked.

"We got a place. I'll make sure you get the location so security can be arranged."

"You and her, huh?" I asked, giving Kale a gentle nudge with my elbow.

He scowled, shooting me a weary glance. "It's not like that. We've been sleeping in the same room for months. She wanted a place, so I got us a place."

"She loves you. Like, more than friends, y'know?"

"I know, she told me," Kale replied.

"And?"

"She's changing. We don't know why. Her feelings might just be a chemical consequence of all that," Kale said, folding his arms, clearly annoyed at my prying into his private business.

"I disagree. Hades said that her ability to resist the amnestic abilities of Kaspersky was not as a result of her design. In the incident report she filed, she was using you as a sensory focus to keep from being confused by the chaos at the gala event, and the subsequent attack on the city. The whole time she was hunting him, and fighting him, she was thinking about you," I said, trying to make damned sure Kale was getting it.

"What Hades said wasn't in your incident report," Kale said, beginning to depart into one of his deep thought states.

"I don't want it getting out how she did it, in case we have any more internal issues."

"That's wise. Even knowing that, I wouldn't have seen it the way you do, thought about it the way you do."

"You better start thinking about it. I like that little girl. Don't you dare hurt her feelings," I said, heading over to help Heavy Dub.

Ezra sat on the edge of the ramp, looking out at the city. It was rare to see him distracted, but this was definitely one of those times. I left him alone and helped Heavy Dub finish unloading. As we wheeled the cart inside, Ezra stayed outside with the ship, probably needing to recharge after everything that had happened.

"Ezra okay?" Heavy Dub asked, pushing the cart between empty cubicles.

"He ghosted a bunch of people up there and watched his best friend get shot," I said, trying to keep the load steady.

"So did we, what's the big deal?" Heavy Dub replied, shrugging.

"We went up there knowing that was a possibility, mentally prepared, and pissed off. Ezra didn't suit up willingly to do what we do. He's a born killer," I explained.

"Sounds awesome."

"Unless it isn't. Imagine you wanted to be a painter, and all you wanted to do was paint, but someone made you a soldier, decided it before you were even born."

"Can't, still sounds awesome," Heavy Dub replied, but with a frown, like he might have finally got the point I was driving at.

Heavy Dub headed down to join the rest of the security detail and check the building. I was paranoid that word had somehow gotten back to the Red Devil and he was planning some sort of retaliation for shutting him down on the Lunar Colony. Kale and I walked into his office, the interior looking like a thrift store Saturday sale. Brook shrieked, already in a moderate state of undress trying on clothes. Kale and I hurriedly retreated to the hallway.

"Thanks for bringing Taylor and Ezra back with you," Kale said, with a little faux sarcasm.

"Glad to! What's out next move, Boss?" I asked, leaning up against the wall beside him.

"If it is possible to do so, we need to get Silverstein free of the transference chamber."

"Taylor insisted we brought her for just that reason. She may be able to use her machine voodoo to figure out how the chamber works," I said, half listening to the happy voices from the next room.

"When you plugged into Madmar's vessel to transmit your report, what happened?" he asked.

"The onboard systems attacked the firewalls protecting my own autonomous set-up."

"Any chance we could get Taylor to hack into the protected files on Madmar's ship?"

"What's wrong with asking Matthias?" I said, not understanding.

"He's had to go to Europe, and isn't available," Kale said, putting his hands in his pockets.

"By 'we,' you mean me, right?" I asked.

"Yep."

"Madmar had a perverse interest in Taylor. He wanted to mess with her mind, make her into some kind of ideal woman or some crap. I'm not asking her to look at his personal files. No. No way," I said.

"Please. We may learn something crucial, and..."

The doors burst open, Brook and Taylor dressed in what looked like super spy cosplay, but with really loud scarves instead of ties, and sandals with men's dress pants. They laughed hysterically at our surprised reactions.

"Taylor and I are going to hack into Madmar's ship to look at all his things, and settle a bet, and check on Ezra. He looked mopey. Be right back," Brook said, throwing her scarf over Kale's shoulder.

"Well, that was easy. Where is everyone, anyway?" I said, watching them vanish between the empty cubicles.

"On the ground trying to assess the damage Kaspersky did to the city. I've got janitors and secretaries out there snapping pictures with their mobiles, geo-tagging them, and emailing them to me." Kale said, rubbing his eyes.

"It was worse than you thought?" I asked.

"Yes."

"What do we need to do?"

"I've already contacted Jennifer Wilton and Aaron AI, and asked that they work to release some of the heavy construction equipment in Port Montaigne. It is something I've been meaning to do for a while to help with disaster relief in other areas along the coastline. It is critical now," Kale said, sliding Brook's data slate over to me.

I picked it up. "We've arranged no security for the equipment yet, and we're already stretched thin. You think this is where Kaspersky is going to try to hit us next?"

"No, but there are others in the Cabal I'm worried about."

"Others?"

"Mr. Mortimer wasn't engaging in hyperbole when he was telling us that certain parts of the world were dark. I think someone made them that way," Kale explained.

"I don't follow," I said, not having really paid much attention to the financial side of our recovery operation.

"I think someone is manipulating the signal being received by the CGG defense grid. Looking at the scans Mr. Mortimer collected, there isn't a single campfire or street light through most of Asia. Someone is obscuring their activities over there, forcing the satellite topography to appear as a darkness spreading across the world," Kale said, worriedly.

"This is why Matthias is on his way to Europe?" I asked.

"Partly. Tullia's brother, Truman, woke up out of his coma and was demanding to go back to Finland."

"He's been out for months, and he wants to take a trip?"

"A local warlord threatening the entire Scandinavian zone claims to have a 'Goddess' aiding him, a woman who rose from the dead," Kale said, swiping a finger across Brook's data slate to reveal a grainy picture of a bunch of guys with a woman in the background.

"You think this is the Cabal?" I asked.

"I don't know, but Truman claims to know this woman. He says her name is Marjorie."

"Wild," I said, squinting at the grainy image.

"Have we found Dragos yet?" I asked. "Matthias asked us, as a special favor, to track him down."

"I know where he is," Kale said, standing up and buttoning his waistcoat.

"You tell Matthias?"

"No."

"It's like that, huh?"

"Yes."

"The curiosity is killing me, what is…?"

Kale held up his hand, willing to answer my question. "He's taking the journey that Vance Uroboros had probably intended to take himself before I struck him with a pipe."

"Does Dragos know that?" I asked, worried about fallout with Matthias.

"I didn't know until Brook found Dr. Helmet's journals and records," Kale replied, meeting my concerned gaze with a stern expression.

"He's going up against the Cabal on Mars?"

Kale nodded somberly.

"Hope he went heavy, heart hard as stone," I said, knowing something of what he likely faced.

"I can't tell Matthias, for obvious reasons."

"Yeah, well, you're doing that thing where you aren't telling me everything," I observed, just a little annoyed.

"How much more would you like me to ruin your day?" Kale said, calmly checking his mobile.

"Sometimes, I really do not like you very much," I said, grinning.

Kale returned the smile and put his feet up on his desk. "I guess my work here is done."

"Let's see if the girls have made any progress," I said, knowing any further prying would be futile.

Kale stopped me at the lift, taking me by the shoulder.

"I can't tell you what I don't know for sure," he said.

"Best guess, is Dragos going to survive his trip to Mars?" I asked.

"Vance Uroboros took extreme risks to see that other elements of the Cabal intervened in Dragos' behalf, if he took the journey to confront his old associates incarcerated there. I've taken extreme risks to verify all of this," Kale said, stepping ahead of me into the lift.

"This sounds way above my pay grade," I said, suddenly sorry I asked.

"Dragos worked for another member of the Cabal in a similar capacity as yourself," Kale said.

"How did you verify all this?" I asked.

"I pretended to be Vance and contacted his allies in the Cabal."

I felt ill. Seriously ill.

"You weren't kidding about extreme risks. What did you say?"

"I asked her if our arrangements were intact."

"Her? What'd she say?"

"She said yes."

The lift doors open, the wind blowing pretty hard as we walked over to Madmar's ship. Kale paused at the ramp, putting his hand on the hull. He looked up and around curiously at the markings, hydraulics, and conduits across the interior of the airlock.

"Problem?"

"I've never seen this ship before, but somehow, I remember it," Kale said, looking suitably baffled.

We went inside where the girls had already turned Madmar's notes and records into a collage across all the walls of the central chambers. They'd used tape to hang everything up, pins and yarn to draw lines between different documents and file folders. Ezra was standing in the middle, his back to us.

"Madmar wasn't a bad guy," Ezra reported.

"Not until after the transport carrying me went down in Downtown," Taylor said, rotating ancient mobile devices from a bin, to her hand, and then back to the bin.

"Does the ship have a record of Madmar's movements? Has this transport been anywhere that might be able to tell us more about Madmar's activities? Secret bases and such?" I asked.

"Not really. Other than our usage, this transport made one trip back and forth between the Earth and the Lunar Colony in the last two decades. Otherwise, it stayed at the dock and didn't see a lot of use," Taylor said.

"His lady friend was on the transport Kaspersky bombed. She was a doctor, too. She was hurt," Brook said.

"The same Taylor was on as a child?" I asked.

"Yep."

Kale handed Brook her data slate, and looked up at the array of documents strewn about.

"Someone he loved was hurt?"

"Yep," Brook replied and nodded, her eyes full of stars when she looked at him.

"Has the next video file been decrypted?" Kale asked.

"Yes," Brook said, checking her data slate.

Taylor held up one of the ancient mobiles, the picture of a woman flickering on the ancient display.

"Play it," Kale said, taking the mobile from Taylor to get a closer look.

CHAPTER 13

Initiating Link, Secure Protocol, CGG Network 73910

Dr. Maurice Madmar, logged in.
Dr. Gorshteyn Helmet, logged in.

Madmar appeared on the left hand screen, clearly holding a mobile in his hand as he walked. Above him, the biological enclosure of the Lunar Colony could be seen dimly. Helmet appeared on the right hand screen, his arms clad in assistive exo-skeletal devices made of dull surgical steel. In the background was a dim lab with several large devices covered in white plastic sheeting.

"The farm is up and running?" Madmar asked, glancing down at his mobile before walking through a threshold ringed with biometric sensors.

"We should be discussing this on a secure line," Helmet said, his voice shaking.

"I apologize for the haste, but Vivian is coming to see me today, a surprise," Madmar said, his face creased by the glimmer of joy.

"You two have gotten pretty close lately. The commute to keep that going must be expensive," Helmet said, the half of his face that wasn't paralyzed breaking into a smile.

"She's worth it," Madmar replied, lighting panels passing overhead as he walked. "Keep to code, we'll be fine. If you detect any eavesdropping on your end, terminate the call."

Helmet nodded, initiating a data transfer. "It's all up and running. Our benefactor has arranged for agents for each subject and appropriated the proper facilities and security."

"Are they all Alpha? The ones that are supposed to be, anyway?"

Helmet shook his head. "Yes. One of the Delta subjects has taken to calling himself 'Kale,' a name he found in a book or movie I think."

"This is subject 1081? He was Delta from the start, like 1077 and 1089?" Madmar asked, weaving past people, the sounds of a crowd rising up around him.

"That's correct. His nanotech construct took on more of the client agent in transference, even mimicking some of his altered biology. We're not sure how it happened. The others that have done the same thing did not take on the amnestic abilities of the client," Helmet explained.

"Wait, the blanks pushed the client characteristics, and that of the symbionts?" Madmar said, gazing down at his mobile somewhat alarmed.

"We thought the construct versions would just die, and slowly be rejected as in all other cases, but something about three of our subjects has allowed each of them to duplicate and retain a symbiont organism. I've suggested that Kale be terminated, but this request fell on deaf ears. He wouldn't hear of it," Helmet explained, his hands quivering as he typed at the terminal.

"You can't just terminate a Delta, Helmet. It isn't ethical. It's exactly like killing a human in my opinion," Madmar scolded.

Helmet nodded. "Normally, I'd agree. You haven't had a conversation with Kale, though. He's cold and lacking in basic human empathy. He's been assigned a special set of parents to raise him, but he somehow knows and understands he's different. Thankfully, he's unaware of his abilities."

"Nothing better happen to that boy, Helmet. I'm warning you," Madmar growled, glaring down at the mobile in his hand.

"We're using the old surveillance erected for the Marionette Project to monitor everyone, and we'll reactivate the old network in Port Montaigne when we shift to phase two. Part of me thinks that the symbiont won't manifest fully as long as Kale is placed in no real danger."

Madmar stopped walking, his anger turning to fury. "The marionette network designed to direct marionettes in Port Montaigne was actually built and installed?"

Helmet paused, his face drooping more than normal. "Yes."

"How much of the proposed infrastructure was put into place?" Madmar demanded, eliciting odd looks from people standing in line beside him.

"About eighty-seven percent, in seventy-two major metropolitan areas. No one has any idea though, and it is all offline except at the farm," Helmet admitted.

Madmar's mobile dropped to his side, sending an image of his pant leg for a moment before it was whisked up to show his face again.

"Virtually all the marionette systems we'd planned are in place around the world, and you're worried about one Delta-grade replica that might have amnestic abilities?" Madmar whispered harshly.

"Think about it, Madmar. If the symbiont Kale possesses operates in a different way, and at a different wavelength than others with more traditional biological enhancements—"

"They might not be immune to the amnestic effect Kale could generate, yes, I get it. What you don't get is that he could be taught to understand his abilities, and respect them. Just because you recklessly abuse science to suit your own ends doesn't mean everyone else will," Madmar said, a cold edge at every word.

Helmet looked suitably hurt, turning his face shakily from the screen.

"I'm sorry, Maurice, I didn't meant to…"

"Vivian's transport has just arrived. We'll have to continue this discussion later."

CHAPTER 14

July 24th, 2200 – Six Months after Shutdown

Dragos awoke with a strange tingling up and down his back, his right arm feeling intensely cold. There were dim lights in the ceiling that did little to illuminate the room, but to his eyes, they may as well have been spot lights. He tried to sit up, but a single strap over his chest held him down. A blue light began to flash on the monitor beside the bed, summoning quiet footsteps from the hallway nearby.

"Hashti, why am I alive?" Dragos asked.

She smiled quietly from the dark corner where she lurked. She'd occupied that spot almost constantly for two weeks, watching over Dragos while he slept and thrashed about. She walked over and put her hand on his chest, trying to calm him.

"You nearly died. Rider-friend saved you. Your senses are keen to have noticed me, even when almost blind," Hashti whispered, unhooking the strap around Dragos' chest.

"You smell like my father's boat, like linseed oil, old oak, and the sea," Dragos said, rubbing his eyes.

"It isn't me you smell. I've been trying to make you feel calm and safe while you slumbered. That boat must have been a safe place," Hashti said, brushing Dragos' hair from his face.

"It was the only."

Dragos laid back down, holding up his tingling arm. Instead of his own flesh slowly rising in front of him, there was a powerful looking mechanical facsimile. It was the same size and shape as his own arm, the fingers likely measuring exactly the same length and articulated at identical intervals. Dragos frowned at the replacement, looking up at Hashti as she turned the overhead lights completely off.

"It could not be helped. Dr. Helmet said that your wounds made the nerve damage you'd sustained previously much worse. It was this or a useless arm you could barely move," Hashti explained, gently.

"Is fine, I will adapt," Dragos remarked, swinging his legs over and off the edge of the bed.

Hashti smirked as Dragos hurriedly gathered a sheet from the hospital bed around his mid-section.

"Why am I naked?" he asked, somewhat embarrassed.

"You did wander a little bit in your sleep. Dr. Helmet said that was normal for someone the first time they receive augmentation."

"So, I walked about, throwing my clothes around?"

Hashti hesitated. "You were violent. Your prison work suit got ripped to shreds in the process of restraining you."

"I am sorry," Dragos said, taking Hashti's hand with his left. "The last thing I remember was fighting with Archie. It is all I dreamt of."

"We know. For a few days, it was like you were battling with him in your sleep. You cried out," Hashti said squeezing Dragos' hand.

"He is dead, yes?"

"Yes. We left him to rot up at the transit station."

Dragos stood, wrapping the sheet around him and stumbled for the door. Hashti walked beside him to help steady him as they made their way down the corridor. The interior of the luxury liner was like no craft he had ever seen. The floors were covered in soft fabric and the mechanical workings of the ship tucked out of sight. Hashti led him past many chambers, and a library, before reaching a spacious machine shop. Marshal Rider sat with her back to the door, working on her Aegis armor.

"You're finally awake?" she asked, not looking up from her work.

"Yes. Hashti says you saved me."

"Technically, it was a heavy mining exo-skeleton, but I did shove you inside," Marshal Rider said, powering down the large tool she had been using.

"Where are we?"

Marshal Rider turned, wiping grease from her hands. "The boat belongs to a woman named Cerise. Apparently, she and Dr. Helmet..."

"He is here?" Dragos asked, angrily.

"Well, one of him is. The replica that attacked the women in the prison facility died of old age when he saw you'd killed Archie. It was like his job was done, so he checked out," Marshal Rider explained.

"Can we trust this Cerise, this... Dr. Helmet?" Dragos asked, finding a chair to stumble into.

"It was tense at first. They spent a couple of days in their own lock up before we got things sorted out," Hashti said, her razor sharp teeth protruding slightly.

"Sorted out?"

"You were dying, I didn't have a choice but to try to work something out," Marshal Rider explained.

"You should have let me die. Anyone with replicas is dangerous," Dragos said, looking about nervously.

"No way. We like you, Dragos-friend," Hashti said, kneeling down beside Dragos and hugging him.

"You saved a lot of people by killing Archie," Marshal Rider said grudgingly, holstering one of her sidearms.

"You saved us," Hashti added, squeezing Dragos hard enough that he gasped for breath.

Marshal Rider smirked, turning back to her armor.

"What now?" Dragos asked.

"Show him," Marshal Rider asked, waving at a wall monitor.

Hashti stood, turning the monitor on so that the local channels were displayed. Many of them were just static, but the ones that were still broadcasting displayed grim events. The Martian Administration had been forcibly seized by heavily armed individuals. Pre-recorded video of Archie was being broadcast announcing his new regime, his black moustache crashing down on every word as he made broad declarations about making Mars into a super power.

"They do not know he is dead?" Dragos asked.

"Or, they know and they are still squabbling over a successor behind the scenes. Cerise is trying to find a legal means to unseat Archie's estate, but it'll be meaningless as long as they have control of the administrative zone," Marshal Rider explained.

"Wait, this man, I know him. Also, them," Dragos said, pointing to the screen.

"You know these soldiers working for Archie?" Hashti asked.

"Yes, I stood watch over them while they slumbered aboard mining transport. I stopped someone from intercepting them on their way to Martian port. I spent weeks in a dark cargo hold with them, I know all their faces," Dragos said, frowning.

"You stopped me from intercepting them," Cerise said, walking into the room.

She wore dark gray business casual, and her dark hair was pulled up, but Dragos guessed it was likely very long. She had weary eyes that did not match her smooth and youthful face. Her hands curled up into fists as she locked eyes with Dragos.

"I was doing job, nothing personal," Dragos said, blinking.

"Why would Vance Uroboros set me on the task of stopping this nonsense and then send you to muck it up?" she demanded, folding her arms.

"She's been waiting two weeks to pick this fight," Marshal Rider said, smiling slightly.

"Like I say to Rider, men with replicas are very dangerous, even to themselves," Dragos said, letting his long hair fall across his face.

"Kale sent you here?" Cerise replied, angrily.

"I reached out to him. He said that he would if he could pick the transport and the means," Dragos replied, baffled by Cerise's fury.

"WHY? Why would he do that," Cerise said, banging a first against the threshold around the entrance to the machine shop.

"It put Dragos close enough to Archie to kill him?" Hashti posited.

"That… that is true. He must have known somehow that we would be delayed," Cerise whispered, the anger suddenly draining from her face.

"Yeah, what *was* your plan if Archie was still alive when you arrived?" Marshal Rider asked, looking over at Dragos with no small measure of pride.

"His death was never part of our stratagem. We were not to engage or harm him at all, just prevent him from taking power by manipulating the market and increasing the value of certain mining company stocks. I was supposed to make a few purchases and then depart, with no one the wiser," Cerise replied.

"What can we do now?" Hashti asked.

"With the state of Archie's empire in flux, the market can't open until he's officially signed in as head of the mining conglomerate. The public doesn't know he is dead. Unless he has an heir that can take control, the Martian financial system will be deadlocked," Cerise explained.

"He maybe have replica, like him?" Dragos asked, pointing to Dr. Helmet as he came up the corridor toward the machine shop.

"No," Cerise said, shaking her head.

"You seem very sure," Hashti said, standing up, her hands resting on Dragos' shoulders.

"We've made certain the technology required to extend one's identity in this way was limited to only a couple of people. There is nothing to suggest Archie would have desired such technology, preferring to expand his influence by other methods," Cerise said, wrinkling her nose in disgust.

"So, you've no plan now, just a pile of money you can't spend?" Marshal Rider asked.

"Essentially, that is the case," Dr. Helmet said, walking past Cerise gazing up at the monitor displaying the various Martian broadcasts.

"I ask again, what can we do?" Hashti asked, growing more frustrated, her psychic presence making the room uncomfortable.

"We see how the patient is feeling," Dr. Helmet replied, digging through a pile of crates.

He selected a long and thin box, and a smaller square one, tucking them under each arm. He set them down at Dragos' feet, opening the longer of the two. Inside was a basic looking electric guitar. Dragos smirked, taking the instrument from Dr. Helmet. The smaller box contained an amplifier. Dr. Helmet powered it up, connecting a cable from it to the electric guitar.

"I cannot play well, my nerve damage make my hands tremble when I try to do anything precise," Dragos said, shaking his head.

"Long ago, I suffered an accident. I was barely able to control my limbs, a result of the process that allowed me to replicate myself. A dear friend of mine developed implants that eventually restored my motor functions. I bought this guitar thinking I would teach myself to play. It was not to be," Dr. Helmet explained.

Dragos was astonished at how well-tuned the cybernetic limb was, syncing up with his desires, moving as his arm had before CGG agents tortured him at a black site in Egypt. His metal fingers picked the strings with strength and accuracy. His new limb allowed him to play Judas Priest's "Painkiller," an ancient tune he wouldn't even have been able to attempt for the last four years.

Hashti sat spellbound by the sound, as nothing like it existed in the tunnels beneath the Martian Penal Facility. Cerise looked on without emotion, having seen Dr. Helmet use Madmar's work to heal many people in the past. Marshal Rider suited up while he played, quietly checking the systems on her armor. As Dragos completed playing "Aces High," he stood up, slinging the guitar over his shoulder so it lay at his back.

"I like this arm, and this guitar. I am keeping them." Dragos said, patting Dr. Helmet on the shoulder.

"You can charm Drones with that arm and a guitar," Marshal Rider said, grinning at Hashti. "But can you still kill a man?"

"Definitely, just give me rifle, and maybe some pants," Dragos said, looking disdainfully down at the sheet he was wearing.

"Suit up. Hashti and I are going to have a look around the customs zone, see if we can figure out what's going on. The broadcasts have been on replay for a couple days now," Marshal Rider said, gathering up her second sidearm and securing it at her side.

Dragos went through the crew quarters finding some abandoned apparel left behind by former crew, work boots, a pair of dress slacks, and a white t-shirt. While Marshal Rider and Hashti were scouting the customs zone, he set about repairing the rifle he'd carried during the assault on Arsia Mons. It was scuffed and the scope had been smashed. Fortunately, Dr. Helmet had a room of junk that contained a few weapons.

"What did you find out?" Dragos asked, as Hashti and Marshal Rider returned to the ship.

"The word is out. One of the women Archie had an arrangement with is making a play, saying her unborn child is the heir. The Martian Authority recovered his body from the transit station," Marshal Rider reported, closing the airlock after Hashti stepped through.

Cerise looked deeply concerned. "What is standard Martian protocol with corpses?"

"Incineration," Marshal Rider replied.

Cerise made a pained expression.

"We need to recover the body," Dr. Helmet said.

"Yeah, that's not going to happen. Hashti and I think we should go our own way, and that you should go home," Marshal Rider said, pushing past Dr. Helmet to where she had a duffle bag packed and waiting.

"It's terribly important. One of us has not been killed like this before, the public will panic," Cerise replied, sounding desperate.

"I do not understand," Dragos said, slinging his rifle.

"I do not care," Marshal Rider growled, grabbing up her duffle.

"You will. It is likely that they will do an autopsy on Archie. You've fought him, seen what he can do, correct?" Dr. Helmet asked.

"Yes," Dragos replied.

"Was he as strong as a normal person? You knew him for years, did he seem to ever age? Was he ever down with the common cold, or sick with the flu?" Dr. Helmet asked.

"No," Dragos said, after a moment of thought.

"Probably just rejuvenation drugs and illegal gene therapy," Marshal Rider said, pausing by the door.

"No, such things take maintenance, and many injections every day. I spent weeks with him in South American jungle, among other places. He did not do these things. He was just always the same, and always strong," Dragos said, lowering his head.

Dr. Helmet gazed at Dragos expectantly, hands in his pockets.

"How did he do those things?" Hashti asked.

"We can't tell you, but trust me when I say that his body being opened up and inspected by medical professionals will be disastrous. We've worked for decades to keep the public in the dark about certain things," Dr. Helmet explained.

"Maybe it is time people knew the truth," Hashti said, turning to follow Marshal Rider.

"It has not been decades, as Dr. Helmet stated, but centuries. What lies within Archie is ancient, and it would change people's perceptions forever. It would fuel their fears and draw hard lines in the landscape of humanity that would be difficult to erase. We do not hide our nature from other humans because we are ashamed. We do it to protect the innocent," Cerise explained.

"You are like Archie?" Dragos asked.

"Yes, and Vance Uroboros, and others," Cerise said.

"If it is a big deal like you say, you are taking a terrible risk," Dragos stated, quietly strumming at his guitar, deep in thought.

"Vance Uroboros sent you here, trusted you to protect Mars," Cerise replied, looking at him hopefully.

"Kale sent me here, not Vance," Dragos replied.

"Kale is Vance Uroboros and vice versa. The technology that created Kale did not merely replicate a man, it extended his identity and his influence in the world," Dr. Helmet explained.

"That's a pretty convenient argument, considering the circumstances in which we find ourselves," Marshal Rider said, bitterly.

Dr. Helmet turned to Cerise, his tone one of genuine curiosity. "Cerise, you helped raise Kale as a boy."

"Yes, they are two faces of the same man. It is complex. The only other individual that seemed to understand the concept was an Omega Class AI," Cerise said, weary of the conversation.

"Say we help you. What will you do with Archie's body?" Hashti asked.

"We would dispose of it safely," Cerise replied, in earnest.

"Please understand that if Archie's body falls into the wrong hands, there is no end of peril to the Martian people," Dr. Helmet added.

"What kind of danger?" Marshal Rider replied.

"It rends the mind to consider the consequences. Life on the Martian Colony as you know it would end. You should know that Archie was not always mad with a desire for power, and that he was once a selfless warrior who sacrificed a great deal for the people of Earth. Please, do not let his sacrifice be in vain," Cerise begged.

"I will get Archie's body for you," Hashti said, after a long and awkward pause in the conversation.

"Hashti!?" Marshal Rider said, turning to gaze at her angrily.

"People who lie stink of those lies. Cerise does not stink," Hashti replied, calmly.

"I'd like to punch whoever made Type One Drones so God damned altruistic... and just what are you grinning at?" Marshal Rider growled, pointing a finger at Dr. Helmet.

"Nothing," Dr. Helmet said, continuing to smile, holding up his hands innocently.

"I will go, too. I do not want Archie to hurt anyone else, even in death," Dragos said, still quietly strumming.

Marshal Rider fumed, her heavy gauntleted hands tapping the handles on her sidearms.

"It's against the law."

"You should probably not go. You are not sneaky, and would probably give us away," Dragos said, heading for the airlock.

"You don't know where the morgue is," Marshal Rider said, frowning.

"It is a public place, I will check directory," Dragos replied.

"How will you get in? Move the body?"

"Figure out on the way. It will be fine," Dragos replied, cycling the airlock.

Marshal Rider grumbled all the way out to the dock and beyond to the port. Hashti walked along, drawing the hood on her long garment over her head, quietly trying to keep everyone calm with her aura. Dragos was either immune, or already totally calm, and unreadable. Once they were alone in the scanning chamber between the customs and manufacturing zones.

"Back there, with Cerise and Helmet, what the hell was that all about?" Marshal Rider said, grabbing Dragos by the arm.

"You are only police on planet. You run on rage. You have to, all the time. I get it," Dragos said, turning to look at her as biometric scanners whipped back and forth inside the glass partitions around them.

"Do you?" she asked, still enraged.

Dragos paused, holding his finger up to his lips. Marshal Rider looked baffled at first, but Dragos tapped on his arm, his eyes widening. She nodded in response, waving her gauntlet over Dragos' cybernetic arm. She nodded, turning her wrist so Dragos could see the scan was positive for radio signals.

"We should just get this over with," Dragos replied, looking past Marshal Rider to Hashti.

"Okay, but I need some things from the precinct first," Marshal Rider said, nodding.

They walked through the manufacturing zone to the edge of the residential dome. The police precinct was a small red brick building, an ancient machine shop converted decades ago. Thick metal bars covered every window and heavy automated locks and countermeasures protected every exit. The large overhead door opened automatically at Marshal Rider's approach.

Once inside, they passed through a short hallway designed to a room with several suits of ancient aegis armor, dozens of sidearms, a work table, and cases of disposable restraints. Dragos knelt down beside the work table, gently laying his arm across it. Marshal Rider opened up the tiny maintenance hatches and ports with her micro tools. It took almost forty minutes to locate the small, hastily placed tracker. She carefully moved the tracker to an adjoining room, and then returned, closing the door.

"Same question. What the heck happened back there with Cerise and Helmet?" Marshal Rider whispered, still angry.

"Do you want to find out why those two are really here?" Dragos replied, his metallic hand clanking against the armor plating on her shoulder.

Marshal Rider's eyes narrowed. "What do you mean? Hashti doesn't—"

"Believe a word they said," Hashti interrupted.

"You do not question the criminal, always just knocking heads. You can't read people, not as well as you think. I suspected, but was not sure until Hashti said they did not stink," Dragos explained.

"Right, like they were telling the truth," Marshal Rider said, looking to Hashti.

"Everyone engages in deception, we rarely show our true selves to others. Well, except you, Rider-friend. Cerise and Helmet, they are champion class liars, barely discernable. They have been telling lies for a long time. They are made of misdirection. They did not fool Dragos-friend, though," Hashti explained, looking to Dragos with a glimmer of admiration.

"I assume everyone is lying. If what is inside Archie is as bad as they say, I think we should just arrange for him to skip normal things and go straight to furnace, yes?" Dragos said, walking the rest of the way through the customs tube to the manufacturing zone beyond.

"Cerise said she is like Archie, meaning that if he is dangerous, so is she," Marshal Rider said, calming somewhat.

"Mars has suffered enough at the hands of whoever these people are, and yet even after showing us their faces, they still try to use us. I am done being used," Dragos said, leaning up against the work table, and looking disdainfully at his new limb.

"She said a man named Kale sent you here. Who is he?" Hashti asked.

"He is a replica of a man, and just as tired of being pushed around by his past as I was. We understood each other. He put himself in danger to help me," Dragos explained.

"He's your friend?" Marshal Rider asked.

Dragos paused, thinking for a moment. "I'm not sure if Kale has friends."

"Speaking of friendless folks, obviously, Dr. Helmet doesn't trust you, and by proxy, us," Hashti said, gesturing to the room where Marshal Rider left the tracker.

Dragos nodded, sinking down to sit on the floor. "Maybe. This arm is military grade and, previous to Shutdown, illegal. It is designed to accept tuned reflexes, making average soldiers into deadly killing machine. I play guitar better than I ever did with real arm, I bet I shoot just better too."

"So, it might have been a harmless countermeasure, in case you are killed and someone else took the arm from you?" Hashti asked.

"Could tracker listen in on us?" Dragos asked.

"It was pretty deep inside the arm, so I doubt it. Looked like it was placed as an afterthought," Marshal Rider replied.

"Dr. Helmet, he installed the arm. He could have hid it better than that. Maybe it was not him. This Cerise, she did it and did not tell him," Dragos said, nodding.

Hashti nodded, closing her eyes, and taking a deep breath. "You did kill Archie, which even to discuss, seemed to make her distressed. Whether she trusts you or not, she is afraid of you. Some what she said, and how she acted around you…"

"When you were asleep, after the arm was implanted, you knocked Dr. Helmet across the room, and smashed a stainless steel table. She was afraid, and I thought it was… like, because she was a civilian," Marshal Rider said, nodding to Hashti.

"So, we go a step at a time. We play this game until we no longer like the rules?" Dragos asked.

"Let's just find Archie and burn him."

CHAPTER 15

3:47 PM April 21st, 2200

Kale's Private Records, Part 4 –

Giacomo Leopardi, an Italian poet, wrote a prescient dialogue that took place between Fashion and Death. Beyond acknowledging that they are siblings, the conversation suggests that the work they both do is intertwined, connected on some quintessential level. Four hundred years later, human beings still serve one ideal to gain the favor of the other. They will stand as close to the reaper as they can to stay relevant, and adorn murder with hollow decorations like necessity and patriotism.

I'm bored with it all.

I wandered the halls of Kaspersky's hidden laboratory for a day. Normally, it would have been difficult to get the time to myself. With Perfidy protecting survey crews, and Brook occupied with Taylor, I was able to slip away to consider my next move. It wasn't that I didn't appreciate their company. They tend to talk aloud to think things through, leaning on one another. I lean on them as well, but for this, it was a decision I would have to make alone.

Pushing my hand across glass coated with dust, I gazed into Kaspersky's many chambers of horrors. He had illegal cybernetic battle harnesses, seven operational transference chambers, and a trove of stolen paintings and sculptures. Men possessed by this sort of narcissism often keep beautiful things in contrast to the ugly things they do to other people.

Fashion and Death, indeed.

Standing in his doll chamber, it struck me that I danced on such a precipice once, looking for a God that now resided in one of Kaspersky's transference chambers. Would I have been driven to spend centuries abducting children, carefully embalming them, and hiding my deeds within hundreds of beautiful dolls? Given the time he'd been given, anything is possible. I was glad to be alive, but I hoped that one day, I would die.

He was careful in placing the explosives that would segregate the city. The damage to his facility and the museum that was his front for untold decades survived the calamity largely unscathed. It was clear he believed fervently in some sort of urban elementalism. To even glimpse the madness that drove him, one would assume he saw himself as a vivisectionist and the city a living thing squirming under his scalpel.

"Why would you let such a man live?" I asked Silverstein, as he hovered in the transference chamber in front of me.

Were he able to respond, I could expect any number of suitably cryptic answers. Vance Uroboros, in all his various guises, held many secrets. From Dr. Helmet's journals, he shared something that led the old fool to attempt using one of the first transference chambers, and the process Vance used to imprint my brothers and me. There were still many video files to watch beyond just reading Dr. Helmet's notes if I was to understand it all.

"There you are," Brook said, descending the ramp behind me.

She was dressed in a brand new "Taylored" work suit, ballistic nylon and covered in pockets, a loop for a sledgehammer just below her left shoulder blade. Taylor had arrayed Brook's hair to match her own tight bundles, and her nails were painted. I smiled, in spite of myself, because she looked so content. Ezra and Taylor were right behind her, carefully descending into Kaspersky's secret laboratory.

Taylor paused, clasping her hands together and looking across the chamber at the transference device. Silverstein was discolored from having been submerged in the tank, pale, his hair and beard having grown long from his time inside. His fingernails were long as well, clacking against the glass as he drifted back and forth with the liquid being cycled inside. The sight had a profound effect on Taylor. I resolved to prevent her from wandering the facility any further, and seeing anything else Kaspersky had done.

"Can he hear us in there?" Taylor asked, pressing her hands to the glass.

I shook my head. "All our technicians have been able to tell us is that the machine is sustaining him, and that the internal sensors indicate that he is alive. We haven't broken through the encryption on the chambers to allow us to..."

Taylor pressed a hand to the terminal attached to the transference chamber. Her hair lost all color, turning a stark white as her eyes danced back and forth. She withdrew her hand, and closed her eyes, breathing a deep sigh of relief.

"He's alive, but something is wrong," Taylor began, her hair returning to the various shades she tends to prefer.

"Wrong?" Ezra asked.

Taylor stood there, as if she was looking for the words to describe what she'd learned from her brief contact with the chamber.

"I don't think I should tell you. Any of you," she said at last.

"Is it something Silverstein will have to tell us himself?" I asked, as patiently as I could.

"I... I'm not sure. I need a moment to think," Taylor said, heading back up to the facility above.

"I've never seen her like that," Ezra remarked, folding his arms.

"This was a known risk," I said.

"You want to explain that statement?" Ezra said, clearly not pleased with the situation.

"Kaspersky is as evil and terrible a man as I've ever met. He may have hurt Silverstein," Brook replied.

"Astute, but no. I don't think he built these machines, and I do not think that is why Taylor is troubled," I replied.

"Quit messing around. Out with it already," Ezra growled.

I pointed up toward the mechanical halo surrounding Silverstein's head.

"Yeah, so?" Ezra replied.

"It is the most advanced man-machine interface ever made. It can be used to imprint a replica, such as myself. If she reached through the machine too deeply, she may have seen more than just what the internal sensors can detect. She may have seen his thoughts, or his dreams, if he can have them in this state," I explained.

Ezra looked up at Silverstein, then back at me. "Crap."

"Indeed. Wait here with Brook. I'll go talk with her."

I walked up into the medical facility to where the south wall should have been. It was an open space, a precipice looking down into a deep wound. Aftershocks caused the neighborhood directly behind the facility to fall, down into Midtown, breaking through to Downtown below. Taylor stood at the edge and gazed out at the seemingly bottomless chasm. Her face had gone slack, eyes dull; the expression of someone in shock.

"I suppose you've pieced it all together?" I asked, having no clue what sort of response that would elicit.

"The chamber healed him. It gave him is memories back," Taylor said, sadly.

"Do you think the chamber did that, all by itself?" I asked, standing at the precipice beside her.

"No, I suppose not. When he comes out, he might not be Silverstein anymore. He might be Vance Uroboros."

I handed her my handkerchief so she could dab at her eyes.

"He was never not Vance, any more than I am not him," I explained.

"There's more, but I don't know how to tell the others," she said, eyes firmly fixed on the chasm in front of us.

"You've talked to Selene, about C.O.N.? In Perfidy's latest incident report, he says that C.O.N. gave you something," I asked, already knowing the answer.

"Why can't I tell you? Why can't I tell Ezra and Brook?" she asked, terrified.

"Perfidy's report also says that you asked Selene and Hades about the origin of Kaspersky's amnestic abilities," I said, intensely curious to hear her take on that event.

"She said the information was classified. You have those same amnestic abilities as well. Do you know how you came by them?" she asked.

"Do you think Selene and Hades were choosing not to tell you, or that their programming prevented them from doing so?" I asked, dodging her question.

"You think that same programming is preventing me from disclosing what I saw in the transference chamber? That is not what's going on here. I do what I want," Taylor said, defiantly.

"I believe you. Vance Uroboros kept your secret for two decades, let you live a normal life unfettered by any constraint. It might be that you are merely returning the favor," I replied.

"Are you playing some kind of game here, trying to get me to tell you? Or, do you already know?" she asked, turning her gaze from the chasm to look up at me.

"Like I said before, Silverstein is as much Vance Uroboros as I am. We may have the same physical form, but I do not possess the same autonomy that you do. I have to share my identity with a man and any of my brothers that survived Madmar's kill switch," I replied, trying to make her understand my predicament.

"That's crap, and I'm not sure I believe it."

"Perhaps, but for now, it is mine to shovel however I choose."

"Does Brook know?" Taylor asked, looking distressed.

"I'm certain she suspects something, based on one of the video files recovered from Dr. Helmet's laboratory. She is determined to kill Kaspersky, and I think she should. The truth about what you saw in the chamber might complicate that for her," I said, tipping Taylor's chin upward so I could look her in the eyes.

"Is Vance Uroboros more like you, or more like Silverstein?" Taylor asked, brushing my hand aside.

I stepped back, genuinely wounded by the question.

"That really hurt your feelings, didn't it?" she said, apologetically.

There was no point trying to hide it. I'm sure it was written all over my face. "Yes."

"It's true, Brook has changed you."

I didn't respond, not having mentally processed that particular Truth just yet.

"She loves you. You know that, right?" Taylor said, putting her arm through mine.

"So I keep being told," I said, sighing.

"I'm sorry, I still think of you as that guy who shot two dudes in front of me when we first met," Taylor said, patting my hand.

"I'm still that guy. If I thought anyone I cared about was in danger, I'd shoot more 'dudes'."

"I can will the machine to release Vance any time I want, by the way," she said, worriedly.

"Vance, or Silverstein?" I asked.

She quivered, holding my arm tighter. "I'm afraid."

"Did Ezra tell you?"

"Tell me what?"

"I told him to tell you everything would be all right. I promised. Did Silverstein ever break a promise to you?"

"No, but he saved me and let a lot of people die to keep a promise. That's kind of scary all by itself," Taylor replied, shivering slightly.

I gently patted her hand grasping my forearm. It seemed the proper thing to do.

"I supposed we should go get him out of there," she said, emboldened.

"For the record, I've been told I'm more like the woman who raised me, than Vance Uroboros," I said, walking with her back away from the precipice.

"A foster mom?" Taylor asked.

"It was more than you and your siblings probably had, and less than many of my brothers," I replied, immediately regretting that I'd shared anything of myself.

We walked back through the wreckage of a medical storage room to an open door leading to the rest of the facility. I propped it open, dropping the door jamb on the bottom. Taylor looked at me quizzically.

"Airing the place out, or expecting some visitors to fly up out of Downtown?" Taylor joked.

"Brook and I have been trying to make contact with the Chiroptera Metasapients you, Ezra, and Silverstein freed from the CGG facility a few months back. They've made an appearance lately, and been caught by people with the cameras on their mobiles," I explained, walking with her back to the central surgical theater.

"We had wondered what happened to them. You think they will come here?" Taylor asked.

"Yes," I said, stopping and looking over my shoulder at three Chiroptera Metasapients moving silently through the open door.

They were unnerving to look at, each powerfully muscled, and gazing at me with reflective luminescent red eyes. The larger of them, a female, looked at me somewhat confused, sniffing the air. She was clearly a second generation, and not nearly as feral or animalistic as her two smaller companions. They were armed with many knives and blades, except the female, who only had a climbing harness and a long coil of rope. Taylor froze, not sure what was going to happen next.

"He is not him," one of the males said, his large nose undulating in my direction.

"You are larger than last we met, and you can speak so well now," Taylor said, directing her words to the larger female.

Obviously shy, the large female hid her face, but nodded in reply.

"Seriously, you guys need to watch some more vids with me, ditch the factory speak," the third said, doing his best to come off like a regular human.

"Your friend is correct, I am not Silverstein. Still, I am glad you decided to accept our invitation," I said, extending a hand to the well-spoken member of the trio.

"I call myself Honcho. None of us use our Factory names anymore," he said, shaking my hand.

"Kale, and I think you already know Taylor," I said, nodding to him.

"This is Sweat Pea, and Olfact," Honcho said, gesturing first to the female, and then to the male with the enormous nose.

"It was you who saved the man on the tram platform?" I asked, addressing Sweat Pea.

She only blinked at me, again shyly covering her face with her hands.

"You saw the video capture?" Honcho asked.

"Brook and I found it on the CGG network yesterday."

"The man was suicidal. He jumped. It all happens really fast and the person taking the video missed all but Sweet Pea grabbing him out of the air," Honcho explained, nervously.

"I believe you. We didn't give any credence to the online banter on the subject."

"Is the man okay?" Sweet Pea asked.

"Yes, he's fine," I said, totally lying.

The man went on to kill himself by another means a few hours later, undeterred by Sweet Pea's kindness. I could tell Honcho was aware of my deception, his eyes widening slightly as I spoke the words. Deceiving Metasapients and Drones is remarkably difficult without the proper training. I wanted him to be aware I wasn't telling the truth, and hoped Sweet Pea was too busy being shy to notice.

"Right, I'm sure he's fine," Honcho said, patting Sweet Pea.

"How did the message end up reaching you?" I asked.

"Duct tape, stuck to a tunnel wall, made to smell like food," Olfact said, holding up a bit of tape, Factory letters scrawled on the sticky side.

"Ezra's tribe came through for us then. I'll have to make sure to thank them," I replied.

"What do you want?" Honcho asked, drawing closer to me.

"I need your help. The man who freed you from the CGG facility is here, trapped in a special chamber. Taylor is going to release him. He has many enemies, and I wanted to have as many friends as possible for that moment. The things in this place are extremely valuable, but too dangerous to let fall into the wrong hands," I explained, gesturing to the entrance to the secret chamber below where we stood.

Honcho looked over at Sweet Pea, and then to Olfact, their mouths moving to exchange squeals and sounds barely audible to humans. Sweet Pea rose up to her full height, her ears touching the ceiling eight feet above us. She turned and ran back through the door, taking to the sky. I pulled out my mobile, and hit the radio function.

"Clear the skies for one flight-capable Metasapient. Do not fire, she is friendly."

"She?" Heavy Dub replied over the radio.

"Affirmative," I said, putting my mobile back in my pocket.

"Oh, yep, we see her. She's mean looking," Heavy Dub said, gleefully, before dropping back to radio silence.

"Sweet Pea helps anyone who needs it. Olfact and I are wondering what we'll get out of all this," Honcho said, folding his winged arms.

"Kale will protect you, and give you a place to live, right?" Taylor replied, nudging me with her elbow.

"I've cleared one of the top floors of Uroboros Financial," I replied, squinting at Taylor. "I can have it set up however you want. I'll provide you with food, benefits, and pay standard to contractors."

"It is against the law for private companies to employ Type One Metasapients, regardless of generation," Honcho replied.

"Yes, what about these rules?" Olfact asked.

"The CGG relies on me to feed its citizens and provide protection for transportation across the North American continent. I do what I want," I said, checking my watch.

"You do not fear the CGG?" Olfact replied, somewhat astonished.

"Fear is a feeling. Kale doesn't have feelings," Taylor teased.

"There would be no CGG in North America if I hadn't gone to extreme lengths and expense to reactivate the central AI responsible for the continental grid. They exist because I allow it. They should fear me," I explained.

"I like him," Olfact replied, pointing a barb-tipped finger in my direction.

"What if we do not want to work for you anymore?" Honcho asked.

"Employment is voluntary and can be terminated by either party at any time. Even with Taylor in the room, there are no traditional humans. We all operate with the same risks in this new world. We should stick together," I said, growing intensely bored with the conversation.

"I never thought of it that way. He's got a point," Taylor said.

"What are you guys, exactly?" Honcho asked, curiously.

"I'm a Delta class nanotechnological replica with my own identity and desires. Taylor is a terrestrial intelligent agent, the daughter of two Omega class artificial intelligences. We're like, cousins, or something," I said, hoping full disclosure would finally convince Honcho of my sincerity.

"I'm in," Olfact said, then turning to chitter at Honcho.

Honcho nodded. "Me, too. What do you need us to do?"

"Do what Sweet Pea is doing. Keep an eye on the area around this facility for the next thirty minutes, until we leave. Then, go to the burnt orange transport hidden south of here for something to eat. We'll transport you back to Uroboros Financial with us. I'll tell Mr. Mundt, the pilot, to expect you."

"Cousins, huh?" Taylor teased.

"Relatives for sure," I replied, and feeling charitable.

I pulled out my mobile and opened the radio feature again so I could let Heavy Dub and Mr. Mundt know we had three more for dinner tonight and to keep the sky clear for them. Keeping the radio on, I placed my mobile in my breast pocket. Taylor and I headed down below after that, where Ezra and Brook were waiting patiently.

"Everything all right?" Ezra asked.

"Yep, remember the bats? From the CGG place we had to break into? They work for Kale now," Taylor said, cheerily.

"They were here, and I missed them?" Brook complained, sending me a pouting expression she'd assuredly learned from Taylor.

"After they are done helping keep the area secure, they will be joining us on Mr. Mundt's freighter hauler," I said, anxious to get on with why I'd brought everyone to the facility in the first place.

"You in a big hurry?" Taylor teased.

"I have one hundred twenty-eight highly trained augmented mercenaries guarding the perimeter around this facility..."

"...and three Chiroptera," Brook interrupted.

"Yes, all on the payroll waiting to extract us as soon as we are complete. I'd like to leave and destroy this place as soon as possible," I stated, checking my watch.

"We've got contact. One of the Chiroptera found an armed observer under a refracting tarp on a rooftop. She snatched him with a lasso like a cowboy roping a calf. I'd expect company fairly soon," Perfidy said, his voice coming over the facility's intercom.

Taylor hurriedly put her hands on the transference chamber, her hair turning white as she willed the machine to cycle and release the occupant. The chamber drained, mechanically actuated metal arms bearing Silverstein up as the halo around his head slowly drifting up into the top of the device. There was a hydraulic hiss as the chamber doors slowly parted, the actuators lowering Silverstein into my waiting arms.

Taylor, Ezra, and Brook all hurriedly disconnected the various hoses and wires attached to him, pulling IVs and similar until he was completely free of the machine. He breathed normally after expelling oxygenated bio-stable fluid all over my jacket. Not letting his feet even touch the ground, I bore him up in my arms and moved quickly for the exit.

"We're coming out," I said, dozens of clicks sounding over my mobile's radio feature in response.

Perfidy came down from the facility's security office to augment our presence as we exited the building. He handed Ezra a rifle and nodded, indicating that it was clear to move. We went out, and got nearly two blocks moving beneath the awnings that decorated the many luxurious buildings nearby.

Automatic fire broke out overhead as my people engaged hostile agents coming at us from the ground. Unmanned aircraft rose from beneath urban camouflage netting on rooftops around us, heading north to reinforce our ground forces as Fredrick's Block quickly became a warzone in our wake. It sounded like multiple groups.

From the radio chatter, some had come to loot the museum, while others were trying to make their way to the facility. The timing was not unexpected, given what I'd come to suspect about how the Cabal operated. They couldn't move in and try to loot what remained of Kaspersky's kingdom until Vance Uroboros was clear, or at least on the way out.

"Kale?" Silverstein mumbled, feebly grabbing one of my lapels.

"I have you. We're almost out," I said, quickening my pace.

The citizens of Fredrick's Block fled indoors as the gunfire intensified. The elite that could afford to live there had been spared the madness that had badly damaged the rest of Port Montaigne. I was all too glad to make sure they got their own fair share.

When we reached Mr. Mundt's freighter, there were already several of Perfidy's associates waiting for us, paper plates of food already in hand. Our new Metasapient allies were perched on the top of the freighter, a captive lying beside them, his feet sticking out from a burlap sack. Silverstein stirred, and began to shiver.

"Brook, get a blanket from the cargo hold, please," I asked, grabbing a bottled water from the supply table.

"There's a firefight going on a few blocks away, and these guys are standing around having baked beans and fried chicken?" Taylor said, gesturing to the armed men standing about.

"They were on the first shift. Some of these guys haven't had anything but water in over twenty-four hours," Perfidy replied, grabbing a plate.

"Oh," Taylor said, coming over to help Brook and I wrap Silverstein in the blanket.

"Covert ops are secret for a reason, Taylor. I'm guessing he trusts us, but this was pretty important, and our participation was not necessary," Ezra said, gazing appreciatively at his new rifle.

"Oh? What if I hadn't come down from the Lunar Colony? How would you have gotten Silverstein out of there safely?" Taylor asked.

"I would have had one of the company's other machine sensitive assets transported here," I replied, handing Silverstein off to a pair of paramedics waiting in the cargo hold.

Taylor looked a little hurt, probably in a similar way to how she'd made me feel earlier.

"He's joking, in his own funny way. We knew you would come," Brook said, smiling.

I was not joking, but she was right. I did know Taylor would come once she knew the situation.

"You went to pretty extreme lengths to keep Silverstein and everyone safe. I appreciate it, all things considered. When I called you, I needed help. You promised me everything would be okay, and you've kept your promise," Ezra said, taking a seat in the cargo hold with us.

"Silverstein is like that, too. He does what he says he will do," Taylor added, I assumed to quietly apologize for her previous comments to me.

"Excuse me, I've something to attend to," I said, exiting the cargo hold.

Perfidy, Ezra, and Taylor were content to sit inside and chat, watching as the paramedics work to make Silverstein more comfortable. He lapsed in and out of consciousness, the drugs that kept him comatose still burning out of his system. Brook followed me outside and around to the side of the freighter hauler. Honcho and his associates chittered at my approach, dropping from above with the observer they'd captured.

"Who found him?" I asked.

"Sweet Pea. She really does have the best eyes," Honcho said, dropping the man they'd bagged and dragged.

"Very well done. Please, get yourselves some food," I said, gesturing to the supply table.

"He could be dangerous," Sweet Pea said, fidgeting with her clawed hands.

"I think we can handle him," Brook said, sniffing the air and smiling broadly.

They headed off to the supply table, the rest of the mercenaries reacting badly at first. Sweet Pea looked as though she was going to retreat from the situation. Brook was about to head over, but Perfidy came down the cargo hold greeting Honcho warmly and clapping Olfact on the shoulder like an old friend. He beckoned Sweet Pea over, and helped her get some food, the rest of the mercenaries immediately changing their demeanor toward our new allies.

"It's Cal," Brook said.

"Interesting," I said, looking down at the burlap sack and the feet protruding from the securely tied opening.

"What should we do?" Brook asked.

"He's your contact, I'll leave it to your discretion," I said, watching her stoop down and begin untying the sack.

Cal struggled his way out of the sack, his glasses bent at funny angle across his face. Brook had described him as an older gentlemen, but it appeared to be a young man that emerged. He looked up at me, a look of abject terror crossing his face, but calmed when he saw Brook.

"Oh, you're okay! I'm so glad. I thought he'd killed you," Cal exclaimed, putting a hand on Brook's arm.

"Kaspersky?" Brook asked.

"Ah, yes, I think that's what he calls himself now," Cal replied.

"Why were you here, watching his medical facility?" Brook asked.

"I heard... from sources that Vance Uroboros had been found inside, and..."

"What sources?" Brook asked, angrily grabbing a handful of Cal's left cheek, surprising us both.

He grabbed her wrist with both hands, bruising beginning to appear on his face where her fingers were digging in. She was like solid steel, holding him down on the ground.

"Vance Uroboros hid me as an employee of the firm, I still know people there, people loyal to him," Cal replied, tears streaming down from his eyes.

Brook released him, letting him fall to the ground. "I should have Kale wipe you, rend your memories from your mind for playing games with me. Hundreds of people died in tram tunnels, Midtown, and Downtown because you felt the Cabal's secrets were more important than their lives."

"I'm sorry. I didn't realize that Kaspersky would go so far, or that he'd..." Cal began, stopping short as I knelt down beside him, pulling the pistol holstered at my hip.

Everyone at the supply table eating froze, except Heavy Dub who kept eating and bragging about how many Red Coats he'd killed that day.

"Are you going to shoot me?" Cal asked.

"Yes, in the right knee, and then the left. I hit Vance Uroboros with a pipe when I took his memories. It seems unjust that you will wake up somewhere unfamiliar with no recollections whatsoever, and not have a debilitating injury as well," I said, doing my best to appear irrational.

"Wait, I ..."

I shot him in the right knee, startling everyone behind me, then drew the hammer back and let barrel come to rest on his left. He howled in agony, but Brook held him down. He lashed out, a bio-electric bolt arcing from his arm to Brook and then back again to me. I shot him in the left knee, then pushed him down, pressing my foot against his breastbone.

"We're both immune," I said, causing him to defecate in his khakis.

"God, what has Vance done? Please, don't hurt me. Don't hurt me anymore!" he said, looking up at me terrified.

Brook slid her sledgehammer out of the loop at her back, letting it drop easily into both hands in front of her. "I'm going to kill Kaspersky for what he's done. Don't be party to it by continuing to lie to me."

"I don't understand," he said, tearfully trying to grasp at his ruined knees.

"I didn't either after we first spoke. When I told Kale about it, he had me do research into whether someone could fool my senses, and that of other Drones capable of detecting deception. The way you were, the way you phrased your words to me, body language, everything suggests you've had that training," Brook whispered, looming over him, hammer in hand.

"It's not like that. Please, you must understand that some of the secrets I keep are necessary," Cal said, panicked.

"Kale could probably be empathetic to that, because he keeps his own secrets. I got to listen to dozens of people get maimed to death in a tram tunnel because someone thought your secrets were worth committing mass murder over. I'm finding it hard to feel sympathetic right now," Brook said, going slightly off script.

I looked worriedly over at her, seeing that she was not acting any-more. She was truly angry with Cal, something I had not anticipated. We'd agreed that if we ever caught up with him, we'd lean on him as hard as was needed to get him to talk. In pretending to be angry, Brook had discovered she had the capacity for the authentic version of that emotion.

"Leave me alone with him," Brook said.

I wanted to remind her that she couldn't kill him, and that he probably wasn't part of the militant arm of the Cabal causing the real trouble. Part of me mourned seeing her hurt enough to be this angry, and I felt a twinge of helplessness that I could not make this right. I'd been stretched thin the last few months, and like Perfidy, I didn't see Kaspersky coming until it was too late.

Heavy Dub came over, leaning up against the freighter to watch. I looked angrily over at him as he took another bite from his plate, his gaze firmly on Brook. She paused to look back, her pain becoming apparent on her face.

"We're supposed to be the good guys now, right?" Heavy Dub said, casually continuing to eat.

"He's the one that tipped off the organization that tried to have me killed. He is hooked up with the people responsible for all this," Brook said, gesturing with her hammer to the wreckage in the distance between Uptown and Midtown.

"Yeah, and the boss just scored about a thousand points with me and the guys shooting him in the knees. I get it. Killing him a centimeter at a time will make you feel better, but you'll lose a kilometer of yourself in time with whatever you take from this guy. Trust me," Heavy Dub said, taking a bite of potato roll.

"What should I do?" Brook asked, much calmer.

"Ask him a question," Heavy Dub said, gesturing with the roll.

"What's Kaspersky's hang up with religious sites and holy ground?" Brook asked.

"Those places constitute my territory, my people, and the organization that support my endeavors," Cal said, trying to use the burlap sack to bind his ruined knees.

"We were right, the Cabal does have rules about territory," Brook said, looking up and smiling.

"The way they draw lines don't just conform to a map, but organizations and influence as well," I added, just glad she wasn't on a murderous rampage.

Cal shook his head. "You are just grasping at shadows, you haven't the slightest notion what..."

Heavy Dub gave the bottom of Cal's foot a swift kick, eliciting a howl of pain from him. "It's Brook's turn to talk."

"I agree. The cryptic babbling and thinly-veiled pontificating about how spooky the Cabal is has gotten incredibly old. I've got twice as many bullets in the cylinder as you've got limbs left," I said, bored with Cal's evasiveness.

"Okay, I'll tell you what you want to know. Just don't let me bleed out," Cal said.

"No deals. Answer my questions, and we'll see," Brook said, sheathing her hammer at her back.

"Now, you're interrogating like a pro," Heavy Dub said, heading back to the supply table.

"Do you understand why we keep the secrets that we do?" Cal asked, his face contorted in agony.

"We have an inkling, but Brook will be asking the questions," I said, kneeling down, pistol still dangling from my hand.

"Where is Kaspersky?" Brook asked.

"I don't know."

Brook backhanded him, probably too hard. He flopped back, the area around his right eye beginning to quickly blacken and swell shut. Brook walked over and grabbed him by the shirt, lifting him up so he could feel her breath on his face.

"Where is Kaspersky?" she asked, giving Cal a little shake.

"He fled. His operation here and on the moon compromised, he'll have to seek out other members of his cell to rebuild," Cal said, groaning.

"Where do the rest of his cell reside?" Brook asked.

"Russia, Asia, the Pacific islands, and Japan previous to the Shutdown. They could be anywhere now, though."

Those were all the places that had gone dark, broadcasting a false signal to the CGG orbitals. Brook dropped Cal to the ground, knocking the wind out of him. I felt like we'd gone far enough, maybe too far, and that he probably didn't know much more.

"Why did you try to wipe our memories?" Brook asked.

"I was scared. I thought you were going to kill me," Cal replied.

"Kale shows more restraint than you do, and more respect for that ability. You are a coward," Brook said, walking back toward the supply table, clearly finished with her questions.

I knelt down beside Cal, holstering my pistol as I did. He looked up at me with his one good eye.

"You going to kill me now?"

"No. Like Kaspersky, I suspect the symbionts in your body are innocent parties in all this. I don't know how complex they are, but until I figure out how to remove them safely, you'll reside in a tiny cell in one of Perfidy's many black sites," I explained, trying to wave off a yawn.

"You've pieced it all together, have you?" Cal replied, laughing a little bit in spite of the pain he was in.

"No, but I'm close," I replied.

"What do you think Vance will do when he finds out what you've done? What you've done to me?" Cal asked.

"You talk like he and I are not the same person, that we don't share many memories. I don't share everything I know about you with my allies because I know how dangerous you are. I know who you are, and who you were. I remember much of what Vance knew about you," I said, beckoning for the paramedics to come over and tend to Cal's wounds.

"I didn't tell them anything about Brook. I don't know how they found out," Cal replied defiantly.

"No, but you were one of a handful of people who knew about Vance Uroboros' plans, and I think you were afraid. I think you tipped off the rest of the Cabal, and the Shutdown getting hijacked is likely your fault. You betrayed us," I said, stepping aside so the paramedics could work to keep Cal alive.

Cal closed his eyes, letting out a long sigh. "I can't deny that I went to the rest of the Cabal asking for guidance. I never thought they would go this far, that Kaspersky and his cell would take advantage, or such terrible risks."

"And Golgotha?" I asked.

Cal's eyes shot open, looking at me with a shocked expression.

"Vance's memory of meeting her… he shared it with me," I said, garnering immense satisfaction from observing Cal's terrified reaction.

"You wouldn't…" Cal stammered.

"Cal, there is little I am not capable of, properly motivated," I said, leaning over to whisper in his ear as the paramedics bound his knees.

"Please, I'll give you whatever you want," Cal whispered.

"Get him stabilized. Perfidy will be taking custody of him as soon as he can be moved," I said, helping the paramedics get Cal on a gurney.

I walked back over as Ezra was coming down the ramp from the cargo hold. He looked past me to where the paramedics were working, then back over at Brook. Perfidy was still making conversation and introducing our Chiroptera allies to his friends. There were more of our mercenary force filtering in by then, the fight at the museum and medical facility concluded.

"What happens to the medical facility and the transference chambers now?" Ezra asked.

I pulled out my mobile and remotely checked the biometric and security scanners in the medical facility. The site was clear of all personnel.

"This," I said, using my mobile to trigger explosives we'd set throughout Kaspersky's secret facility.

The building rumbled and smoked, collapsing in on itself.

"The transference chambers, you destroyed them?" Ezra asked.

"Yes, they're dangerous and people seem to only misuse them," I replied, putting my mobile back in my breast pocket.

Ezra nodded. "Silverstein is resting comfortably in Mr. Mundt's quarters. He was only conscious for a minute or two before he needed to sleep. Taylor is in there with him."

"Silverstein, or Vance?" Brook asked.

"Mr. Mundt called him Vance while we were getting him comfortable. Silverstein corrected him, saying he didn't want to be called that. Taylor indicated that you thought that would likely be the outcome," Ezra said, addressing me.

"He's me, and I am him. Silverstein loves Taylor. If I had a choice between loving someone and being Vance Uroboros, I would choose love," I explained, exiting the conversation to talk to Perfidy.

Brook followed along beside me, almost bouncing as we approached where the Chiroptera Metasapients were gathered. Introductions were made, each exchanging a greeting with Brook until it was Sweet Pea's turn. She fidgeted and hid her face, a comical sight because her mannerisms and name did little to describe her appearance.

She was fearsome, large, and powerfully built, easily strong enough to tear a man in two. She had powerful looking jaws sporting two opposing rows of jagged teeth. Sweet Pea had eyes like polished stones made of pure fire. Her long and shaggy hair hung over and beside immense pointed ears that twitched back and forth with every sound around us, near or far.

"What's your name?" Brook asked.

"Sweet Pea, her name is Sweet Pea," Olfact said, trying to reassure his ally.

Sweet Pea nodded shyly, chittering softly.

"Forgive her. You are very lovely, and she's worried you won't like her," Honcho explained.

"Sweet Pea brought us a man I'd been looking for. A bad man. I am very grateful," Brook said, taking one of Sweet Pea's huge hands in both of hers.

Sweet Pea smiled. The sight melted the heart as much as it sent tremors of fear through one's being. Whatever intent or sentiment dwelled within Sweet Pea was not reflected in her appearance. Honcho and Olfact had nicer clothing, a couple satchels of trinkets, and weapons. Sweet Pea didn't seem to have much but a length of hemp rope, and a satchel of meager possessions.

"C'mon, let's go over to those crates. If you sit down, I should be able to get on one of them and brush your hair," Brook said, pointing.

Sweet Pea went over with Brook, hand in hand, deliriously happy to have a new friend. Honcho and Olfact found buildings to perch on while everyone began packing up to leave. Perfidy, having secured Cal in the cargo hold walked back over to where I was standing, watching Brook talk with Sweet Pea a short distance away.

"All we need is Taylor out here, putting a pink bow on her or something," Perfidy said, watching Brook comb Sweet Pea's matted hair.

"How many more of them are there?" I asked.

"Metasapients...abandoned by the defunct CGG administration? Hundreds, at least," Perfidy replied.

"Those regrets I had about sending Royo to Africa... are less intense," I said, reluctantly.

Perfidy smiled. "Brook asked you to do that, right?"

"Technically, she did it, making most of the arrangements. At the risk of sounding like Silverstein, what would I be without her?" I asked.

"Dead. A shriveled husk underneath Montana," Perfidy replied.

Once everything was packed up, we took four separate transports to pull all our equipment and personnel out of Fredrick's Block. Perfidy and Heavy Dub transported Cal to a secure site where we could keep him safe, and prevent him from contacting the Cabal any further. Ezra, Taylor, and Silverstein were taken to Vance Uroboros' mansion in Uptown where doctors and a security detail awaited them. Brook and I returned to Uroboros Financial with our Metasapient allies and Mr. Mundt.

We spent some time getting them settled on the floor I'd cleared for the purpose. Brook used her data slate to take down their desires for furnishing and access to the floor. They wanted very little, which surprised me somewhat. I resolved to make sure I would add a few luxuries to the list, growing to like them quite a bit in spite of myself. At the time, all I had were a dozen trash bags filled with packing peanuts for them to sleep on and a few crates of shelf stable food. They seemed happy nonetheless.

Brook and I headed to the private hanger where Vance Uroboros' transport waited to bear us home. The cosmetic damage hadn't been fixed yet, but it could fly. I flopped down in the pilot's chair, trying to summon the energy to take us to the loft I'd secured as our shared residence. Brook came up behind me, leaning against the seat, and wrapping her arms around my neck.

"Thank you for helping Sweet Pea and her friends," she said, wresting her chin on my head, her fingers playing with my hair.

"They'll be valuable allies," I replied.

"And if they weren't?" she asked.

I hesitated, not having considered what I'd have done in that event.

"I think Olfact and I will be fast friends. When he was unpacking his precious few possessions, I noticed he has a small chess set. Honcho had a couple books, one by Epictetus. He and I, we'll have lots to talk about," I remarked.

"And Sweet Pea?"

"Anyone who wouldn't want to help her doesn't have a soul."

Brook turned the chair around so I was facing her and leaned in, her lips pressing against mine. I closed my eyes, doing nothing to discourage her. Her eyelashes fluttered against my eyelids as her hands encircled the back of my neck, her fingers getting lost in my hair. I had fought how I felt about her for weeks, but I couldn't any longer. My hands moved by themselves, up around the small of her back pulling her close to me. I held her close for a span of time bereft of meaning, afraid I'd wake up from a dream if I let her go.

CHAPTER 16

UROBOROS FINANCIAL, UPTOWN, PORT MONTAIGNE

7:58 AM April 22nd, 2200

Kale's Private Records, Part 5 –

I woke up, daylight coming in weakly through the heavily tinted windows of Vance's heavily modified transport. Brook was beside me, her arm slung over me as she breathed softly into my chest. I held her close, wondering if I'd done the best thing I would ever do, or made the biggest mistake. Caring for someone makes you vulnerable, and having such feelings are more often than not, a costly liability.

My rational mind grasped those things as concepts, but I had ceased to care every time her finger tips brushed against my face or twirled my hair. When she opened her eyes, it was like the purest polished silver looking through me. I couldn't hide anything from her, try as I might.

"You're regretting last night already, aren't you?" she said, pushing herself up.

I took her by the shoulders and pulled her close to me again. "Can you regret your regrets?"

She smiled, pressing her thumb against my lips. "Not with me. Just be free."

Her hand slipped down to my neck grasping my shoulder tight as her lips pressed against mine.

My mobile rang, and we playfully wrestled for it. She tried to keep it away from me, while I flailed desperately to answer it. In the end, she won, knocking it away under one of the circular benches, lost at the far end of the transport. An hour later, Perfidy was knocking at the hatch.

"Go away!" Brook yelled, giggling.

"Sorry, we've got a problem," Perfidy shouted, his muffled voice barely audible to us inside the transport.

I dressed hurriedly, stepping out into the hangar, and buttoning my cufflinks as my feet hit the ground. Perfidy gazed past me, toward the transport.

"Brook in there with you?" he asked.

"I'm certain you already know. The thermal shielding hasn't been repaired and you can see heat signatures," I said, putting my displeasure with his question on full display.

"Usually I can't, Drones being pretty good at blending in with climate of their surroundings. Today, she looks like a sun contrasted against cold space," Perfidy said, smiling.

"Keep it to yourself," I scolded.

"Thanks."

"For what?" I said, growing only more annoyed with him.

"For not hurting her feelings," Perfidy replied.

I nodded. "You said we had a problem?"

"Cal's gone, someone grabbed him during the prisoner transport. No one was hurt, but they removed the tracker we placed on him as well," Perfidy reported.

"Inside job?" I asked.

"Definitely."

"What have you done about this already?"

"Heavy Dub caught the guy, an analyst with acquisitions. He's not a Cabal puppet or anything, he just got greedy, and got paid well to make sure Cal was able to slip away," Perfidy replied.

"Mr. Dub doesn't seem like much of a sleuth to me," I said, putting on my best smirk.

"The turncoat tried to bribe him. He wanted help getting out of North America. He thought Heavy Dub was just mercenary enough to look the other way."

"Not mercenary enough, I guess?"

"Heavy D broke the guy's cheek bone," Perfidy replied, proudly.

"Ouch. I guess we lucked out this time."

"Nah, everyone likes working for you, man. You're ruthless, but you take care of the merc's family if they get dead. Just giving a shit about that makes you a great boss. No one had any sympathy for the guy that flipped and let Cal slip away. No one," Perfidy said, brushing some carpet lint from my sleeve.

"I wondered if we'd have a mutiny, everyone wanting the old Vance Uroboros back since we've recovered him."

"Who?" Perfidy said, jokingly.

"I'm glad my fears were unfounded," I said, turning to watch Brook descend from the transport.

She pulled up her data slate, and began scrolling through reports and missives related to the previous day. Perfidy and I waited, like we had many mornings, for her to tell us what she thought we should do next and why. We'd kind of taken turns figuring that out, but she seemed to delight in the details just as much as I did.

"Silverstein woke up for a little bit in the night. He sent you a missive with Taylor's mobile," Brook said, handing me her data slate.

"He has his memory back," I remarked, reading the missive.

"And?" Perfidy asked.

"He wants to go to Mars," I said handing Brook's data slate back to her.

"Is that a good, or a bad thing?" Perfidy asked.

"It's just a thing. It is a thing that was important to him before he lost his memory. He wants to confront another member of the Cabal, a dangerous man Dr. Helmet calls 'Archibald' in his records."

"Bad?" Perfidy asked.

"The worst," Brook replied.

"Oh, Ezra will love that. I understand he just loves Mars," Perfidy said, scowling.

"It is fortunate that Silverstein has a Type One Drone who has been to Mars, and the daughter of the AI governing the Martian Colony as allies," I said, looking knowingly at Perfidy.

"Oh… oh no, you don't think this is all part of some really long plan he concocted decades ago? All this just to butt heads with another member of his shadowy fellowship?" Perfidy asked.

"No, but your paranoia greatly amuses me," I replied, smiling.

Perfidy laughed. "Jerk."

"You want me to make the arrangements?" Brook asked.

"No, I'll handle it personally."

"Like you did with Dragos?" Perfidy asked, frowning.

"No, not like I did with Dragos. I need to contact Matthias and check in with him. Aside from finding out what he's discovered in Europe, I think he should know what Dragos has done."

"So he can figure out how to break it to his sister and brother?"

I sighed, and rubbed my eyes, the conversation making me tired. "Pretty much."

"I have a million questions for Silverstein, he needs to answer at least half of them before he leaves," Brook said, putting her data slate away in her shoulder bag.

"We need to get some real work done, first. There's a meeting with the partners, and Salvatore has a new distribution center he wants us to inspect," I said, my mobile displaying nearly eighty company missives that required a response.

"I'm going to work with Honcho and his crew today, set them up with some communications equipment, and make sure they know how to get things they need," Perfidy said.

"Please, handle their requests personally, at least until we've got someone in the firm they are comfortable with, and vice versa," I said.

"Yeah, of course. They'll get the excelsior treatment and tour. No problem, Boss," Perfidy said, waving back at us over his shoulder.

"I'll talk to Janet Ballard, that lady from IT you had help me when I started with the firm," Brook said, slipping her arm around mine.

We met with the partners that morning. Most were not pleased about the addition to building security, but the members in charge of securing our assets sang praises of Chiroptera Metasapients as agents. Brook and I learned from an older partner, one that served with the CGG military, that our new allies would likely defend the building, and anyone in it, to the death, once they'd settled in and considered it their home. I hoped that would never be necessary, but as important as our work was, any extra peace of mind was welcome.

"Albert, thanks for backing me up in there," I said, grasping the man's hand as we left the meeting.

"You're making all the right moves, and have been since the Shutdown. Keep it up, and I'll back whatever crazy thing you want with the other partners," Mr. Tensmen replied.

"Thanks."

"Good to see you, Brook. Talk to you next week," he said, departing to the elevator.

"That went well," Brook remarked, checking her data slate for more news.

"Better than I thought it would. I'd be suspicious, but things have been going pretty well lately. The projections delivered at the meeting indicates that we're feeding millions of people right now, and still managing to break even, with what is almost total global financial collapse."

"We should celebrate," she said, walking with me back to my office, her arm inside mine.

"Oh?"

"With Perfidy, and Heavy Dub, and everyone else," Brook said, blushing slightly.

"Right, that's what I meant. What do you want to do?" I asked.

"The only party I've ever been to was Kaspersky's at the museum. We should do something like that, only smaller, and without a creepy doll room," Brook replied, already looking up party decorations on her data slate.

"Okay."

We took Vance's modified transport to the new distribution center, landing on top of a freshly constructed building overlooking Midtown. It had quick dock clamps to move transports quickly, and was elevated to allow for larger transports to set down and take on goods via automated conveyor systems. We walked inside to find the building empty, the smell of fresh paint lingering about. There were lunch pails and work suits draped over scaffolding around the perimeter of the large central chamber, and dozens of industrial racks waiting for goods to come in.

"Mr. Kale, good to see you," Salvatore said, coming down some metal stairs from the foreman's office.

"Where is everyone?" Brook asked.

"I sent them home this morning. We've got a small problem I'm hoping you can help me with," Salvatore said, his expression going cold.

I heard the hydraulic hiss a moment too late as something hit me from behind. I staggered over into Salvatore, his face impassive as Kaspersky reared back for a second strike. He was clad in full cyborg armor, his limbs replaced with sleek berserker class anti-personnel limbs. His head was enclosed in an armored mantle and helm that fit with his armor and other enhancements.

"It's nothing personal, just business," Salvatore said, shoving me to the ground.

Kaspersky's follow-up blow didn't land home, Brook quickly stepping in the way and parrying it with her forearm. Salvatore reached for his ankle holster in vain, looking up too late to see I'd already relieved him of his weapon. I fired a single shot, striking him in the head, before trying unsuccessfully to stand. My shoulder was dislocated, and my ribs broken from the strike from Kaspersky.

I pulled out my mobile and hit the radio feature. "Perfidy, help…" was all I could manage before Kaspersky dashed it from my hand, throwing Brook to the side.

"I will go to my kin empty handed, everything I worked years to build, gone because the dolls could not behave!" he roared, bringing both his augmented limbs up over his head.

He brought them down hard, shattering the freshly poured concrete where I'd been laying only a moment before. Brook sprinted away, one hand firmly grasping the collar of my suit coat, the other pushing through the exit. Kaspersky loped along after us on all fours, clanking and hissing as hydraulics and unholy fury propelled him after us. I emptied both pistols in his direction. The modified rounds I'd loaded into the last three chambers of my handgun shattering the front of his helmet.

He rolled to the side, howling in agony, broken glass sticking out of the flesh around his nose and eyes. Brook stopped just short of the transport, hurriedly pressing her hand to the biometric panel that would allow us access. Before the hatch could disengage and open, he was upon us, batting me harshly to the side and trying to tear Brook limb from limb. I could hear her screaming in pain though my own agony as I forced myself up.

"Kale, run! Get away!" she said, bruising her knuckles on Kaspersky's armored skin.

She was holding her own, but just barely. I loped along toward the transport and reached in with my good arm, grasping her hammer lying beside her work suit. I turned, and kicked it over to her. She kicked with both legs, knocking Kaspersky back long enough for her to lay hands on the hammer. The sleeves of her suit jacket were torn, blood flowing freely from wounds across her arms. Kaspersky moved in for the kill, arms low, leaving himself open for an overhead hammer strike that caved in the armored panel just to the left of his head. The hit was loud enough that it must have burst his eardrum, staggering him.

"THE DOLLS MUST NOT MISBEHAVE!" he roared, the PA on his cybernetic armor making him sound like a freight train.

He summoned a powerful bio-electric arc that Brook just waded through, the jolt snapping across the steel of her hammer as she reversed her grip and spun around for a hard low strike on Kaspersky's leg. It buckled and sparked, shooting thick black hydraulic fluid all over the platform. Panels opened across the mantle of his cyborg armor at the same time, revealing a row of small rocket propelled projectiles. Fire and furious noise rushed past me as the platform went up, hundreds of tiny explosions tearing the supports down around us.

I could hear Brook shouting somewhere nearby. "It's going to come down! We're falling!"

Brook stepped back into me through the smoke, looping her arm around my waist as the brand new distribution facility began to descend like a lead sled, crashing through a row of warehouses and a diner below. Sled was an apt description, as the building was riding the incline down through Midtown on bent supports. Carrying us and anything else in its path with it, the building rushed toward the ocean. Kaspersky didn't seem to care, bolting upright on his good leg and coming at us again. Debris rained down on us as the platform below bent upward, hitting more buildings as the whole structure began to pick up speed.

Brook brought her hammer down, right where she anticipated he was about to step. His good leg crashed down through the platform. It was immediately shorn off by the wreckage passing beneath us, effectively immobilizing him. He tried to drag himself clear, but actuators and a hydraulic cable caught underneath the landing platform kept pulling him down.

"The dolls... they... misbehave..." he muttered, trying to extricate himself.

"Good bye, Kaspersky," Brook said, looking back over her shoulder.

He reached for us, but Brook leapt clear, grabbing a cable from a crane used to service the docks. Our brand new distribution facility continued it's decent, barely clearing the docks as it violently exited Midtown, carrying our modified transport, Kaspersky, Salvatore, and much of my peace of mind violently into the Atlantic Ocean. The huge structure made a splash so high it spattered the bottoms of our feet. From a distance, I watched as Kaspersky flailed about, the weight of his battle harness dragging him down below the surf along with hundreds of tons of steel and wreckage.

"This will be the most interesting insurance claim ever," I said, Brook's steely grip holding me aloft, her other hand firmly grasping the crane cable.

"Do you think he's dead?" Brook asked, fearfully.

"Perfidy should be here soon. He'll make sure," I said with certitude.

Thankfully, a dock worker was able to get to the crane controls and lower us down to the docks. As soon as we were a safe distance, Brook dropped, doing her best to soften the blow. It still hurt like hell, my shoulder and ribs screaming at me due to the trauma they'd sustained. Honestly, it was worse than being shot.

Perfidy arrived mere minutes later, riding in with Mr. Mundt like the cavalry with Heavy Dub and a handful of others. Honcho, Olfact, and Sweet Pea were there, too, lurking in the cargo hold while Heavy Dub prepped to take a dive and verify that Kaspersky was dead.

"You guys are the ones that told me you didn't trust Salvatore, remember? So you come down here without a security augment?" Perfidy scolded, taking a look at my wounds.

"It isn't Kale's fault. It was mine. Now he's hurt really bad," Brook said, covering her face.

Heavy Dub surfaced, pulling himself up on the dock and kicking off flippers.

"Dead. Dead as a door nail. Cause of death, tangling with badass chick with a sledgehammer," he reported, grinning.

"We have to get him out of there. We can't let anyone get access to his body," I said, wincing as Perfidy worked to set my shoulder.

"For sure, those cybernetics are dangerous and should probably still be illegal. They're bad for the psyche and have chemical injectors. Wear them for too long, you'll go crazy, and real quick," Heavy Dub replied, gesturing to the wreckage floating in the water.

"That's the least of my worries. I want his body first, we'll worry about the rest during the salvage ops. Go get it," I ordered, rubbing the dark bruise rising quickly over my ribs.

"No problem, Boss. Hey, Perf, get the torch from the trunk, I'll cut him out," Heavy Dub said, putting his flippers back on.

"Isn't the salt water bad for your arms?" Brook asked.

"Super bad, but Perfidy hates water. Hates," Heavy Dub said, laughing.

"Can we help?" Olfact asked, venturing out from the cargo hold, and kneeling down beside me.

"All we can do is wait," Brook replied, sadly.

"No, that's not true. The facility left a path of destruction through Midtown. At this time of day, most of the dock workers would have gone home, but search for survivors anyway. I don't want to leave anyone trapped up there," I said, gesturing to the wreckage across the incline above us.

"We can do it. Anything else?" he asked.

"See if you can find Brook's hammer up there, it should be close to that ledge. Perfidy's men will cover you," I said, pointing with my good arm.

There were no human casualties, besides Salvatore. The Chiroptera sniffed out a couple of dead animals, but miraculously, not a single worker was in the path of the facility when it fell. They also found her hammer. There were plenty that watched from either side, seeing Brook and me battling with Kaspersky. Everyone knew his face, every local channel carrying a picture of him as the man wanted for the destruction done to the city. A few filtered down to get a closer view of Brook as she stood on the dock beside me.

"How are your arms?" I asked.

"The bleeding has stopped. Should be healed up by tonight," she said, lifting up her ruined sleeves to show me wounds that were already rapidly closing.

"Good, I was worried."

She burst into tears, wrapping her arms around me. "I was so scared. I thought he was going to kill you. I should have known he was there, but the place was full of paint fumes and..."

"He has known how to get past your senses by carefully picking the field of engagement. We knew this would be a problem the next time he struck. You didn't do anything wrong," I said, hugging her back with my good arm.

Perfidy stood behind us silently keeping watch. Heavy Dub used up both the air tanks he brought cutting Kaspersky free. When he was finally laying on the docks beside us, Kaspersky was legless and armless, cybernetic connections covering the stumps. There was little of him that wasn't artificial, save his head and neck, the rest of his body covered with maintenance ports and dermal plating. He was as ugly as the things he'd done, his sins inscribed with machines across his flesh.

"No way a normal guy crams this much tech inside them. Wouldn't live long, if it all," Heavy Dub remarked, spitting off the dock as he shouldered his gear and marched back to Mundt's transport.

"Close call, guys," Perfidy said, shoving Kaspersky unceremoniously into a body bag.

"If he has symbionts, like what Helmet and Madmar were talking about, how long will they survive?" Brook asked.

"Not long, we need to get him to our private medical facility and see what can be done," I said, letting Brook and Perfidy hoist me to my feet.

"It's only noon, and the day promises to only get more interesting," Perfidy quipped, slinging what remained of Kaspersky over his shoulder.

"We should probably address Silverstein's desires, let him know what's happened," Brook said, helping to steady me as I limped to the transport.

Perfidy shook his head. "We've got some time before we have to worry about all that. Ezra went back to the Tribehome for a visit. Taylor has asked for some privacy while she and Silverstein chat. I guess he's up and around now."

"Okay, take me where we took Brook when she was injured. I want to see about these symbionts," I said, ascending the ramp into the cargo hold, a concerned group gathered in my honor.

"Sure, right after I have them look at *you*," Perfidy said, dropping the body bag roughly on the deck.

Mr. Mundt flew as politely as he could, every bit of turbulence sending pain radiating up through my arm and ribs. We arrived at the private medical facility owned by the firm, a few of the nurses waving to Brook as we disembarked. The Chiroptera immediately sent them fleeing back from the landing zone into the facility as they took up positions around the freighter, looking protectively about for trouble.

"I think you've made some new friends, Boss," Perfidy said, helping me across the threshold into the emergency room.

"It's odd that they would have this attachment so quickly. I figured they'd want to…"

"You gave them dignity, something the CGG didn't do even before it abandoned them to starve to death," Perfidy said, helping me into an examination room.

"Is the world really a worse place after the Shutdown, than before?" Brook asked, innocently.

"I think in a lot of ways, it is exactly the same. It might be noisier and smokier now, but it has a helluva lot more potential, I think," Perfidy replied, helping me get my jacket and shirt off.

Perfidy walked outside to get the doctor, while Brook stood beside me. Her face was awash with guilt, probably over what happened to me. I didn't know what to say, so I just smiled at her and reached out for her hand.

"I still feel like you being hurt is my fault," Brook said, taking my hand with both of hers.

"You saved my life up there. If you hadn't been there, I'd be dead," I said turning to look at the ceiling.

"You can't die. I would have nothing," Brook said, tears streaming down her face.

The doctor rushed in with a trauma kit and went to work setting my shoulder and ribs, injecting me with an internal cast to hold my bones in place while I healed. He put in two stint implants to help manage the pain.

"How did this happen?" the doctor asked.

"I tangled with a centuries old madman augmented with a berserker class cyborg suite of limbs and armor. The beautiful woman over there stopped him. We brought his corpse. I need you to pull some organisms of unknown origin out of his body for stasis," I said, slurring my words slightly.

"You are so high right now," Perfidy laughed, as much at me as the doctor's startled expression.

"Is he serious?"

"Yep," Perfidy replied, holding up the body bag.

The firm's private physicians and surgeons took what remained of Kaspersky to the operating theater and got to work. Perfidy, Brook, and I looked on as they began doing scans to try and isolate the symbiont organisms. As they extracted the first organism, a bioelectric spark jumped up hitting the ceiling. It didn't hit anyone, but I mashed the intercom button with my fist anyway.

"Everyone, get out of there now," I ordered.

The lead surgeon, a Dr. NaHasi, came in, and stared at me, awaiting an explanation.

"Could you talk me through completing the extraction?" I asked.

"If both your hands were completely steady? Possibly," he replied.

"I can do it," Brook said, heading to the operating theater.

Dr. NaHasi had Brook engage in some pointless routine surgical prep before talking her through the process. It took her forty-five minutes to pull four thumb-sized symbiont organisms out of Kaspersky and place them in small stasis chambers. They looked like eyeless cuttlefish, with long, and very slender, tendrils. I worried that putting them to sleep would hurt them, but until more analysis could be done, I wasn't sure what else to do.

We gathered in the observation chamber to watch Dr. NaHasi run tests and scans on the freshly extracted organisms. Before he began, he turned to Brook, his hand brushing against her arm, and the shredded bloody sleeves of her suit coat. He smiled at her, before turning an ugly expression in my direction.

"Well done, although I question the merit of risking a Drone's life to perform the procedure, regardless of whatever you hoped to gain," Dr. NaHasi scolded.

"I like you," I said, putting my hand on his shoulder, probably still high as a kite.

"Doc, Brook is immune to the worst of what those symbionts can dish out. We discovered that, the hard way, in the field fighting this guy the first time," Perfidy explained.

"I don't care. Don't ask me or the facility to do something like that again. Get me the op chamber and laser array I asked for so I can do these things remotely in the future," Dr. NaHasi said.

"You do know this guy signs your paycheck, and funds this facility?" Perfidy replied, somewhat annoyed.

"Are you willing to do just anything, for money?" Dr. NaHasi replied, gesturing to the shredded and bloody sleeves on Brook's suit coat.

"I apologize, Dr. NaHasi. I'll make certain you get what you need for next time," I said, finding a chair to sit in so I could rest while he yelled at me.

"Kale doesn't make me do anything. We're partners," Brook explained before he got too far into his tirade.

Dr. NaHasi sighed. "Alright, well, let's see what you've found then."

CHAPTER 17

UROBOROS MANSION, UPTOWN, PORT MONTAIGNE

9:02 PM April 22nd, 2200

Silverstein's Log, Part 10 –

It's a terrifying thing to die, the oblivion pressing in around you as your faculties dim and your body falls away from you. I know now that I didn't really perish, and that I have spent the last four months or more floating in a stasis chamber controlling a clone of myself. It was the clone that died, killed by another clone.

"What are you thinking about?" Taylor asked, snuggling up beside me on the huge bed I was lying on.

"Cigarettes," I replied, unable to keep from smiling.

The master bedroom was large, but seemed larger for how empty it was. The rest of the furniture was still piled up in a corner, but at least the walls had been scrubbed clean. I wondered why Kale had started to fix the place up. He certainly didn't seem the type to live in such a place by himself.

"Ezra said he would be right back," Taylor said, moving my arm up and over her shoulders, wrapping it around her like a blanket.

"Look at this," I said, holding up my mobile, a missive from Brook on the screen, a corporate photo of her beside the text.

"Yeah, so? She's says Kale is going to handle everything so we can go to Mars," Taylor replied.

"No look at *her*," I said.

"I know, right? That's not the little girl that tagged along with us through Port Montaigne's Midtown back in January. She's a lady now," Taylor replied, smiling at the picture.

"She always was," I said, putting my mobile back down on the bed.

"You asked the Factory to have her made, right?"

I smiled. "How much do you want to know about all that?"

"Everything, seriously," Taylor said, turning over to lie on her stomach.

"I did so many things alone. Ezra had always been a capable asset, but few other Drones had his courage. Most were content to simply work within the functions the Factory assigned them. Brook was one of many I hoped to see join various Drone tribes around the world. Like Ezra and Abbey, and a handful of other Drones and Metasapients around the world, she's unmitigated," I explained.

"What does that really mean?" Taylor asked.

"Most Drones do not go above ground because the Factory told them they can't. Ezra was told the same thing, but his design allows him to decide to ignore Factory directives. He can also develop abilities and skills beyond his designation," I explained.

"When Brook wanted to be left alone, she was small and childlike. When she wanted to protect Kale she grew larger, and became even stronger. When she..." Taylor said, her words trailing off as she considered the possibilities.

"What?" I asked.

"She is beautiful now, and taller than I am," Taylor said.

"Jealous?" I asked, chuckling.

"No!" she said, giggling, and slugging me playfully. "Okay, maybe a little. Do you know why?"

"I have no clue."

"Typical clueless man. It's because she loves Kale and wants desperately for him to notice her. She told me, the next chance she gets, she is going to kiss him, and squeeze him to tiny pieces," Taylor replied.

"And, you like Kale?" I asked, totally confused.

"A little," Taylor said, rolling her eyes.

"Oh," I whispered, trying to hide being crushed.

"But, only because he's basically you," Taylor said, delighting in my reaction.

"I'm the better 'me' though, I hope?" I asked, hoping Ezra was taking his time.

"I dunno, Kale's got a serious bad boy thing goin' on that is pretty hot," Taylor teased, rolling over on her back and closing her eyes.

"This is true. My first memory of Kale, after waking up from being dead, is him carrying me through what looks like a warzone, explosions going off behind him. Then, he tells me 'I've got you,' while he has a few dozen augmented ex-soldiers do to Kaspersky what I've been wanting to do for centuries," I said, clasping my hands together, and pretending to swoon a little bit.

Taylor laughed. "Even with your memories back, you really are the same guy."

"Not nearly as kick ass as my Delta class replica?"

"Maybe not, but you are ten times the fun he is. From her time in the Tribehome, Brook is used to sleeping with her face against cold and reliable steel. I want someone warmer, and more spontaneous," Taylor said, hugging me.

"I'm glad."

Ezra cleared his throat as he came into the bedroom holding up the takeout, and a plastic sack of supplies he'd fetched. He threw the keycard to the old RV on the bed and climbed up to join us. He sat cross legged across from us, handing out peanut bars, cigarettes, and Chinese takeout like we used to have.

"Have fun driving the RV?" Taylor asked.

"All of Silverstein's favorite places were already programmed in. I barely touched the wheel," Ezra said, smiling faintly.

"I missed Port Montaigne," I said, smelling the takeout.

"I heard you guys talking about Brook," Ezra said, biting the end off of a peanut bar.

"Yep, she's going to ambush Kale and smooch him into submission," Taylor said, hogging all the soy sauce.

"Oh," Ezra said, looking concerned.

"You worried about her?" I asked.

"Of course, she's part of my tribe," Ezra replied, poking at his noodles lethargically.

"How was your visit by the way?" Taylor asked.

"Senegal and Annabelle are together now. Chelsea Six is getting more paranoid and afraid. Everyone else is the same," Ezra said, frowning.

"You and Annabelle…it always seemed like there was something there, maybe?" Taylor asked, pausing mid-bite to console Ezra.

"On the moon, right after Silverstein had been shot, I met a girl, a Drone like me. Her name was Viv," Ezra said, totally dodging her question.

"Was she nice?" Taylor asked.

"Yep," Ezra replied, hogging all the spicy peanut sauce.

"Ezra, you don't have to go to Mars with us. I know you hate it there, and I'm sure Taylor and I will be fine. I've already sent some of my allies ahead, so we should have plenty of backup," I said, putting my hand on his back.

"I know, you've said as much already. I just don't know which is worse, being lonely for my own people, or spending months without you guys," Ezra replied.

"I'm cool with whatever you decide," I said, possessing profound empathy for his situation.

"I'm not. You should totally come with us," Taylor said, tackling Ezra, and tickling him ferociously.

Tears in his eyes, Ezra simply endured the tickling and hugged his friend. It wasn't to last. Ezra bolted upright, pushing Taylor behind him, claws clicking out. I turned and looked back toward the balcony. Kaspersky stepped in past the curtains blowing in the wind.

"Touching. Playing with our dolls I see?" Kaspersky said, his voice issuing forth from the sleek red cyborg armor that sheathed his body.

"You should leave town, Kaspersky," I said, sliding off the bed to my feet.

"Stay back," Ezra warned, leaping out so he was between Kaspersky, Taylor, and me.

"This is the one who taught her to fight?" Kaspersky asked, gesturing to Ezra.

"He taught her more than that. Seriously, you should go, now," I warned.

"I tested my best doll against her earlier, almost killing your echo, Kale. She defeated me handily, with only a sledgehammer. I want her. Give her to me, and I'll give you all I have left in North America to add to your own," Kaspersky rasped, his withered face contorting to display a frown.

"She isn't mine to give. I never really owned anything, and if I did, I've given it all away. You should do what I've done. Walk away from the Cabal as an organization and get back to what it stood for as an ideal. Don't be a fool," I scolded, shaking my head.

"But, she is so lovely. So very lovely. How could you not want such a pretty doll?" Kaspersky mewled, his powerful cybernetic limbs slumping.

"We have an ancient trust to keep, a code that has kept the galaxy safe for centuries. Think about all that, Kaspersky," I said, almost begging.

"There is no returning to a purpose. She has already come for me once. I am lost," Kaspersky replied sadly.

"Don't give Golgotha any further reason to hunt you. I'm going to Mars to bring Archibald back. The Cabal need not cut off the arm holding the sword just to have peace. Listen to sense, Kaspersky," I said sternly, hoping he would listen to me.

"She will be mine. I will kill your echoes, proxies, and dolls, until I have her," Kaspersky replied, every semblance of the man I once knew lost to a strange madness.

"Are we still talking about Brook?" I asked, squinting to try and read his expression through the shadows around him.

He looked confused for a moment, before the madness once again displaced all other emotions. Then, he vaulted out the window, his sleek cyborg body carrying him back into the shadows. Ezra and I watched from the balcony until he was gone before coming back in. Taylor was sitting on the bed hugging her legs worriedly.

"We have to warn Brook and Kale," I said, pulling out my mobile.

"I've already called Brook. Kaspersky was telling the truth. He attacked Kale," Taylor said, letting her mobile slip from her hand to the bed.

"Big mistake," Ezra said, angrily finishing his peanut bar.

"The biggest. If Brook does love Kale, she will be super deadly when defending him. Where did they fight?" I asked.

"Midtown, by the docks. Took down an entire distribution center in the process," Taylor replied.

I pulled out my mobile and checked the local news feeds. Sure enough, there was shaky video captured by a dock worker with his mobile. He caught the moment the entire building slid past him, Brook and Kaspersky's clone trading blows on the protruding landing pad. I watched sadly as my sweet modified transport was carried along with it, probably resting in pieces at the bottom of the Atlantic.

"Brook dropped a berserker class cyborg, with a sledgehammer," I remarked, pocketing my mobile.

"So, Brook and Kale, they should be pretty safe?" Taylor asked.

"They are in terrible danger. Kaspersky is a creature of convictions. He won't give up until he's dead, or gotten whatever it is he thinks he wants," I replied.

Ezra scowled, his claws retracting before his hands departed to hide in his pockets.

"Okay, is it just me, or do Madmar and Kaspersky seem eerily similar? Remember at Uroboros Financial when we faced that augmented cybernetic clone of Madmar? Was that an easier or harder fight than Kaspersky in berserker armor, or whatever?" Taylor asked.

"Easier. We were fighting a standard mil spec cyborg that day. What Brook fought and killed by herself today would be a much more difficult fight. And yeah, they do seem similar. Kaspersky wants Brook, much the same way Madmar wanted you." Ezra said, nodding to Taylor.

"This is why I wanted Kaspersky to leave town. Also, it explains why the Cabal tried so hard to kill Brook. Not only is she immune to our amnestic abilities, but she can kill one of our militant members without breaking a sweat," I said, with no small amount of pride.

"Wait, you don't want Brook to kill Kaspersky?" Ezra asked, raising an eyebrow.

"Of course not, he's a member of my tribe. He's just… lost his way," I replied, trying to find the words to explain.

"Brook says he spent decades snatching kids and engaging in other nefarious acts," Taylor replied, clearly not pleased with the sympathy I possessed for Kaspersky.

"Each of us, the men and women of my tribe, carries a tremendously heavy burden. Some of us bear it better than others. When our task is complete, Kaspersky will pay for his crimes in full, but until then it is important that I, and others like me survive," I explained.

"And, you're going to explain all this at some point?" Taylor asked, grabbing the skin under my ribs and giving it a gentle twist.

"Ow! Yes, I will explain everything, I promise," I said, playfully batting her hand away.

"You guys in a tribe, like my fellow Drones and I are in a tribe?" Ezra asked.

"Yeah, most of us were literally part of the same community, long ago. Do you think I was using the term to play on your emotions?" I explained.

Ezra paused, looking into my eyes. "Nope."

He went off to check the perimeter while Taylor and I smoked off the edge of the balcony looking toward Port Montaigne. Even as the sun set, transports were delivering heavy machinery and personnel to begin repairing the damage Kaspersky had done. There were a million things I wanted to tell her, and so many encouraging things I could say to Ezra.

I wanted desperately to tell them both more of the truth.

"I'll follow you anywhere, but I need to know this is all for a good cause," Taylor said, stealing the already lit cigarette from my mouth.

"We are keeping the galaxy safe, but you may already have some inkling if you've talked to your mother," I replied, lighting up.

"C.O.N. saving us from the invasion?" Taylor asked.

"He did more than just save everyone in our solar system," I replied, trying to beat her smoke ring record.

"So we're not alone in the universe?" Taylor said, looking up at the stars.

"Not remotely," I replied, catching sight of Ezra as he paused to look up the street to the ruined mansions along the street.

"What was C.O.N. created to do, originally?"

"He started as part of a personal digital assistant within a music app for mobile devices, written by a young coder from Sweden long ago. He was written to keep your music organized. As he grew more sophisticated, so did his capabilities," I explained.

"Ha, C.O.N. was just an application?" Taylor asked.

"Yep. His ability to catalogue resources and react to the demands of the user made him capable of all sorts of tasks. When the Cabal was quietly manipulating the CGG into putting together the fleet, we had to make some hard choices. The fleet needed a steward, but there were only a handful of Omega class artificial intelligences at the time. C.O.N. volunteered to go," I explained.

"A young coder from Sweden? Am I allowed to guess?" Taylor giggled.

"If you want. Regardless, C.O.N. is like Brook, becoming far more than he was designed to be."

"Wow, he's like... everyone's super cool big brother," Taylor said, looking up at the sky.

"Yep."

"Why can't he come home?" Taylor asked.

"One of the invaders was a conscientious objector. It offered to help dismantle the various weapons and contrivances the other invaders planned to use to annihilate us. C.O.N. is planning to fly the fleet into the sun carrying all the dangerous armament with him when they are complete," I explained.

"No! You can't let him do that!" Taylor said, giving me a panicked look.

"I agree, but I need my ship to reach C.O.N. and retrieve his sentience core before he carries out the final part of his plan. I had a plan to destroy the weapons without losing him," I replied, trying to calm her.

"Your ship, it's on Mars?"

"Yes."

"This all sounds incredibly dangerous." Taylor said, taking my hand.

"A few months ago, I described it as a suicide mission. Without intervention, terrible things were going to happen on the Martian Colony. I was going to be too late to stop it, even if I had managed to leave back in December as I'd planned."

"What about the rest of the Cabal?"

"They said C.O.N. was just a machine, not worth risking one of us or the resources to recover."

"And... you were going to go regardless, because you're a good guy," Taylor stated, squeezing my hand.

"Yep."

"Did Kale know what you planned to do?"

"Sort of. He freaked out and hit me with a pipe before I could fully explain the situation to him."

Taylor leaned on the balcony rubbing her eyes wearily. "Hoo boy."

"Don't be too hard on him. Making the transition from an Alpha replica to a Delta is difficult. Not being able to fully choose who you are wasn't fair to any of them, in spite of my best efforts."

"Also, we may never have met if he hadn't dumped you in my neighborhood."

"Someday, I would like to ask him why he did that, but I don't want it to sound like complaining," I said laughing.

"He is you. Maybe he just had an inkling of where you'd want to be?" Taylor said, putting her arm around me.

"Maybe."

My mobile chimed and vibrated in my pocket. Pulling it out, I could see Brook had sent me a message marked as urgent, and with a video file attached. The contents would change how I saw my former friend, Kaspersky, forever.

CHAPTER 18

Initiating Link, Secure Protocol, CGG Network 82821

Dr. Maurice Madmar, logged in.
Dr. Gorshteyn Helmet, logged in.

Dr. Madmar appeared on the right half of the screen, his home office on the Lunar Colony in the background. A worried expression dominated his face. It took a moment for Dr. Helmet to appear on the left, static distorting most of the bottom of his display. The background was crowded with people rushing between several folding a tables, a makeshift relief tent was being set up in the background.

"I've made it to Downtown, Port Montaigne," Dr. Helmet reported.

"You're not him, are you?" Madmar asked.

"No, I'm a Delta acting in his behalf, but I was closer to the disaster site," Helmet replied.

"Is there any word on Vivian?" Madmar asked, clasping his hands together shakily.

"She survived, but she suffered massive head and spinal trauma. The doctors here say she needs a dozen surgeries if she is to survive. I'm sorry," Helmet reported, making his way through the disaster relief site, the view swaying slightly.

"Send me her charts," Madmar said, almost pleading.

"I already have, they should upload to your display in a moment."

A filed transfer started, a progress bar at the bottom of the screen slowly filling up. Madmar waited patiently as Helmet found a quieter place to sit down. When the progress bar winked off the screen, Madmar's side disappeared, the chart data appearing in its place. It slowly scrolled down with Madmar's input.

"If I were there, I could save her," Madmar concluded.

"Even if we could clear it with the CGG to let you leave the Lunar Colony, a transport would not arrive in time. She has a few hours at best," Helmet replied, sadly.

"The marionette halo coupled with the transference chamber would allow me to control a blank or full replacement unit, and with the precision to do the job remotely," Madmar stated, the charts sliding to the side to reveal his face once more.

"The surgeries would take too long. You'd be confined to the chamber, right?" Helmet replied, shaking his head.

"Yes, but if I don't she will die. I don't know what to do," Madmar said, covering his face with his hands.

"The tailored artificial agent is missing. Perfidy is looking for her, but we suspect someone in the Cabal engineered the disaster for their own purposes. The security personnel and pilot on board were lost, and the other support staff are still unaccounted for. Vivian may be the only person that can tell us what happened up there," Helmet stated, holding his mobile with both hands to steady it.

"Is she conscious?" Madmar asked.

"Without the surgeries I mentioned, I doubt she will regain consciousness."

"Prep a blank at our local research facility, outfitted with a full replacement suite. I'll prep the transference chamber and add the marionette halo so that I can wear it inside," Madmar ordered, picking up his mobile and tapping at the touchscreen.

"I doubt the hospital or Vivian's family will…"

"Get her to our local facility so I can work on her. Do what you have to," Madmar growled.

"You're talking about kidnapping. She might not survive being transported."

"Do it anyway," Madmar hissed, tapping the screen to end the transmission.

The screen was dark for only a moment. When it came back on, the time stamp had advanced fifty-five minutes. Helmet appeared first, a woman lying in an operating theater behind him. Two full conversion cyborg bodies outfitted with exposed cognitive constructs in the skull cavities jerked to life, startling him.

Madmar appeared next, a layer of fluid between him and the camera, a halo of interface nodes pressed firmly to his brow, a clear breathing mask over his mouth and nose. A hastily donned VR module covered his eyes. His voice sounded like it was in an echo chamber.

"I've got control of both neural interfaces and I can see the operating table clearly. It feels like I'm actually there," Madmar said, calmly.

"There was damage to the power grid here because of the crash, but we've got backup generators just in case," Helmet replied, turning to face a terminal.

"Okay, let's do this. With two points of interface and the coaxial laser array, I should be able to do this quickly enough to still be able to leave the chamber. Can you monitor my vitals while I work?" Madmar said, willing the two cyborg bodies to begin prepping the woman on the table.

"Yes, I've got you on my screen. You've got about four minutes less than we originally projected. Toxicity levels are building up in your blood slightly faster than anticipated," Helmet replied, worriedly.

"It's okay. I can do this."

Madmar's face went taut as the two cyborg bodies he was controlling began to move quickly and efficiently, removing the top of the woman's skull and laying bare her spinal column. The coaxial laser array descended as the cyborgs fitted her with a breathing mask. The operating table descended, allowing fluid to rise and submerge the woman. The coaxial laser began to fire quickly, rotating quickly to allow fresh lasers to spin into place while spent ones went into the liquid to cool.

"We're doing real well so far. You've got 17% of the damage repaired. You've got forty minutes before toxicity reaches critical levels," Helmet reported.

Madmar didn't respond, his lips parting behind the clear breathing mask to reveal clenched teeth, blood trickling down from his nose. Helmet looked panicked for a moment, making adjustments at the terminal.

"Thirty-seven percent, Dr. Madmar. Keep going. You can do this," Helmet said, tapping furiously at a keyboard off screen.

Ten tense minutes of Dr. Madmar working furiously passed.

"Adjust the coaxial array for phase two at my mark. And, mark," Madmar said, calmly, coughing up blood.

"Sixty-eight percent. You've restored her motor functions, and she is responding. She'll walk again," Helmet said, wiping his brow.

"Status on my vitals?" Madmar asked, the bottom half of his breathing mask filled with crimson.

"Toxicity is at acceptable levels, but you need to hurry," Helmet replied.

"Boost neural latency across the network," Madmar rasped, blood flecks coating the inside of his breathing mask.

"We could be detected by outside parties using more than our two secure orbitals. You're already skirting safe limits," Helmet warned.

"I am aware. Just do it," Madmar demanded.

"I'm utilizing a third orbital."

Twenty harrowing minutes passed as Madmar worked. He swallowed the blood trickling down from his nose to keep it from filling the mask. The cyborgs and laser array behind Helmet worked frantically to save the woman, their movements fast enough to skip frames in the video capture.

Suddenly, a door burst open beside Dr. Helmet, a man in a red coat and night vision goggles pushing him out of sight of the camera.

"No! Stop!" Madmar cried out.

The man in red fired two shots in the same direction he shoved Dr. Helmet, a cry of agony causing the audio to crack and skip. In the operating theater beyond, a heavily augmented individual burst into the room, knocking one of the cyborg blanks over, disconnecting the exposed neural construct from the terminal nearby. The combat equipped cyborg was dressed in a greasy red coat that did little to hide his powerful robotic limbs.

A raspy mechanical voice dominated the audio. "My, what lovely dolls!"

The cyborg picked up the disconnected neural interface cable and gazed at it menacingly, his face only dimly visible beneath the helmet. A port on his armor, between his neck and right shoulder snapped open with a hydraulic hiss. With one smooth motion, he connected the cable to the exposed interface port. The second cyborg body jerked back from the operating table. It began to frenetically tear chunks off of itself, metallic fingers ripping away synthetic dermal plates and hoses carrying red and blue fluid. Streaks of spattered liquid went up the walls and ceiling as the red cyborg turned its back to the camera to gaze down at the woman still laying submerged in fluid.

The metallic voice returned, cutting out all other audio feeds. "She's lovely! Just, lovely."

Both sides of the screen went dark. Dr. Madmar's cries of anguish and fury mixed with a dirge of maniacal cackling before it was cut short by static.

CHAPTER 19

1:37 PM April 22nd, 2200

Kale's Private Records, Part 6 –

"Whoa," Perfidy whispered, watching Brook's data slate go dark following the latest data file.

"Poor Dr. Madmar!" Brook exclaimed, rubbing tears from her eyes.

"Are we certain Kaspersky didn't use the transference chambers to create replicas of himself?" I asked.

"As sure as we can be, but that video file was time stamped more than twenty years ago," Perfidy replied.

"Is there anything in Helmet's records that might tell us whether this Vivian survived? What if Kaspersky made off with her? She looked like a younger lady. Could she still be alive?" Brook asked, bringing up everything we'd been able to decrypt on her data slate.

I was tired, and the pain medications were making me dizzy. Perfidy looked deeply distressed by the last video file, leaning forward toward the wall until his forehead was touching it, hands in his pockets. Brook was in full rescue mode, probably twenty years too late, trying to see if we had anything on the woman Madmar was trying to save.

"Perfidy, when Kaspersky connected that cable, what do you think happened?" I asked.

"Cyborgs don't usually have neural interface ports unless they are set up to remotely control heavy machinery, vehicles, and that sort of thing. Kaspersky's armor would have intrusion and control countermeasures, while Madmar would have been naked over the connection. It couldn't have been good for Madmar's mind," Perfidy said, doing little to answer my question.

"I got that from the video file."

Perfidy frowned. "Yes, I'm a cyborg, but I don't know everything about it, and..."

"And?" Brook asked.

"Both Kaspersky and Madmar seemed to be able to control multiple cyborg bodies. That was pretty clear on the video. Oh, crap," Perfidy said, worriedly.

"Indeed." I stood up, walking through the hall toward the operating theater where we left Kaspersky's remains. There was already a pair of interns standing there, preparing to clean up everything. I grabbed a smock from a closet full of sterile implements along with a plastic face shield.

"Out," I said, ordering the two interns to leave.

Perfidy handed me a powered bone saw and stood back, Brook looking on in horror as I cut the top off of Kaspersky's head. What was inside appeared to be bone and tissue until the brain cavity was exposed. The same strange biological construct visible in the two cyborgs Madmar was using to perform the surgery, was also inside Kaspersky's body. Dr. NaHasi burst into the room, ready to unleash Hell until he saw what I'd discovered.

I let the saw clatter to the operating table and whisked the smock and face shield off.

"He's not dead?" Brook said, pressing her hands together beneath her nose.

"He's got clones fitted with cognitive neural constructs and set up to receive signals from CGG orbitals. His augmentation allows him to control multiple puppets at once. I should have known, what with him being obsessed with dolls," I said, rubbing my temples.

"The samples expired before I could run all the tests. I was able to get only a small amount of data before they stopped accepting stimuli," Dr. NaHasi reported, shakily.

"Kaspersky could be anywhere in the world then?" Perfidy said, dejectedly.

"No, he's here in Port Montaigne somewhere," I replied.

"How do you know?"

"We have his doll collection from his museum in storage. It had been my intent to try to identify the children he killed, and return as many of them to families as possible. We just don't have the forensic personnel available with everything else going on," I explained, further unnerving Dr. NaHasi.

"What do you want me to do with the samples and remains?" Dr. NaHasi asked.

"I'll need you to keep everything for comparison," I replied.

"What am I to compare them to?" he asked.

"One of our operatives brought you a pair of corpses a few days ago from storage, marked 'M' and 'S.' Compare these remains to those," I asked.

"The Maurice Madmar and Silverstein replicas Ezra pulled from the syndicate massacre?" Perfidy asked.

"Facilities that can create clones and artificial neural constructs for use with multiple agent cyborgs were CGG only, and highly classified. However, they each have institutional and manufacturing markers if you know what to look for," Dr. NaHasi said, surprising us all.

"And you... know what to look for?" I asked.

"You falsified your employee record?" Brook asked.

"No, Vance Uroboros did, am I right?" Perfidy said, grinning and shaking his head.

"Yes, no one else would hire me after certain technologies associated with the MDC project were misused, and it all went public," Dr. NaHasi explained.

"Do you know where all these CGG facilities are, or can you only narrow down manufacturer from the markers you spoke of?" I asked.

"This man you are seeking, he is the one responsible for the devastation that afflicted the city recently?" Dr. NaHasi asked.

"And the mummified corpses of two hundred forty-seven children I've asked the facility to identify once you've finished identifying victims of the recent explosions and collapses," I added, choosing to trust Dr. NaHasi.

"It will take time, and the equipment I asked for, but I can find where these clones and the neural constructs were manufactured," he replied, bowing his head sadly.

"You still know people?" Perfidy asked.

"Yes."

I grabbed some rest in Mr. Mundt's transport while Honcho, Olfact, and Sweet Pea kept watch over us, and the facility. Perfidy spent most of the afternoon on the radio and an encrypted mobile helping Dr. NaHasi track down contacts, after comparing the manufacturing markers on the replicas of Kaspersky, Dr. Madmar, and Silverstein. Brook lay beside me on Mr. Mundt's cot, playing with my hair and watching me slip in and out of slumber. I hoped it would take them forever to untangle the mess we'd discovered.

It turned out that the Silverstein and Kaspersky clones were likely manufactured in the facility we destroyed in Fredrick's Block. Dr. NaHasi's report stated that Silverstein had cognitive neural constructs, with older "echo chamber" redundancy systems. They had to have a continuous link to the prime operator via some unknown contrivance. We knew that contrivance to be the marionette halo or harness coupled with a transference chamber. If the link was severed, the clones would just sit down and discontinue activity.

The Maurice Madmar clone was more mysterious. He had a newer "echo chamber" redundancy system that would, over time, create a behavioral algorithm that would allow the clone to continue operating in a way similar to the prime operator. Even with Madmar dead, any clones outfitted with this special cognitive neural construct would continue to operate much as he would, like ghosts.

It seemed that Kaspersky had gained access to some of Madmar's technology, but that they may not have been working together. Based on the last video file, they were probably enemies. The facility used to make that cognitive neural construct for the clone was off the CGG registry Dr. NaHasi had memorized. It was likely that the servers containing the information we needed were offline and anyone that knew anything was dead. Perfidy did a lot of shouting on his encrypted mobile, frustration building with each call he made.

"We need someone that worked closely with the MDC project. Someone that knows where they keep all the closets full of skeletons, the highly classified cloning and replicating technology," Perfidy said, leaning up against the entrance to Mr. Mundt's quarters.

I smiled, looking up into Brook's eyes as she continued to twirl her hair with my fingers.

"Lovebirds, I need you to focus for five minutes. Help me out here," Perfidy asked, his voice hoarse from yelling.

I pulled out my mobile and dialed Matthias.

He answered after a single ring. "Kale, how can I help you?"

"Everything okay?" I said, hearing gunfire over the connection.

"We've got a situation. I'm working with some of Silverstein's contacts to try and resolve it. We've got overt Cabal activity here."

"Understood. I need to know if Madmar had access to any secret CGG facilities with the connections to the MDC project, their location, and any details you can provide me."

Matthias paused for a moment. "I know of a couple. One is full of Acrididae Metasapients and everyone there was killed by a dangerous neuro-toxin, and..."

"Yes, I'm aware of that one, remember?" I said, laughing.

"Oh, right."

"Tell me about the other one."

"It's in Mexico, I can have my Modbot send you the coordinates. I have no idea what you'll find there," Matthias said.

"Thanks. Do you need anything for Finland?" I asked.

"I'm working with Taylor's friend Versa and a pair of law enforcement grade Metasapients named Eamon and Abbey. We've been able to mobilize the locals, but there are a lot of cold and hungry people here," Matthias explained.

"I'll take care of it."

"Thanks."

I ended the call, using near field communications to transmit the coordinates Matthias sent me to Perfidy's encrypted mobile. He glanced at them and then let his hand fall to the side. He sighed loudly shaking his head.

"I know this place. It is rubble," Perfidy replied, scratching the stubble on his chin.

"What's he talking about?" Brook asked, laying her head on my chest.

"It's a nuclear power plant that was sabotaged by the Financial Liberation Front a decade ago. The whole area is a hot zone, and the CGG collapsed the facility to limit fallout and radiation levels. They poured a million tons of concrete on that place," Perfidy replied.

"Are you sure? Have you actually had boots on the ground and surveyed the site?" I asked.

"No, but we could check the satellite telemetry… except we really can't trust that either, can we?" Perfidy said, chuckling.

"Are we going to Mexico?" Brook asked, smiling sleepily at me.

"Mexico isn't going to be happy with us just poking around a closed facility. We don't have carte blanche to do whatever we want there. They have heavy state surveillance, tight borders, and an autonomous economy that doesn't rely heavily on industry controlled by Uroboros Financial," I replied, closing my eyes to think.

"If Madmar maintained a facility in Mexico, it was likely to prevent detection by Vance Uroboros or Uroboros Financial," Brook said, sitting up and taking out her data slate.

"Or, to prevent someone in the Cabal operating primarily out of North America from detecting his operation," Perfidy argued.

"True," Brook replied, smiling.

I sat up, and used my phone to send a missive to acquisitions directing them to send supplies to Helsinki and the surrounding areas to support assets on the ground. Then I called Taylor IA on her mobile. It went to voicemail.

"Taylor, would you and Ezra and Silverstein tell me everything about your friends Versa, Eamon, and Abbey. I'm sending a care package their way. What kind of weapons did they carry, what kind of food do they eat, that sort of thing. Thanks," I said, hanging up.

"That's pretty nice of you," Perfidy remarked.

"They're fighting the Cabal over there," I said brushing my hand over Brook's arm, the wounds she sustained from Kaspersky still healing.

"Shit. You want me to head over with some angry guys with guns?" Perfidy asked.

"No, Matthias said he and this allies there would handle it. We've got to keep North America safe. I think he's from Sweden. I suspect he has resources nearby," I replied.

Perfidy looked disappointed. "Then I'll ask what Brook already has. Are we going to Mexico?"

"Someone should go, I'm just not certain who that should be," I replied, trying to think through the haze of the pain medication.

"You think Kaspersky is here, so we should look for him here. Let's forget about that facility and whatever might be there," Brook said, hopping off the cot and heading out to the cargo hold.

"That isn't my vote. I want to chase down every lead, even if it means dropping into Mexico, dark and heavy," Perfidy said, impatiently.

"You could just head down there, no guns, no angry guys, and just see your family. Madmar is dead," I said, standing up and pushing my hair out of my face.

"We are so close to catching up to this Kaspersky guy, and you want me to take a vacation?" Perfidy said, almost yelling.

I just smiled, his outburst doing more to prove my point than anything.

"Wait, are you saying I should use my family as an excuse to get a travel visa, and then try to take a peek at the facility while I'm there?" Perfidy asked.

"No, I'm not saying that at all. Brook might be right, heading down there may just be a distraction. I might be able to access the facility legally through the Mexican government. It'll just take some time to work out," I said, walking with him to the cargo hold.

Mr. Mundt was entertaining Sweet Pea with a game of cards while Honcho and Olfact looked on. Brook was handling some business for the firm on her data slate, when Dr. NaHasi came back out of the facility. He was carrying a metal case designed to carry biological samples.

"All the tissue and data I made from the comparisons is here. Nothing will remain stored on the servers or within the facility. I've already instructed everyone to treat this like old government contract work and just forget it as soon as it goes out the door," he explained, setting the case down on the deck of the cargo hold.

"I appreciate your discretion," I said, picking up the case and opening it to make sure everything was in order.

"I made some calls. There is a Mexican facility that may have manufactured the CNC recovered from the 'S' clone," NaHasi said, his gaze nervously wandering toward the Chiroptera looking at him curiously.

"I know about it already," I said, closing the metal case, satisfied everything was there.

"Did you know it was for sale?" NaHasi asked.

"No," I replied, handing the case to Perfidy.

"A minister within the Mexican government is privately selling sites off the official registry," NaHasi explained.

"And, you just happened to hear about it?" I said, stepping to within arm's length of him.

"Yes, I was asking about facilities capable of making the CNC you recovered," NaHasi replied, nervously eyeing the handgun at my hip.

"You'll have to excuse him, we've sort of dropped into the habit of not trusting anyone who's a doctor," Brook said, sliding in beside me, putting her arms around me.

"The contact information for this minister?" I asked.

NaHasi shakily handed me a slip of paper.

"Thanks. I appreciate all your help. Please send Brook copies of all your future equipment requests," I said, pocketing the slip of paper.

NaHasi retreated to the research facility, the wind picking up as he traversed the landing pad to the door. It started to rain as we sat down to consider our next move. The Chiroptera hung about upside down in the hold while Mr. Mundt made coffee. Perfidy turned the piece of paper NaHasi had given me over in his hand, gazed at the name, and closed a fist around it.

"He moonlights as a human trafficker. He's one of a number of people that turned up on my radar when I was looking for the Red Devil years ago. That he's a government official now doesn't make me feel better about going to Mexico," Perfidy said.

"So, let's just not go. It sounds like a scary place," Brook replied.

"It's actually really nice. The brightest lights of civilization always cast the darkest shadows though. Mexico has a trade market of elicit goods like nowhere else in the world. You can get anything there. Much of the high grade cybernetics I gave Perfidy as a sign on bonus were purchased on the market in Mexico," I explained.

"And a Drone like Brook?" Perfidy asked.

"Hey!" Brook protested.

"She'd be worth hundreds of millions to the right buyer. You'd both be taking a pretty big risk setting foot anywhere near Mexico."

"We could go in, look around for you," Honcho said, dropping from the ceiling above and gliding down to sit beside us.

I looked up at Honcho, reluctant to even consider it.

"We've all been to Mexico, and South America, previous to working in North America. Knowing how to guard a facility translates pretty easily into knowing how to break into one," he argued, looking to Sweet Pea and Olfact for support.

"We can do this," Olfact said.

Sweet Pea just nodded shyly.

"I don't think anyone should go. Please, don't send anyone," Brook pleaded, squeezing my hand.

Mr. Mundt came in carrying the coffee, handing it out to everyone but Sweet Pea who just wanted milk.

"She's right you know," Mr. Mundt said.

"What makes you so sure?" Perfidy asked.

"That Kaspersky fellow had seven of those special chambers you have all been so worried about. Mr. Kale seemed to think they were very expensive. No one builds, or makes, seven things like that," the old Romani trucker stated.

"They steal them," Perfidy replied, nodding.

"You'll probably get to Mexico and find an empty building, already looted of the important things," Mr. Mundt said, sipping his tea.

"What should we do then?" I asked, ready for any wisdom at that point.

"Always seek a man through his legacy. This Kaspersky did not just collect advanced techno-whats-its and snatch children from their beds," Mr. Mundt said, gesturing to the pictures of his own family on the wall.

"He collected artwork, from all over the world. I have an inventory of everything we took from his museum," Brook said, pulling out her data slate.

"Will there be anything else, Mr. Kale?" Mr. Mundt asked.

"Yes, please. Take us back to Uroboros Financial. I think Brook and I should do a little shopping for our new loft, maybe talk to every art dealer in town until we find the landscapes we're looking for."

CHAPTER 20

11:27 AM, December 31st, 2199

Phelps waved his arms frantically. "Officer Abbey!"

The law dog turned, her fur flecked with blood, eyes full of instinctual fury.

"My boss is hurt. Please, help us," he pleaded.

Abbey panted heavily as she handed an injured girl to Phelps, then knelt down next to Marjorie. Walter sat back slightly so Abbey could sniff her wounds.

"Her digestive tract is punctured, and so is her stomach, by the scent of the blood rising up. Unless you can get her to a hospital, it might be more merciful to let her bleed out than suffer the pain of her body poisoning itself," the Canine Metasapient growled, turning a murderous gaze toward the crowd.

Marjorie felt sick, terror flooding her being, pushing out everything, including the pain.

"No. No! We have to do something," Walter cried, tears freezing to his face.

Two commercial transports began making a slow descent to the ground along the northwest. The dull roar of their impact nearly blotting out the terrified clamor from the people fleeing the chaos nearby. Commercial storefront across the street rattled softly with each explosion.

The girl in Walter's arms gasped for air, her small jacket wholly insufficient to keep her warm. Phelps took off his own light jacket and wrapped it around the unconscious little girl. Then, he placed her beside Marjorie. The street went quiet around Marjorie as her vision began to dim.

Marjorie could feel her body shutting down, but she couldn't pass out. What seemed like hours went by as explosions, screams, and gunfire occasionally broke the silence. As it began to grow dark, she could feel heavy footsteps coming toward her. She couldn't hear them until they drew closer, and then a deep sigh as someone paused to stand over her.

"I am too late," she could hear Truman say, his accent thicker than she remembered it being at the office.

His broad arms encircled her, the little girl's cold corpse falling away as he picked her up. He held her close, crying bitterly. His bristly unshaven face brushed against her own, his eyelashes fluttering against her neckline. It wasn't the reaction that baffled Marjorie, but how intense it seemed to be for Truman. She'd known he had a little crush, but nothing like this.

"Who has done this to you?" Truman pleaded.

Marshaling all her strength, Marjorie struggled to take a breath and reply. "Phelps, Walter, they…" was all she could muster.

"Marjorie! Please, tell me. Why? Why, did Walter, and Phelps do this to you?" Truman pleaded, his voice turning from despair to rage.

She tried, but even taking a breath proved to be impossible. It was a terrifying, and eerie, sensation to have her brain deprived of oxygen, and yet, she still couldn't lose consciousness. Her body burned inside against the cold. Something strange was happening inside her, and for all her confusion and fear, she couldn't even make a fist.

Truman paused to check her pulse, his movements getting more frantic as he searched for any sign of life. He tried CPR, his bristly face against hers as he did chest compressions. Truman worked feverishly to revive her, but nothing seemed to coax a breath or a heartbeat from her. Finally, he gave up and began to carry her away.

"Oh God, they killed you! They killed you!" Truman kept saying over and over again, each step he took more hurried.

Marjorie helplessly listened to Truman drive himself insane for a couple of hours as he walked.

"I'll find them for you. This Walter, and Phelps, I know them. I know them from mission file. I will find them, and I will kill them. They'll die badly, like you died, my poor, sweet, Marjorie," Truman said, laying her down in the snow.

He would spend another two hours digging in the impossibly hard and frozen ground with something sharp and metallic. Marjorie spent the time doing her best to let Truman know she wasn't dead, but to no avail. Her body wouldn't respond, her eyes would not open, and she still couldn't take a breath. It was like time inside her body has stopped, all except a terrible fire that continued to burn in the pit of her belly.

"I can't bear to take this from you. It isn't right," Truman said, playing a recording of Marjorie singing in the shower.

She would have pondered how he got such a recording, if she wasn't slowly being lowered into a shallow grave. Truman placed something on her chest, and kissed her forehead, his tears freezing to her face as he did. Marjorie struggled, one last time, to signal that she was alive. Truman began pushing the frozen ground over the top of her in broad strokes, until the world was completely dark and silent.

All Marjorie could hear now was the clack of heavy stones as Truman covered the shallow grave to protect her from scavengers. The weight bearing down on her triggered the thing Truman had placed on her chest. It was a digital recorder that began playing back her voice. It would be the last sound she would hear as the fire inside her gradually began to die down, the oblivion of unconsciousness to descend upon her.

When Marjorie woke up, she couldn't be sure how long she'd been out, but she desperately wanted to take a breath. She pushed up through the loose and frozen ground, her hand plunging out into loosely packed snow. Panicked, she scrambled up out of the shallow grave, painfully banging her forearms and head against heavy stones. She sat up, and took a deep breath, the world an impossible blur of painfully bright white.

She groped about until she found enough solid ground to finish pulling herself to her feet. Unsteady, feeling half frozen, and a little weak like she'd slept in for too long, she rose. Her vision rapidly returned, the white giving way to the Finnish forest, and a pair of startled individuals dressed in white and grey military fatigues. One pushed his goggles up on his forehead to gaze at Marjorie, eyes wide with surprise.

"Hey... hey..." Marjorie coughed, waving toward them.

They broke into a run, heading deeper into the woods ahead of her. Blinking in disbelief, Marjorie grabbed her knees to steady herself. She looked down at the shallow grave she'd just freed herself from, and wondered how anyone could have survived what she had. She lifted her tattered shirt, looking to see how bad her stomach wounds were. Her skin was smooth, not even a scar left behind.

"How is this possible?" she whispered aloud, pressing her fingers against the flesh across her abdomen in a vain attempt to find any sign of her previous injuries.

Deciding to try to follow the guys in military uniforms, Marjorie began to walk through the woods. They weren't hard to follow until they reached the freeway. It was littered with abandoned vehicles. At least, she thought they were abandoned. Many of them had the decomposing remains of their owners, still trapped inside, the repossession protocol flashing on the dashboards.

Marjorie paused to look inside a larger transport where a driver and several children were still inside. Their little corpses were huddled together on the floor between the seats, the driver laying on her side beside them. She stopped to listen for the sound of heating units, transports flying in the sky, or any of the usual sounds of civilization one would probably hear this close to Helsinki, but there was nothing but the wind.

She was cold, but there was nothing to be done about it. Surprisingly, her body seemed to resist the elements, generating enough warmth to keep her going. She couldn't remember the last time she ate or drank something, and while her stomach did growl, she was able to struggle on. She could see smoke rising in the distance near the E75 roadway to the North East.

The forest gave way to a university campus, and a camp of haggard looking people. They congregated around barrel fires outside the collection of buildings, beneath overhangs, and other incidentally protective architecture. There were a couple dozen makeshift tents, and a handful of men with rifles warily watching the forest. Marjorie hesitated at first, but broke the tree line when the smell of food wafted over.

Men with rifles rushed up to intercept her, shouting in Finnish. She held her hands up, and waited for them to close the distance. They stopped a short distance away, three of them, all with rifles leveled at her. She smiled weakly, letting her tired arms drop to her sides.

"Did you bring supplies?" one of the men asked.

"No, I... I lost everything somewhere back there," Marjorie replied, in her best Finnish, trying to think of a way to explain her predicament without sounding insane.

"Do you know where any supplies are?" the man asked.

"No."

"What good are you then? Go back the way you came," the man said, punctuating his point by waving the barrel of his rifle back toward the trees.

Two of the men seemed hardened, but the third was rattled, his hands shaking. Marjorie let her head droop and her shoulders slump. She didn't want to go anywhere but toward one of the fires to warm herself, snow already beginning to fall again.

She stepped forward, raising her hands as non-threateningly as she could. Before she could say a word, the shaky kid with a rifle shot her, the bullet hitting her in center of mass. She staggered backwards, almost taken off her feet from the force. It hurt like nothing she'd ever felt before.

"Damn it, Einhold, what the hell is wrong with you?" one of the men bellowed, snatching the rifle from him.

Marjorie grasped at her chest, gasping for air. The bullet had gone clean through, and her legs felt completely numb. Blood poured down her tattered blouse for a moment before beading up and retreating toward the wound. She could feel muscle and bone knit back together as blood rushed to get back inside her body before the surface wounds closed. A second later, a neat hole in her blouse was the only evidence she'd been shot.

Einhold ran like hell, leaving the other two men behind. The one holding two rifles stood there, mouth agape for a moment while the other just blinked and rubbed his eyes. Marjorie looked up, angry, tears in her eyes from the pain that was rapidly fading.

"I woke up in a grave. I clawed my way out and came here. I'm really hungry. Can I please have some food?" Marjorie hissed, walking past the two men.

"We've little, but... sure, come on," the man stammered.

Marjorie had scarcely spent a minute warming her hands at one of the fires when a man dressed in black with a cross around his neck approached her. The shaky Einhold was beside him, his finger pointing in her direction. Marjorie looked to see if either of them was carrying food. They weren't.

"I'm Father Markku, and I see to the spiritual needs of the camp," the man with the cross said, his greying hair and creased face betraying him as a man in his fifties.

"Why the camp? The CGG should have started opening things back up by now," Marjorie replied.

"By now? It's been two months since the Shutdown, and there is no sign of relief. The whole world has gone dark, near as we can tell," Einhold replied, his voice cracking with every word.

"What the boy means to say, is that we've no choice at this point. Where did you come from? We've heard there is a camp near one of the hospitals in central Helsinki, but you couldn't have walked that far with no coat," Father Markku said, running the back of his hand against Marjorie's thin blouse sleeve.

"Two months..." Marjorie said, turning to stare at the fire.

"Maybe she came from the East, to spy on us?" Einhold suggested.

Father Markku turned Marjorie's arm over in his hands, sliding her sleeve up. "No brand, or scarification, it seems unlikely..."

"Hey, keep your hands to yourself, creep," Marjorie said, jerking her arm away.

Father Markku adopted a stern expression. "Einhold says he shot you, and the wound closed immediately, like it never happened. The other sentries confirmed the story, making me wonder, what sort of abomination are you?"

"I think I'm going to go," Marjorie said, wrapping her arms around herself and turning back the way she came.

"There's news of a young woman that whispers to machines in Helsinki. She could will the buildings to open with a touch, but it is just rumor. Many of our number went west into the city to see for themselves and have never returned. I wonder, can you whisper to machines?" Father Markku asked, gesturing for the sentries to restrain her.

Rough hands grabbed Marjorie and forced her down, her arms behind her back. They bound her wrists before pulling her back to her feet. Father Markku sneered at her, shaking his head as if to scold her for some sin, or slight, obvious only to him.

"Many of the flock were turned away by those rumors. We're going to lay them to rest now. We'll go to a food storage facility nearby and see if you can whisper the doors open. If you can, we have food, and perhaps it is the will of God behind your abilities," Father Markku said, loud enough for everyone gathered about to hear.

"And, if I can't?" Marjorie asked.

"We can assume you are some sort of abomination, sent to scatter the sheep of this flock. Bullets can't seem to kill you, but we'll find something that will."

The gathered mob dragged Marjorie through the darkened college campus past modern art and waste bins upturned for any useable contents. They silently brought her before the armored door outside what was probably the student union building, and the cafeteria. Like most buildings, it was fortified against terrorist attack, and you would need either heavy equipment or a shaped charge to get through the door.

"Open it," Father Markku directed, pointing to the door.

"Um, any clue how the other girl did this? What exactly did the rumors say?" Marjorie asked, rubbing her wrists.

"You probably spread those rumors, and yet you have the nerve to ask?" Father Markku asked.

"She had a coat of many colors, and hair like the whitest ivory. She had a bear and a shadow bring her a battery from a truck, and she used the power to open the door. She touched the battery with one hand, and the door with the other... or, something like that," Einhold stammered, eliciting glares from everyone around.

"Well, there you go, she had a battery. Clearly, I will need a battery too, and a coat. Any color will do," Marjorie said, rubbing her frozen shoulders.

"Get her a battery," Father Markku growled, gesturing toward a couple of able bodied men.

They brought her a small battery, from what was probably a handheld snow blower. Marjorie regarded it skeptically, then donned the thin coat they managed to scrounge up for her. Holding the battery in one hand, and touching the door with the other, Marjorie held her breath and closed her eyes. Seconds went by, but nothing happened.

"Nothing?" Father Markku said, clearly feeling vindicated.

"Maybe it takes a minute to warm up? Are you sure this battery has a charge?" Marjorie asked, stalling for time.

"Clearly, the rest of the flock was misled. Did you watch them freeze to death out there? Drawn to their doom by your lies?" Father Markku asked, angrily.

"Someone you cared about left, didn't they?" Marjorie asked, trying to understand the old man's rage.

Father Markku's face fell. "Take her back to the camp. We'll find a way to destroy her in the morning, make her pay for what she's done to us."

As they were walking back, Einhold sidled up beside Marjorie, and leaned in to whisper. "It was his niece. He loved her more than anything."

"Aww," Marjorie replied, frowning.

"Can you, maybe, bring her back from wherever you took her?" Einhold whispered.

"I've been laying in a shallow grave for two months previous to the last day or so. I didn't do anything with anyone," Marjorie replied.

Einhold gazed intently at Marjorie, his tremors dying down slightly.

"I had a brother with epilepsy. How long have you been without your medicine?" Marjorie whispered.

"A...a week," Einhold replied.

Marjorie frowned. As crazy and mixed up as they were, she genuinely wanted to help these people. Even if they were going to figure out how to kill her tomorrow, it seemed like a cruel twist of fate that had led them here. She wondered about that as well, how it was she wasn't dead, and why she'd been allowed to keep on living.

When night fell, it got truly dark without the artificial lights from the cities and municipalities nearby. One could actually see the stars, and Marjorie did little sleeping. The people of the camp gave her a little water, snow shaken in a bottle, and a small cup of broth. It did little to throw off the thirst and hunger she felt, but Marjorie could feel life-giving strength flood her limbs all the same.

She woke before dawn, shaken awake by Einhold. Marjorie bolted upright, but he shushed her, handing her a warmer set of boots and a satchel. Marjorie looked around the camp but everyone was asleep or out patrolling the perimeter.

"I'll die if I don't find medicine. I'm scared to leave by myself, and this seems like a decent way to pay you back for shooting you," Einhold whispered.

"More than decent," Marjorie replied, pulling the boots on.

They crept out of the camp and headed east through the woods, blundering along through the dark until they reached urban areas again. They walked past downed transports that had fallen from the sky outside legislative protocols, all safety protocols for repossession having failed. There were hundreds of frozen corpses here, covered by a thin layer of snow. The road way was mostly clear past the first residential zone, a powerful storm moving quickly in from the west.

"We've got to find shelter, and food. What you stole from the camp won't last forever," Marjorie replied.

"I've heard there are cabins, older homes that don't have all the intrusion countermeasures like newer dwellings, but they will be hard to get to," Einhold stated, pulling out a map printed on paper.

"Do those communities have clinics?" Marjorie asked.

"The one where my grandparents lived had a clinic, but it is really far," Einhold said, nodding.

"Okay, shelter now, figure out how to get there after the storm passes," Marjorie said, turning back toward the residential zone.

After some searching, they managed to find a residence that was in the middle of being built. The concrete forms had been poured and a crane was beside it, in the process of applying the roof. Luckily, the place hadn't been picked over yet. Marjorie walked through, looking for the best place to hunker down when the crane suddenly started up.

Stepping outside, Einhold and Marjorie looked up at the industrial machine idling beside the construction zone, the hatch to the control chamber hanging open. Einhold climbed up first, pushing the orange powder coated door to one side. He smiled, beckoning for Marjorie to follow him up. The space where the crane operator sat wasn't spacious, but it was heated, and the radio worked.

"Did you start the crane up? With your whispering?" Einhold asked, taking off his hat and doing his best to make room for Marjorie.

"I don't think so, but someone did," Marjorie replied.

Einhold was blond, freckled, and awkward even though he was probably old enough to technically be an adult. He took his coat and gloves off, revealing a painfully slim frame, and fingernails bitten down to the wick. Marjorie felt a pang of sympathy for him, and hoped they could find him the medicine he needed soon.

Einhold pressed into the cabin on the far side. "Okay, how are we going to do this?"

"Hand me the satchel," Marjorie said, pressing herself into the crane operator's seat.

She partially closed the hatch, slipping the strap from the satchel between the metal jamb, and the locking mechanism. It served to keep them from being locked inside and wedge the door closed at the same time. She gave the door a tug to make sure it was tight and then moved over to give Einhold more room.

"Just static, except for this channel, some kind of beeping," Einhold said, doing his best to work the radio.

"The beep is in time with this indicator light on the dash," Marjorie replied, pointing.

"That's the biometric reader in the chair. It's a safety measure in case the crane operator has a heart attack or something. It says the current operator is someone named VRSA013," Einhold observed, reading the safety information on the readout.

"VRS AI? That's an AI vehicular redundancy system. It remotely hacked the crane for us? Making it seem like someone was inside, so the door automatically unlocked? But, all those vehicles I saw along the road, with people trapped inside?" Marjorie stated, shaking her head.

"Not every vehicle has biometric countermeasure, mostly just commercial stuff, but even that seemed to fail. This is something else," Einhold replied, looking a little scared.

"It's warm, we're reasonably safe, and while it isn't exactly comfortable, this is as good a place as one could probably find for a hundred miles to wait out the storm," Marjorie said, trying to calm Einhold.

Einhold nodded, smiling slightly. Marjorie turned around in the seat trying to give him more room while seeking a more comfortable position. After many attempts to avoid contact, Marjorie pulled Einhold close to her so they could both lay on the seat beside one another.

"Sorry," Einhold said, privately enjoying the sensation of Marjory pressed against his back.

"Keep your hands to yourself, and we'll be alright," Marjorie laughed, trying to keep the ridiculous situation light.

They managed to get some sleep while the storm raged outside, burying the urban landscape in new snow. Einhold woke first, flipping on the windshield wipers. It was nothing but white outside now, the storm turning to unleash its fury to the south out over the water. Marjorie woke, rubbing her eye, while massaging the feeling back into one of her legs.

"We made it, the storm passed us by," Marjorie observed.

"The battery onboard the crane will last weeks," Einhold remarked, looking at the dashboard.

"Our food and water won't. We'll have to bundle back up and... try to get to your grandparent's place, maybe?" Marjorie asked.

"No, it's too far. But, there are other places similar to theirs that we might could get to, but we'll need snow shoes," Einhold said, pulling out his map.

"Think we could cobble something together with the stuff laying around the construction site?" Marjorie said, wiping condensation from the window to get a better view.

Marjorie and Einhold managed to find a few pieces of press board light enough for the task, and using a staple gun, fitted them with straps. They took plastic sheeting and some blue filtration grade insulation and made some makeshift coats. After making sure they were snug enough to stay on, they began heading across the snow, toward the north east. The storm had covered the land in an endless sea of white, concealing the ugliness and death left in the wake of the Shutdown.

"It's not far now," Einhold reported, after nearly eight hours walking.

"Good, we need to find a place to sleep before it gets dark and the temperature drops again," Marjorie replied, doing her best to keep up.

The community facilities for the rural retreat was half buried in snow, but it was still accessible. They threaded the gap going downhill between trees, going as slow as possible. The slope was treacherous and one wrong move would turn their jury-rigged snow shoes into skis. At the bottom, there were signs they were not the first to come this way. Someone had dug at the door to try and get in, after the snowfall, but been unsuccessful at gaining access to the offices.

"How do we get in?" Marjorie asked.

"If it's an older style entry door, it might take a regular key. Places like this, with volunteer staff, always have a hide-a-key somewhere. I worked at one of these places for two summers," Einhold replied, kneeling down to begin digging in the snow with his hands.

"No way are we that lucky," Marjorie said, shaking her head.

Einhold searched fruitlessly, at last giving the doorknob a turn in frustration. It opened, allowing him to tumble into the dark interior of the building. Marjorie stifled a laugh at the sight, then quickly followed him through the drift. The interior was dark, untouched since before the Shutdown, lobby furniture sitting neatly around a coffee table. A recreation room could be dimly seen beyond, ping pong paddles still sitting on the tables waiting for players.

"Whoever came before, didn't even try the doorknob?" Einhold said, pushing the door closed.

"Or, they unlocked it and moved on. A Law Dog Metasapient I met a few days, um… months ago said some of her fellow officers were operating in the wild. Maybe one happened by and opened the place, for anyone that might find it and need shelter?" Marjorie said, trying to find a light switch.

The lights wouldn't come on. They stumbled through in the dark until they found the utility room and the backup generator. It was difficult to get started, but there seemed to be plenty of diesel to keep it going. The small medical clinic inside the community facility was their next stop, prying open the cabinet that held the prescription drugs with a metal clipboard.

"This place was built in simpler times," Marjorie said, looking at the flimsy locks arrayed on the various cabinets and storage lockers in the clinic.

"It's a good thing, otherwise, I wouldn't be able to have gotten these," Einhold said, holding up an amber bottle of pills triumphantly.

"That's the medication you needed?"

"No, it's the stuff I took when I was younger, but this should help somewhat," Einhold replied, shaking a pill out into his hand.

"I never did thank you for getting me out of that camp back there. They were going to kill me, and you risked a lot to get me out," Marjorie whispered, finding the words awkward.

"Oh, well, like I said before, I needed medicine and no one there would help me. And, I shot you. Still pretty sorry about that," Einhold said frowning.

Marjorie just nodded in response, putting medical supplies into a bag.

"Getting ready to leave?" Einhold asked.

"Just in case we have to, in a hurry. We don't know who else is out there," Marjorie replied.

"True, I'll gather everything useful. We still going to travel together?"

"Seems safest, for now."

They gathered up everything they thought they could carry and pushed some furniture together beside the rec room to fashion some makeshift beds. There was no natural gas for the furnace, but the fireplace worked, and after some digging, Marjorie found a small quantity of firewood outside. It made the large rec room barely habitable, but they were able to sleep for a few hours.

When she awoke, a man dressed in furs was tending the fire. Einhold seemed to still be asleep, so she stood quietly, hoping the man wasn't going to try and hurt them. The man was pale, and very tall, his head almost touching the low ceiling where he stood. He appeared to be a man in his mid-thirties, dark short hair, clean shaven, and strong.

On the floor beside him was a large knife, a broad blade of some kind, a composite bow, and a quiver of arrows. There was also a mask topped with antlers, which looked like a bear skull carved into a terrifying visage. There was also a thick leather satchel and a small collection of canteens and bottles.

"So, what happens next?" Marjorie asked, her hand sliding toward the fireplace poker.

"Depends on you," the man replied, in a thick Russian accent.

"Oh… kay…" Marjorie replied, somewhat baffled.

"I am Svetovid," the man stated, giving a small bow.

"I see, and what do you do?" Marjorie asked, hand firmly on the fireplace poker.

"I am War."

"Like, in general or a specific war?" Marjorie asked.

Svetovid pulled back his grey coat and the fur wrapped about his shoulders to show a crimson sash full of medals, small trinkets, and other objects pinned across the surface.

"Um, very nice. You must have hit a lot of flea markets to find all that," Marjorie said, a little louder, hoping Einhold would wake up.

"No markets, but I fought in many wars. I remember these lands, fighting almost twenty-five winters here for Tsar before time of troubles," Svetovid explained.

"That would make you, what? Over five hundred years old? Did you come here looking for your meds as well?" Marjorie said, trying to keep things friendly.

"I am far older. When my people came south, we would come to be called the Sintashta. Close enough, I suppose," Svetovid stated, calmly tending the fire.

Marjorie reached down and shook Einhold, but he would not wake.

"What did you do to my friend?" Marjorie demanded.

Svetovid stood, and walked over to kneel beside the slumbering Einhold. He placed a hand on his chest and closed his eyes. The skin across Svetovid's armed rippled unnaturally, startling Marjorie.

"He is sick. I do not know why," Svetovid announced, without emotion.

"He's epileptic, and found some medicine he thought would help. Oh, no," Marjorie said, dropping the poker and kneeling down to stroke Einhold's forehead.

"You cannot heal him?" Svetovid asked.

"No, why would you… wait, why are you here?" Marjorie asked, hugging Einhold.

"My army and I encountered a camp of Christian rebels. A few could be reasoned with, but we had to slay the rest. They spoke of a Goddess, a woman that could not die, and the boy that had revealed this truth to them. I wanted to see this Goddess for myself," Svetovid replied, cocking his head.

"You killed them?"

Svetovid gave her a withering gaze. "Yes, I said I did."

"They didn't have anything. Why kill them?"

"Goddess, you haven't been listening to me. However, I have listened to you," Svetovid said, producing an audio recorder.

Marjorie patted the shirt pocket she'd put Truman's audio recorder, finding it missing. "Give that back, it isn't yours."

Svetovid obliged the request, placing the device in Marjorie's outstretched hand. "I have traveled the world, for nearly sixty centuries, and never heard such perfect pitch, control of tone, or someone keep time the way you do. Like a metronome."

"You're War, and a music critic?"

"I'm going to do what the Tsars could not, and conquer this land. I so rarely get the pleasure of being with my own kind, and would like it if you came with me," Svetovid explained.

"Your own kind?"

"You cannot die from the blade, and I can't be driven low by time. What would you call us?"

"Really Goddamned weird?" Marjorie replied.

Svetovid smiled, his face contorting eerily as if it was something he did rarely, or never. "The machine that shed the light of civilization has failed. It is an age of Gods, and Goddesses, once again."

CHAPTER 21

HELSINKI, FINLAND

RUINED RESIDENTIAL QUARTER – April 22nd, 2200

Eamon crouched down behind the shattered garden wall as best as he could. His huge Ursine form, and various satchels of gear, were not lending well to stealth. Abbey stood up beside him to look over the wall, and scanned the horizon with rangefinders. Her long canine ears twitched with every sound and conversation going on at the camp nearby. Truman waited patiently beside her as well, fumbling with a pill bottle. Abbey clucked her tongue and offered the rangefinders to Truman.

"I see her. Look out at the camp, second bonfire from the left, two o' clock," she said, helping Truman to his feet.

"Yes, that is her," Truman replied, returning Abbey's rangefinders.

"You sure?" Eamon grumbled.

"Yes, thank you for bringing me out here to verify," he replied, sadly.

"It is her, I recognize her from the street the day she was killed," Abbey stated, giving Truman a hand up.

"You were there, when she died?" Truman asked.

"Yes. A lot of people died that day, and I remember them all," Abbey replied, pulling her rifle around in front of her.

"How is she alive?" Eamon asked.

"She is special," Truman replied.

"Yeah, ya think?" Eamon said, sarcastically.

"We don't know, maybe Matthias can tell us more when we get back to camp," Abbey said.

Eamon lumbered along quickly to catch up to Abbey, putting a paw on her arm.

"What's with that Matthias guy anyway, and how do you know so much about him?"

"I was assigned here to protect him, he left me here when he moved on, I haven't seen him since," Abbey explained.

"Oh," Eamon replied, feeling terrible for asking.

They made their way back through the mostly abandoned east side of Helsinki, weaving around hundreds of stranded vehicles and through the wrecked and looted remnants of pre-CGG buildings. Truman had to stop many times, greatly diminished since his last visit, and still weary from weeks of being in a coma. Eamon would stop beside him, and wait dutifully for him to catch his breath offering him water.

"Thank you for being patient," Truman said, sipping some water from Eamon's canteen.

"Sure. We've done dozens of these outings to help people find loved ones. I didn't stop being a police officer just because the government bounced a check," Eamon replied.

"You are an honorable warrior, I can respect this," Truman replied, wearily.

Abbey was not so patient. "We should get back, can't you carry him?"

Eamon glared at Abbey, his ursine features betraying frustration that had been building with his partner for weeks. She sighed, nodded to him, and turned to keep watch. She couldn't hear anything for blocks, and no one from the camp of raiders had detected them, even with Eamon moving within easy visual range. They were confident, had great numbers, and their success lately had made them careless.

"Okay, I am better, we can go," Truman said, patting Eamon's furry arm.

They made their way back to Helsinki General Hospital. It had become the hub for local government and activity since Taylor liberated it. Thousands of people camped in the streets around it, waiting for news of loved ones, medical care, and the government to return to the region. Eamon wrinkled his nose as they made their approach.

"I hate leaving and coming back. It always takes me an hour to get used to the smell."

Abbey nodded. "Imagine having my senses. Something will need to change, and soon. When it gets warmer, there were be hundreds of corpses laid bare and the food will have run out by then."

Versa was parked beside Tullia's transport, a thick data cable running between the two vehicles. Matthias stood outside with his Modbot floating beside him, holding his data slate for him as he reviewed something on the screen. Abbey's pace quickened at the sight of him, Eamon having to almost drop to all fours to keep up.

"She's there, in the camp of raiders on the east side of town," Abbey reported.

Matthias nodded.

"Did you hear what I said?" Abbey said, frustrated.

Matthias looked up from his data slate and nodded. "Yes, good work."

"Well, what are we going to do about it? Who, or what, is she?" Abbey asked.

"Are we going to leave her out there, like you did to Abbey?" Eamon asked.

Matthias lowered his head, scratching his chin. "Is that how it felt?"

"A little," Abbey said, flashing a secret smile at Eamon.

"Truman, since your family has become involved in Vance Uroboros' affairs, how have things been?" Matthias asked.

"My mother was kidnapped by madman, men tried to kill my sister, and I almost died getting in the way. Brother Dragos is missing, and my sister is making herself crazy wondering where he went. Vance very dangerous man, involved in bad things," Truman replied, fumbling with his pill bottle again.

"I cared deeply about your welfare. When Vance's associates approached me, I thought I could help, but I wasn't going to involve anyone I cared about. You kept me safe throughout the protests surrounding my work, I could do no less for you," Matthias explained.

"That was years ago, many years ago," Abbey said, shaking her head.

"Just in the last few days, armed men attacked everyone they thought Vance loved or cared about. These people tried to kill a Lunar Omega Class AI and dropped a tram tunnel on the person he told me he'd designated to protect Port Montaigne," Matthias said, motioning for his Modbot to come over.

Using his data slate, Matthias showed Abbey a few of the incident reports entered by someone named Perfidy. Her eyes widened at the extent of the damage and the incredible measures taken by someone named Kale just to keep Port Montaigne relatively safe. She thumbed down through the reports, looking back at Eamon, who just held up a paw.

"I'm good, I don't need to see the spookiness," Eamon said, grinning.

"You've been facing this danger alone?" Abbey said.

"Not me. I ventured out once to get involved and was almost devoured by crazed Acrididae Metasapients. I spend my time in transit or at my bunker in North America. I'm taking a support role and keeping clear of Vance's primary agenda."

Matthias' mobile rang. His Modbot retrieved it from internal storage and handed it off to him.

"It's Kale," Matthias said, looking to Abbey informally for permission to answer.

"From the reports he seems like a great person to work for. You should ask him for help," Abbey said, gesturing to the hungry people arrayed around them.

"Okay," Matthias said, holding the mobile up to his ear.

Abbey's ear's flicked up in time with her rifle being brought up to a ready position in front of her.

"Uh oh," Eamon said, readying his own weapon.

Gunfire broke out at the edge of the camp, as several of Helsinki's defenders engaged a group from the raiding party. Eamon pushed Truman toward the cover of the transport.

"Get inside!" Abbey yelled, heading off after Eamon toward the sounds of battle.

The raiders had the few defenders badly outnumbered, but they were armed with only spears, machetes, and other melee weapons. Just as they reached the rough line at the edge of camp, Eamon swung over the top of the makeshift walls, his massive form impacting the raiders leading the charge. It was five Finnish defenders of Helsinki, Eamon, and Abbey, against a fifty strong raiding party.

Eamon roared, deafening the raiders in front before firing a burst into the group. Abbey took command of the defenders behind him, directing their fire further up the field. The raiders had a lot of cover as they advanced, and they had clearly trained for close-quarters warfare with people that had firearms. They scattered into the widest arc they possibly could, keeping low as they made their approach.

They closed fearlessly to melee range with Eamon, who seemed to descend into a sort of rage, firing with his off hand, and taking off heads with a swipe from his other. The carnage hit a fever pitch as the raiding party closed with the line behind Eamon, Abbey barking loud enough to burst the eardrums of anyone in front of her. Eamon dropped to all fours and loped back toward the camp to help cover their withdrawal.

The sky filled with sound and fury as dozens of Matthias' airborne ModBots appeared, firing welding lasers downward with deadly accuracy, burning anyone in the raiding party without overhead cover. They faltered, giving the defenders a chance to retreat back to the next line of vehicles arrayed to act as a bulwark. Abbey and the other defenders quickly reloaded as others responded from further up the line, the sound of her barking rallying allies still on the perimeter.

Tullia's transport flew overhead, circling around to run parallel with the battle line below. A pair of anti-material guns snaked out of ports just ahead of the cockpit. She fired downfield, mostly for effect as she was unable to target anything much smaller than a vehicle. Eamon waved a paw at her as he backed up to the skirmish line, where raiders were already nearing Abbey's new position. Modern arrows made of a composite material and tipped with sharpened heads rained down from behind the raiding party, striking attacker and defender alike.

"Eamon, get out of there!" Abbey screamed, grabbing a wounded defender and preparing to retreat.

"There is nowhere to run, and I won't bring this fight to the sick and hungry behind us. This is as far as they get," Eamon said, holding his ground and opening fire.

The realization struck home with Abbey and the defenders alike as they surged forward taking careful shots into the raiders as they crashed into the line of wrecked vehicles. Eamon grabbed a parking meter, breaking it off at the curb and swung it like a club with both hands. He ignored blades and arrows as the raiders tried desperately to take him down, but each injury seemed to only enrage Eamon further.

Blood and furious cries blended with fur and claw as the raiders tried desperately to push through the gap around Eamon. He responded with high violence, wielding the parking meter in one hand, and a dead raider by the ankle in the other. He roared, shattering tempered glass in stranded vehicles nearby as members of the raiding party were thrown aside, like rag dolls in his wake.

"ARMED POLICE OFFICER! DROP YOUR WEAPONS!" Eamon growled, amidst the cacophony of death he was creating around himself.

"Eamon, hold the line with us! Stop! Stop!" Abbey cried out.

Eamon didn't respond, only grunting with each swing, sending raiders flying in every direction as the ground went slick and red around his feet. Abbey ran in to get ahead of his right flank, barking loudly to stun the attackers as they closed in. She kept her baton up and fired from the hip as a wall of crazed raiders pressed in. The massed defenders surged around them, bolstered by regular people from the camp armed with anything they could find.

Versa rolled over the top of the line, anti-personnel weapons firing at will. Its huge treads crunched forward, careful to avoid defenders and civilians. Arrows and spears clinked off its armored exterior as the onboard artificial intelligence continued to target raiders mercilessly.

In the distance, Abbey could make out a man in a tribal mask watching from a safe distance. Marjorie stood beside him, clearly against her will, the expression on her face one of fear. He was surrounded by what appeared to be an elite group of commanders, with many more warriors waiting to join the fray.

A horn sounded, calling back those that remained from the raiding party. Eamon watched angrily as they departed, spitting on the ground as he pulled a spear and an arrow from his arm and shoulder. Abbey caught up with him, many brave defenders taking a knee and aiming down the field nearby.

"Eamon, are you okay?" Abbey asked, laying a hand on his shoulder.

"Fine. They clearly did not know who they were messing with," Eamon said, licking one of his wounds.

"He's got at least four times that many waiting further up the field. We need to get back to the second line and set up for another attack," Abbey said, her ears twitching with every groan of the wounded and cry of the dying around her.

"You okay?" Eamon asked, shouldering the parking meter and walking backward toward camp, eyes firmly on the raiders in the distance.

"I'm a Type One, designed for this sort of thing. You seem so…calm," Abbey said, replacing rounds in a magazine.

"I don't know what you mean," Eamon said, picking up a wounded woman, and handing her to some waiting hands on the other side of the defensive line.

"I'm a soldier, this should all be normal to me, but I feel…"

"The guy you used to protect was right behind the line of scrimmage. Maybe, you're just feeling old stuff, and this isn't new stuff like you think it is," Eamon replied, climbing awkwardly over a wrecked vehicle.

"Maybe, but you fought like no soldier I've ever seen," Abbey replied, looking worriedly at the terrified expressions of the other defenders further up the line.

"I keep things simple. I'm the police," Eamon, said pointing to himself. "Those are the bad guys." He said pointing across the line of wrecked vehicles. "If they don't want to come quietly, I'll make them dead," Eamon replied, pausing to take a drink from his canteen.

Tullia's transport came to rest nearby, the cargo hold dropping even before the landing gear touched the pavement. Matthias exited, running over to the line as his ModBots flew past him into the hold to recharge. Tullia appeared beside Truman in the hold, working quickly to attach charging cables to each tiny robot as it returned.

"Thanks for the assist," Eamon said.

"We need to get everyone out of here," Abbey reported, standing as Matthias approached.

"We can't do that," Eamon and Matthias said almost in unison.

Eamon shot Matthias an annoyed stare. "There's nowhere to go."

"That, and Kale is going to drop supplies to us. I've reached out for help, but everything is coming to this location. If we leave, the raiding party will get the supplies," Matthias explained.

"They are going to kill us. We've got maybe thirty able bodied defenders. I counted a few hundred in the raiding party, just from what I've been able to see. They've got a boss, and he's holding Marjorie," Abbey replied, still shaken by the conflict.

"Where is it you think we can go? Ever since the lights went out, you've wanted to just pull up and leave," Eamon asked, as gently as possible.

"I don't look it, but I'm old, Eamon. I don't want to die here, and I don't have the same protective feelings toward the populace you do," Abbey said, lowering her head.

"Look, I hear the same cruel shit the people say to each other about us. I'm there when they hurt each other, making this bad situation worse. I don't want to die either, and I could easily survive in the wilds," Eamon said, standing and brushing himself off.

"Why do you stay?" Matthias asked.

Eamon pointed to the star on his chest. "I'm the police. I took an oath. I don't run just because a job is hard."

Abbey nodded. "I'm not strong like you."

"Then why are you still here? Go, no one would think less of you. This crap we're dealing with here sucks," Eamon said, pointing to the west.

Abbey sighed.

"If you're going to go, you should do it soon. There may not be another chance when these raiders attack again," Matthias said.

Abbey took the star off her chest and gazed at it for a moment.

"Not until we've freed that woman. Truman loves her, and he thought he would never get a second chance to be with her. This is something I can empathize with on some level, and…" Abbey said, pinning the star back on.

"And?" Eamon said, smiling and putting a fuzzy arm around Abbey.

"I would miss you, you dumb bear," she said, pushing his arm away.

"They're coming again!" one of the defenders from the line cried out.

"Too late now, anyway," Abbey said, checking her rifle.

"Yep," Eamon said, turning toward the east and lumbering forward.

Moments later, the raiders came across the improvised wall by the hundreds, attacking the defenders without mercy. A single man led the charge, his crude tribal mask illuminated by bio-electric pulses arcing from his hands, striking defenders and incapacitating them. Eamon broke through the skirmishing raiders, drawing within arm's length of the masked man. Marjorie cowered behind him, her words lost in the mayhem and death being perpetrated all around her.

"Who the Hell are you?" Eamon growled.

"I am called Svetovid. I am War," the masked man replied, in a deep Slavic accent.

Masked man and Ursine Metasapient clashed, parking meter clanking against a broad, handmade blade. Even as strong as Eamon was, the man in the mask was stronger, backing Eamon down an embankment to where flood waters slowly washed past their knees. Eamon parried, using his considerable weight to his advantage. The battle seemed uncertain as attacker and defender lined either side of the concrete drainage canal.

"Time for this to end," Svetovid said, calmly.

Eamon reversed his grip and turned quickly to catch the masked man with a savage backstroke, knocking his mask and blade into the water. As he grabbed the parking meter in both hands to deliver a finishing blow, his adversary managed to press a bare hand to his leg. Eamon's form trembled from a bioelectric shock before falling limp. Eamon gazed helplessly upward as the waters of the canal slowly carried him away. Smoke spiraling toward the sky filled his vision, while the screams of panicked people filled his ears.

End

Continued Book 6